TYLER
RIDING HARD SERIES, BOOK 4
Copyright © 2017 by Jennifer Ashley

Cover Design and Interior Format

© KILLION
THE KILLION GROUP INC.

TYLER

RIDING HARD

THE SERIES

JENNIFER

NEW YORK TIMES BESTSELLING AUTHOR

ASHLEY

ALSO BY JENNIFER ASHLEY

CHAPTER 1

———

*W*ELL, HELLO TALL, DARK, AND SEXY.
The cowboy was way out of place in this backstreet Dallas bar full of bikers. Jessica pretended to be busy wiping trays while she checked him out—dark hair, tall body honed to satisfaction, blue eyes that could drop a woman at ten paces.

He looked around warily, assessing the slightly smelly, tattooed men around him before he took a seat at the relatively empty end of the bar's counter. His black cowboy shirt stretched across hard shoulders, and jeans cupped the finest ass Jessica had seen in a long, long time.

Jess set down her tray and made her careful way to him, ignoring the glare from Elijah, the thickly muscled leader of the bikers, that said she should ignore him. She didn't work for Elijah—she worked for the bar, no matter what he thought.

"What can I get you?" Jess asked, putting a little more warmth into the question than usual.

The cowboy looked up as she spoke, caught her gaze and held it. Then he smiled.

He had a smile full of fire and sin, his blue eyes heating as he ran his gaze down Jessica's tight black

T-shirt that said *Bike Me.* From there he moved to her arm of lacy ink, and up to her face and curls of dark hair she tried to tame into a ponytail.

"Hey there, sweetheart," he said, his voice deep and rumbling. "Damn, I'm glad there's something pretty to look at in here."

Jess tried to avoid his intense stare by moving her gaze to his throat, but that didn't help. He had a tanned, strong neck that led down to the open top button of his shirt, which in turn led to a glimpse of his chest.

Jess zipped her eyes to his face again. He was watching her with a piercing focus, and when Jess looked at him fully, his smile widened.

Her heart thumped, but she tamped down her reaction. The cowboy was a charmer—she recognized that right away. Probably he smiled like this at every woman from here to San Antonio, or wherever he was from. He had a Central Texas accent—less broad than a West Texas, less Southern than an East.

Trouble was, this bar was for locals who didn't like strangers, and bikers who didn't like cowboys. The local boys figured Jessica belonged to them. Jessica had once been married to one of their own, and they were proprietary.

"You didn't answer my question," Jessica said. The quicker the cowboy drank his drink and took off, the better. "What do you want?"

His sinful look deepened, and Jess's face scorched. "From the bar," she added hastily and then heated again as he kept on grinning. Realizing he'd turn everything she said into innuendo, Jess asked, "Beer?"

"Sure," the cowboy answered, not looking away from her. "A beer would be great."

Jess grabbed a glass and poured a draft from the tap. She didn't ask what kind of beer he wanted because it was rare she served anything but the straight commercial brand in the kegs.

As Jessica set down the mug, the cowboy gave her a nod of thanks, his eyes crinkling in the corners. They were kind eyes, full of warmth that said he could be friendly, a guy Jessica wanted to get to know.

Of course she wanted to get to know him—she'd love to—but there was no room in her life for wishful thinking. The cowboy would leave and head back to wherever, and Jess would go on working and home to her kid. That was how it was.

"Where you from?" she heard herself asking as the cowboy sipped his beer.

What was she doing, talking to a heartbreaker? But Jessica was naturally interested in people, wanting to know all about them, even though that knowledge sometimes burned. *Friendly,* people called her. *A real sweetheart.* Dominic always said, *Too trusting, Mom,* and Dominic was usually right.

"Riverbend," the cowboy answered. He pitched his voice low, leaning forward as though he and Jess could have a private conversation in the crowded bar.

"Where's that?" Not a strange question. There were so many little towns in Texas that even Texans hadn't heard of them all.

"Hill Country," the man said, pride in his voice. "West of Austin."

That explained his accent. Hill Country people

were smug about where they lived, and no wonder. It was one of the most beautiful pockets of Texas, and they knew it.

"I hear it's pretty out there," Jess said wistfully. "I've never been."

"Well, when you get the chance, come on down. Riverbend's the friendliest town in Texas—that's what the sign in front of it says anyway." He laughed, a rumbling sound that tingled in her spine. "Well, it has a few assholes, but I'll tell you who they are."

Jess found herself smiling back. She opened her mouth to ask why a cowboy from a great little town was slumming in a biker bar in Dallas when Elijah stood up.

The cowboy's smile faded, and he changed from teasing flirt to watchful outsider in a heartbeat. He gave Jessica a warning look, as though encouraging her to take cover and be safe while whatever was about to happen went down.

Five bikers rose to join Elijah, who was large, thick-bearded and thick-haired. His eyes held an evil glint, which went with the rest of his evil personality.

The bikers and Elijah moved to surround the cowboy, two of Elijah's guys standing directly behind his stool. "Time to go," Elijah said.

A sensible man would have shrugged, set down his beer, and walked quietly to the door, maybe even apologize for disturbing everyone and saying he didn't want trouble.

The cowboy met Elijah's stare with a level one of his own. "I just started my beer," he said without worry. "Had a long day, boys. Maybe you caught our show?"

The bikers' expressions turned to ones of puzzlement. "What show?" Elijah's second-in-command asked. "Costume party?" His friends laughed at his feeble humor.

The cowboy was unfazed. "Mesquite Arena. We're stunt riders. We got another show tomorrow. I can get you tickets if you want."

This stymied them. "What kind of stunts?" Elijah asked.

The cowboy rested an elbow on the bar, the arm stretching the black shirt full of powerful muscle. He gave Elijah and company an unconcerned look, as though ready to make friends with them all. "Trick riding, fights, shoot-em-ups. Kids love it."

Sounded like something Dominic would enjoy—he loved anything to do with horses, even if he'd never ridden one. But only if Jessica could afford to go, which was unlikely.

"Show us," Elijah said, folding his arms. "Do some stunts, cowboy."

The cowboy chuckled and shook his head. "I'd need a horse."

"How about the fighting?" another asked. "Come on. Let's see some good shit."

"How about I buy you a round of brews instead?" the cowboy offered.

That should have softened up the crowd, and in fact, one or two of them started to nod, as though maybe this guy wasn't so bad.

But Elijah, who was a brutal bully of a man, bent a vicious glare on the cowboy. "Do it or get out, mother-fu—"

The word ended in a grunt as the cowboy, faster

than fast, was off the stool, swinging his beer mug straight into Elijah's gut. The cowboy followed that by ducking down, rolling more swiftly than a man should be able to move, and coming up on the other side of Elijah's men.

Half the bar stared in amazement, a few guys laughing as Elijah straightened up, his shirt and jeans soaked with beer, but a buzz of anger drowned out the mirth. As a pack, Elijah's bikers went for the cowboy.

The cowboy moved on quick feet, his motion a blur. He'd left his hat on the bar, and one of the bikers grabbed it, whooping like he'd won a prize. He turned with it in his hands, to find himself face to face with the cowboy, who wasn't smiling anymore.

The blue eyes held controlled anger, as though he could stand there and pick them off one by one. Too bad he wouldn't get a chance, because a dozen men were between him and the door.

The cowboy and the biker with his hat stared at each other a second, then the cowboy's fist flashed out and caught the other man upside the head.

As the biker dropped to the floor, the cowboy caught his hat and ran toward the barstool where he'd been sitting. Elijah's guys surged on him, but the cowboy vaulted himself upward, landing with his butt on the countertop, and used the momentum to slide down it, right toward Jessica. He grinned at her as he went by, touching his lips, making her realize her own were parted in shock.

Elijah and his thugs hurried to the end of the bar, ready to catch the cowboy when he came off. The cowboy didn't let them. He swung his legs behind the counter and hopped down, landing right against Jessica.

Jess had the sensation of a hard body flush with hers, strength in every inch. He was tall, but not so tall it was a chore to look up at him.

He gazed at Jessica with dark blue eyes full of a strange emptiness, before he caught her around the waist, yanked her to him, and brought his mouth down on hers in a fierce kiss.

Jessica's never-strong leg gave way, but the cowboy held her in place, his arm as solid as a steel bar, his strength renewing her balance. He kissed her like he had all the time in the world, his lips skilled, promising plenty of wickedness if they ever got out of this bar.

Heat swam through her, Jess's mouth responding to his before she could stop herself. She drank him into her—his nearness bringing scents of leather and outdoors. He tasted of beer and spice, sparking feelings she'd thought dead forever, reminding her she was still alive.

The cowboy gave a start as her lips returned his pressure, as though he hadn't expected her to kiss him back. The two of them hovered in a silent moment, the noise, stale air, and stench of too many sweaty men fading, a bubble of warmth and *rightness* enclosing them.

The cowboy drew back, looking down at her as seconds ticked by. His eyes fixed on her, something in the blue depths dancing out of Jess's reach.

Then he released her, smiled his melting smile, and spun away. He deftly rolled over the side of the bar opposite where Elijah and his guys had halted in confusion and made for the space that had cleared to the door. The cowboy ran into the night, hot Texas wind pouring into the room in his wake.

Elijah and his crew went after him.

Jessica leaned on the counter, fighting to stay upright, touching her fingers to her tingling lips as her heart banged so fast she could barely breathe.

She should be outraged that a perfect stranger had kissed her. But it had been glorious. For the first time in years, Jess had felt connected to another person, wanted.

She'd been groped plenty in this bar, a hazard of the job, and she'd learned to shrug it off. She knew these drunken guys didn't really want *her*, and while she'd been married, they'd been too afraid to even touch her. They only wanted to show her that they could have power over her if they chose—or so they thought.

This had been different. The cowboy had looked at *Jess*, not as a body to be touched as she brought him a drink, but as a woman, a person he maybe wanted to know better.

A shout went up outside, one of triumph. Cold swamped her. *Holy shit,* they'd caught him.

Jessica gulped air as she came out from behind the bar, impatiently skirting the tables on the way to the door. The cowboy had moved through the room as though the furniture didn't exist, but Jess bumped her hips and knees on what seemed like every chair.

By the time she reached the parking lot, Elijah's boys had the cowboy cornered against the garbage bins and were closing around him.

"Call the cops!" Jess yelled behind her at Buddy,

the bar's manager, who'd finally come out of his office, and then she hurried across the parking lot.

Much of the homicide in this town came from bar fights that raged out of control. Alcohol, anger, the wrong person in the wrong bar saying the wrong thing—tempers flared, fists flew, and weapons came out. Jess knew for a fact that most of the guys who came to this bar carried knives, some pistols. It might be the twenty-first century, but the Wild West wasn't dead, and Dallas was one of its gateways.

Elijah's guys now had the cowboy pinned against the side of the giant metal trash container. The stink was brutal.

Jessica ran at them, her sneakers squishing in puddles of muck she didn't want to look at. "Leave him alone. *Elijah!*"

The big man swung around, his tight biker's vest a black smudge in the shadows. His fist was balled up, ready to fly into the cowboy's face. The cowboy had his chin up, as though stoically prepared to take it.

"Why?" Elijah demanded of Jess. "You his whore? I saw him kissing you. I'll take care of him, then I'll see to you next."

Elijah threatened Jessica often, almost habitually, though he'd never actually done anything to her. He was her ex's best friend and considered it his job to keep an eye on her. He'd taken the breakup personally. According to Elijah, Jessica should have stayed and put up with her husband's abuse, no matter what. It was what wives were supposed to do.

The fact that Jessica had total custody of Dominic outraged Elijah as well. But Jessica's ex was in prison for assault, and he wasn't getting custody, ever.

As soon as the threat left Elijah's mouth, the cowboy came alive.

He dropped in a flash from Elijah's thugs who held him, spun, and elbowed the chest of his nearest captor, his other fist catching Elijah square on the jaw.

Elijah roared, blood spraying from this mouth. His knife flashed in the parking lot's lights as he sliced toward the cowboy's throat.

But the cowboy wasn't where he'd been a second ago. He ended up behind Elijah, foot lashing out in a roundhouse kick. At the same time, he punched another biker, and twisted around to elbow yet another in his gut. He went back to Elijah, coming under the man's reach to bash fists into his face and then backing off for a kick that took out Elijah's knife.

The cowboy might have made it if there hadn't been so many of them. If he and Elijah had fought one on one, he'd have walked away victorious.

But the bikers were loyal to Elijah, they were drunk, and now they were mad. They were used to fights between rival gangs, which could be free-for-all wars, with men dead at the end of it. Jessica's ex wasn't in prison for hitting *her*—he'd been convicted for putting another biker into a coma.

The cowboy fought valiantly. He pummeled and kicked, and guys went down, but the odds were vastly against him.

Jessica ran forward. She grabbed arms and hauled fists back, losing her footing plenty, nearly falling.

She earned glares and snarls of "What the hell, Jess?" but she was glad to divert their attention. One man swung at *her*, but Jessica had become expert at dodging blows, and she only felt the wind of his fist.

Sirens sounded—Buddy must have made the call. Three squad cars sped along the road on the other side of the chain-link fence, heading for the parking lot.

Jess feared it was too late. The cowboy was on the ground, men in motorcycle boots kicking him, fists connecting with his face, gut, ribs. He'd folded himself up, head tucked under muscled arms, trying to protect himself from the worst of the beating.

As the cop cars came racing around the last corner, Elijah shouted an order. The guys put in their final kicks or punches, and then faded away. Motorcycles started up and slid off into darkness, escaping before the squad cars burst into the parking lot. The spotlights from the cops' cars swept through the lot, landing only on the fallen cowboy and Jessica crouching next to him, trying to make sure he was still alive.

———

TYLER LOOKED UP INTO THE face of an angel.

An angel with unruly dark hair falling from a ponytail, a deep frown, and fantastic ink. A half sleeve of tatts ran from elbow to shoulder on her right arm; her left arm bore curlicues that laced around her shoulder and trailed down under the collar of her tight T-shirt.

Tyler wanted more than anything to find out

where those curlicues went, maybe while kissing them.

Right this minute, he was flat on his ass, his body throbbing. He took a deep breath, which was tough, but he exhaled in relief when he didn't feel stabbing pain in his sides. They might not have broken his ribs after all. Carter would have killed him for that.

The bartender wore shorts, which meant that the legs folded near Tyler were bare. Slim but muscled, the legs of a woman who was on her feet a lot, carrying the weight of the world. Strong arms too, strength in the fingers that touched him, though those fingers shook a little. Her eyes, dark like her hair, held worry, and behind that, resilience—a woman who'd seen much and was intent on surviving.

"You all right?" she asked through the rushing in his head.

"No," Tyler slurred. "But thanks for asking, sweetheart."

Cop cars, three of them, filled the parking lot. The bikers were long gone, smart enough to flee. Tyler was the only one left to answer for the trouble.

The woman helped him sit up. A cop crouched next to them, but Tyler remained half leaning against the woman, liking the soft cushion of her. He might feel like shit, but he could make the most of the situation.

The cop asked them both what happened.

"What happened is I said the wrong thing in the wrong bar and got my ass handed to me," Tyler said, trying to grin, wincing when his mouth pulled on a cut.

The pretty bartender scowled. "He was minding his own business, and Elijah lit into him."

The cop nodded knowingly. Apparently, he was familiar with Elijah and his ways.

"You want to go to the hospital?" the cop asked. He'd shone a light into Tyler's eyes, got him to follow his fingers, asked his full name, routine emergency tech stuff. Tyler knew the drill.

"Nah," Tyler said, trying to move without wincing. "I've been hurt worse falling off my horses. It's my job." He started to get his feet under him, groaned, and leaned back on the bartender. She was gorgeous—why was he in such a hurry to get up?

The cop and his partner got their hands under Tyler's arms and gently but firmly helped him stand. Tyler tested his legs and arms, patted his sides, wiggled his swollen fingers. Nothing broken, fortunately.

But he was banged up. Tyler put his hand to his face and found his cheek swelling, blood from the cut on his lip. His hands were a mess, and his clothes were stained with both his blood and that of his enemies.

"Why don't you get back home?" the cop said. He spoke in a heavy Dallas accent, one that said this was *his* town, in all its chaotic glory. His suggestion wasn't really a suggestion, and Tyler knew it. "Sleep it off, go to the ER if you're still hurting in the morning."

"Yeah, will do," Tyler answered.

They asked if he wanted to file a complaint against Elijah or have the man picked up for assault, but Tyler shook his head. Rounding up Elijah probably wouldn't do any good, and Tyler just wanted to get back to his hotel room and rest. He had a show tomorrow.

The cops didn't seem surprised Tyler let the incident go, which told him that Elijah was a serious pain in the ass to many. They talked to him a little longer, making sure he really was all right, then they got into their cars and left.

The bartender remained by his side. She came up to his shoulder—just tall enough to rest her head there if she wanted. Her hair smelled sweet, and her hand on Tyler's chest would be warm and light. He remembered the taste of her lips, the tightening in his heart when she kissed him back, and the heat that started in other places besides his heart. He wouldn't mind kissing her again.

She gazed up at him, not in longing, but in worry mixed with anger.

"You should have asked them to take you home," she said. "Or to a hospital. Elijah's boys beat you up good."

Translation—Tyler looked like hell. Great. He felt for his keys, glad to find them still in his pocket, and glanced around for his truck. It sat under the one light in the parking lot, alone and shining, untouched.

He shook his head, wishing the movement didn't make him dizzy. "Don't worry, sweetheart, I've had worse than this in a tussle with my brothers. And *we* mostly like each other. Besides, I didn't want to leave my truck." He looked down at her, knowing that if he didn't go, he wouldn't resist the urge to slide his arm around her and pull her up for another kiss. He wanted to see if the second one would blow him away as much as the first. "What about you? You all right? I saw you in that fight, throwing guys around like a superhero."

She flushed, her eyes starry. "Sure, I was. Elijah's a bully, and it wasn't a fair fight."

"I appreciate that. I really do. Hey." Tyler stuck his fingers into his back pocket and brought out three battered pieces of cardboard. "These will get you into our show tomorrow. We're on at eleven-thirty. You have someone you want to bring?"

She looked suddenly grateful, a real smile breaking through. Damn, she was hot when she did that. "Yes, my son, Dominic. He's nine, and he'd love it."

A son. Good—Tyler liked kids. No mention of a husband or boyfriend. More good, though that didn't mean one wasn't lurking in the background.

"All right, then. Guess I'll be saying so long." Tyler should walk away now, head for the truck, and heave himself into it. His feet wouldn't move. "What's your name, darlin'?" he asked. "I want to know who I'm saying good night to."

"Jessica," she answered, her voice like music. "Or Jess."

"Jessica. That's pretty." Tyler tried to give her his flirting smile, but it pulled at the side of his lip, which smarted. "I'm Tyler. Tyler Campbell. If you come to the show, ask for me. Your son can meet my horses, and my brothers. One of them's famous—Adam. He's a movie stuntman."

And safely married and happily in love with his wife so he wouldn't be stealing Tyler's ladies anymore. Grant and Carter were also married, so Tyler didn't have to worry about them either. It was great being the only single Campbell on the stunt team.

"Thanks," Jessica said, clutching the tickets.

Tyler hoped, truly hoped, she'd use them. He'd introduce her son to his family and show the kid the horses. Then Tyler would suggest he take them out for a nice lunch. Maybe Jessica would smile at him for real again. After that he'd suggest he and Jessica go out to a fancier dinner, just the two of them …

Right. She looked like a woman who wanted to hook up with a beat-up cowboy.

"Good night," Tyler made himself repeat. "See you there."

He leaned down with difficulty and retrieved his hat. One of the bikers had stomped on it after it had fallen in the struggle, right into an oil puddle. He gazed at the hat in resignation, gave Jessica a rueful smile, and headed for his truck.

Limped for the truck was more like it. Tyler might not have broken anything, but he was battered and bruised and had pulled more muscles than he knew he had.

He clicked the remote to unlock the driver's side door and levered himself inside. There he sat, leaning back against the seat, eyes closed, while he willed pain to die down.

When he opened his eyes again, he found Jessica standing next to his door. She was way better looking than his dingy hotel room, so he decided to sit still and enjoy her.

"Hey, sweetheart," he croaked.

"Move over," Jessica said in a firm voice. "You're not driving anywhere. *I'll* take you home."

CHAPTER 2

———

TYLER STARED DOWN AT JESS for a split second with those sexy blue eyes, then he slid over to the passenger side without argument, leaving the keys in the ignition.

Jessica awkwardly climbed up and inside. The pickup was big, a guy's truck, the driver's seat pushed all the way back to accommodate long legs. Tyler watched while Jess adjusted the seat so could reach the pedals. She didn't touch the mirrors, not wanting to hear any lashing out that she'd messed with their perfection.

Tyler said nothing, only stiffly strapped on his seatbelt. Jess put on her own seatbelt and then turned the key. The truck throbbed under her, the engine powerful. It felt good, like a motorcycle ready to go.

Jess wasn't used to driving pickups—she had a motorcycle and a small car—but she figured out which gear was where and how sensitive the pedals were while Tyler leaned back and closed his eyes. Finally, Jess carefully maneuvered the truck out of the parking lot and into the street, only hitting an inch or so of the curb.

Tyler didn't admonish her. He groaned slightly when the truck bumped, but no cursing, no telling her she was clumsy and stupid.

"Where to?" she asked as she glided the truck down the shabby back street.

"Aw, damn," Tyler said in a faint rasp, trying to put a laugh in there. "I thought you meant you'd take me to *your* home. I have the shittiest luck."

A vision flashed through her of the two of them in her small bedroom, the cowboy filling her bed with his warmth. Heat flashed through her, the vision potent.

But no, he didn't mean it. He was teasing. Jess had just met him, for crap's sake.

"Where are you staying?" she asked, as though she hadn't heard him. She shot him a worried look as he pressed his hand to his abdomen. "You sure you don't want to go to the ER? There's one close."

"No." Tyler shook his head against the seat. "I've been hurt so many times I know exactly when something's wrong and when it isn't. I'll be okay after I lay my butt down." He let out a grunt as he stretched out his legs. "I'm staying at a place called the Lone Pine, just off the 635. Not far, and nothing fancy." He popped down the visor and peered at himself in the dusty mirror as he gingerly touched his face. "Aw, man, Carter's gonna kill me."

"Who's Carter?" Jess asked. Maybe he had an Elijah in his life too.

"My brother. My older brother. I have three of those. One younger. Ross. I like *him*."

"Carter will get mad at you for fighting?"

"Nah, not for fighting." Tyler brushed a swelling

cut on his cheek. "For messing up my face. Though I'm supposed to be a bad guy this time. Carter's always a bad guy—he prefers it—but I go either way, depending on how many we need on which-ever side." His eyes narrowed and he slammed the visor back up. "I'll wear a bandana. Or work my bruises into the show."

"What do you do in your show?" Jess asked, interested and wanting to keep him talking. He had an amazing voice, deep and gravelly and at the same time smooth like the richest coffee.

"Stupid things." His laugh was short. "Falling off horses and jumping back on, shooting at each other—fake shooting. I do a lot of acrobatics. Kind of my specialty."

That explained his athletic body and easy grace. "No wonder you could move so fast in the fight then," Jess said in admiration as she took the ramp onto the I-30, heading east. "It was wild."

"I still got my ass kicked pretty hard," Tyler said without rancor. "Hey, if you're driving me, how will *you* get home? I'd offer to book you a room at the hotel, but you said you had a kid, and I'm thinking you'll want to go back to him." He waved the problem away. "Don't worry. I'll call you a cab or something."

Jess took her eyes off the traffic to glance over at him. Why the hell was he being so *nice*? No guys were ever nice to Jess, not since her dad had left so very long ago, not since they'd decided she wasn't worth the trouble.

She swallowed. "I'll take you up on a cab back to the bar. My bike's there. Buddy—he's the man-ager—will make sure no one messes with it." She'd snatched up her purse and phone when she'd told Buddy she'd better make sure the cowboy was all right. Buddy had waved her off, saying he'd close up the bar early now that all his patrons had taken off. No one there liked cops.

Tyler studied Jess a moment while oncoming cars washed white light across his bruised face. "Why do you work there? That place is a dive. Dangerous."

"What's a girl like me doing in a bar like that?" Jessica tossed back at him. "Answer—*I need the job*. Why the hell else would I be there? Plus they provide insurance. Crappy insurance, but better than nothing."

"I get that." Tyler gave her a nod. "You have a kid. It's tough raising them on your own."

He put a questioning tone on the last words, but he'd guessed right. "Yeah, I'm divorced," Jess said, happy it was true. "My ex is in prison. Another reason I work at the dive. People don't always want to hire me when they find out my husband is a con. Like he'll break out and come after me." Jessica shivered, knowing that Cade was capable of doing just that. "Elijah got me the job, actually. The bar owner owed him a favor. And probably money. It's not a bad job—as a bartender, I'm paid more than the waitresses and I get tips."

Working behind the bar meant she wasn't running around with a heavy tray, which was dangerous for her. Too many potential falls, plus a risk of dropping a ton of glassware, which she'd have to pay for. She could stand and pour drinks all night though—most of the people who came into the bar ordered beer anyway.

Tyler stared at her. Not as if horrified because she had an ex-husband in prison, but with concern. "I don't like you owing anything to that Elijah shithead."

"I don't either," Jess said truthfully. "But—"

"And don't tell me he's great once you get to know him," Tyler growled. "I've dealt with guys like him before. He's not."

"I know that," Jessica said, breaking through his words. "If you let me finish, I was going to say Elijah is my ex's best friend. He's not going to touch me. They have a code of honor." She finished with a twist of lips.

Tyler huffed out a breath. "Yeah, I bet."

"Hey, I'm tough and know how to take care of myself," Jess said in irritation. "I've been doing this for a while."

Tyler held up his hands. "Fine. If you want to keep being a superhero, you go right ahead. I watch those movies. The ladies in them are seriously hot. My brother did stunts for a couple of them."

"Oh, yeah?" Jess asked, interested, but she couldn't help grinning. "For the ladies?"

"Funny. But yeah, Adam says they use guys to do women's stunts. He can tell you all about it. Adam's full of himself so he can go on—yackity, yackity." Tyler mimed a mouth talking with his hand.

Jess heard his pride for his brother though, and his fondness. "You like your brothers."

"Sure, they're good guys." Tyler looked out the window as they merged onto the loop of the 635, heading south. "When they're asleep. Only time they shut up."

But he worked with them, fought with them,

joked with them. Jess felt a pang of envy. She had no family anymore, except Dominic, whom she loved with a fierceness that scared her sometimes.

"You have kids?" she asked.

Tyler's laugh filled the truck. "Me? No. No kids, no wife. Carefree bachelor. If people still call it that."

Jess noticed he didn't say "no girlfriend." She bit the inside of her mouth so she wouldn't ask.

"My brothers are married," Tyler went on, unprompted. "Adam married his high-school sweetheart, and Grant married the girl he lusted after in high school—not the same thing. Carter married Grace, and he'd been jonesing for *her* since they were in grade school." He shook his head. "I guess no one does anything in Riverbend schools except look for marriage partners. Carter already has a daughter—sweet little thing—and Bailey and Christina—my sisters-in-law—had kids earlier this year. Bailey a boy, and Christina a girl. Grace now is ready to pop with her firstborn. I'm about to be an uncle four times over."

Jessica's heart burned. It sounded nice, brothers and sisters-in-law, nieces and nephews, connections Jess was never going to have.

"Congratulations," she said.

"Huh. Means I'll be stuck babysitting a lot, I'll bet." Tyler shook his head, his groan of pain a little softer. "Here it is, sweetheart. Take this exit, and the first driveway into the lot."

Jessica followed his directions, pulling into a Texas chain hotel that was nice, not the seedy dives her ex'd had them stay in whenever they rode out of town. *Nothing fancy,* Tyler had said, but it was a hell of a lot nicer than some apartments she'd lived in.

Tyler waved her to a place in the dark lot, saying he didn't have to be dropped off at the front door like a baby. His room was just up a flight of outside stairs around the back.

Jess parked and turned off the truck, sliding out of it and hurrying around to the other side to help Tyler down. He was already prying himself out of the passenger seat, dropping to his feet. Jessica slid an arm around him, bracing herself to hold him.

He came unbalanced as he landed, his weight crashing into Jess and her weaker leg. Tyler caught himself, but not before he'd pressed the length of his hard body against Jessica, sending pins and needles of energy from the top of her head down the backs of her legs.

Tyler straightened up, but he kept his arm around Jess's shoulders. His blue eyes were dark in the night, his smile as hot as his touch.

"Thank you, darlin'," he said in all sincerity. "You all right? I fall like a ton of bricks."

"I'm fine." Jessica straightened, felt shaky, and ducked out of his embrace to steady herself on the cold side of the pickup. "Like I said, I have a son. I catch him all the time."

"Yeah, but he can't be as big and ugly as me. Come on, sweetheart, I'll get you that cab."

Jessica didn't like the dart of disappointment that went through her. Yes, she needed to get back to the bar to pick up her bike, and she needed most of all to go home to Dominic, who'd be asleep by now. His babysitter was good at seeing he went to bed on time.

But for some reason she wanted to linger here

with Tyler. Talk to him. Ask him more about his brothers and sisters-in-law, how they'd gotten together, what he'd meant when he'd said Grant lusting over his wife-to-be in high school wasn't the same thing as having a high-school sweetheart. She wanted to ask him about the brother called Carter, who would be furious at Tyler for getting bruises on his face, but who'd fallen in love with the woman who was now his wife way back in grade school.

Most of all, she simply wanted to hear his voice, as warm and comforting as a Texas summer wind.

There was a wind now, hot with a touch of humidity, bringing with it the smell and noise of the city. The 635 ran heavy with traffic even at this hour, cars and trucks swishing by only a few yards from the hotel's parking lot.

I'm feeling good because he's being nice to me, Jessica told herself. *He's being nice because we just met. Everyone in Texas is taught to be polite to strangers. That's all this is.*

Tyler, unaware of her inner dilemma, took a step, heading for the hotel.

His leg folded up under him, and he ended up sitting on the asphalt, banging back into the wheel of his truck. "Fucking hell," he muttered.

Jessica bent over him, hand on his shoulder. "You okay?"

"Shit." Tyler's face was twisted with pain. "I'm fine—just … Damn it. Help me up, darlin', will you? I look like an asshole—a drunk asshole. Wish I *was* drunk. It would hurt less." He caught her hands and got his feet beneath him. "One, two, *three* …"

He used Jessica's weight, the truck, and his own strength to heave himself up, which pulled her against him. He regained his balance with enviable ease, but once more, Jess smashed into him, and once more, it was a joy.

She shivered as his arms came around her, then again when he let her go almost immediately. He was only keeping himself upright, not hugging her. Still, it was hard not to like his strong embrace, his hands on her back, the warmth and scent of male and the night.

Tyler stepped away without apologizing, and rested his hand on the truck. "If you would help my clumsy ass up those stairs, I'd be forever grateful. I already gave you tickets to the show, but I'll give you more if you want. Plus lunch for you and your son. On me."

"You don't have to bribe me to help you." Jess kept her voice light. Her heart turned inside out with his offer for lunch, though she knew damn well he wasn't asking her on a date. He meant he'd give her money or coupons that would let her take Dominic out for fast food or whatever.

"Well, that's good." His eyes crinkled with mirth. "Makes a change. It's this way. Not far."

Tyler draped his arm across Jess's shoulders without embarrassment, leaning on her a little as he hobbled forward. Jess got her weight under her, her legs shaking as panic welled inside her. What if *she* stumbled? They'd both go down in a tangle in the parking lot, Tyler's warm weight on top of her.

And this would be a bad thing ... why?

After a few steps, Jess realized that supporting Tyler wasn't as difficult as she'd feared. He had an easy balance that kept him light on his feet, even as hurt as he must be. His body against her was solid but supple. What he called clumsy, Jess called a good day on her feet.

"Do you usually have to bribe people to help you?" Jessica asked as they half staggered across the parking lot.

"Yep. People fall all over themselves to do shit for my older brothers, but I'm too far down the food chain. I'm just Tyler, the reckless one."

"Are you reckless?" That sounded nice. Jess hadn't been reckless since she'd been much younger, and she'd paid for it. Now she was responsible, dependable, working in a tough bar to make ends meet because no one respectable wanted to hire a young woman with her issues. Recklessness was a long time ago and far away.

"I'm the wild one," Tyler said with an ironic note in his voice. "Couldn't you tell?"

Jess shrugged, liking how the movement brushed her shoulder against his chest. "Because you took on a bar full of bikers? Yeah, that could be considered reckless. Or do you commit crimes too?"

That would be her luck. She was tired of guys always on the lookout for the cops. Not what she wanted around Dominic.

Tyler's laughter vibrated down to her toes. "Not lately. Ross would crush me. I mean I stay out too late and party too much. I don't pay attention to business. That's what Carter says, anyway. He's all business—well, he pretends to be. But he had a messed-up youth, so he's obsessed with keeping the rest of us on the straight and narrow."

This Carter sounded like a hard-ass, but Jess

knew guys who'd been in jail in their younger days and worked their fingers off to never go back there again. She didn't blame them, but it made them intense.

"If he had a messed-up youth, didn't you too?" They'd reached the stairs. Tyler grabbed the handrail and hoisted himself up, his arm still around Jess. She clutched the rail on the other side, the two of them hauling themselves up each step.

"Naw, I had it great," Tyler said without rancor. "Except for losing my dad when I was little. That was tough. But I had Adam and my mom, the rest of my brothers, my friends. Carter's adopted. Mom saved him from a life on the streets. She's like that."

It sounded too good to be true, like a TV show based around a huge loving family. Sure, they fought, but their problems could be solved with a brief talk and a lot of hugging by the end of the hour.

"Carter's lucky," Jessica said. They reached the landing, and Jess supported Tyler while he grabbed for the next railing.

"Hey, that's what *I* always say. When we were younger, I'd say that to his face. He'd say yeah, he knew it, then we'd start hitting each other. Don't ask me why. We still beat up on each other; we just do it in front of people and charge admission."

Their show. The tickets burned in Jessica's back pocket. She would go to the rodeo arena and see it, she decided. Didn't matter about work—tomorrow was Sunday, her day off. She longed to see Tyler riding or whatever he did, watch his body in action.

That is, if he could stand up by tomorrow. This

man was in no condition to ride a horse or even walk very far.

Tyler almost fell on the top step. He caught both of them with his hand on the balcony rail, Jess stumbling into his side.

"Whoops," Tyler said as though he thought it all very funny. "Let me dig out my key before we slide back down the stairs."

His body was strength itself in spite of the way he teetered. He held up Jess and himself both while he slid his hand into his back pocket and pulled out a card.

"If I can remember my room number, we'll be good."

He started down the balcony lined with doors and windows, arm firmly around Jess.

No man had walked with his arm around her in a long time. Guys, including her husband, had wanted to go to bed with Jess, but they didn't want to *be* with her. No hand holding, or buying her stupid gifts for no reason, calling in the night just to hear her voice. None of that romantic shit for Jessica. It was a booty call or nothing. She was a body for them to enjoy, not a person to fall in love with. In the last few years, they hadn't even wanted her for the body in their bed.

Jess could pretend for the next few steps that Tyler had his arm around her for more reason than helping him stand. She let herself imagine that they'd been out on a date, and now they were back at his hotel room, both excited about where this might lead.

Tyler stopped in front of a door, key hovering. "Think this is right. *Yes.*" The card made the electronic light glow green, the door clicking open when he turned the handle.

Tyler didn't release Jess even then. They scooted through the doorway at the same time, sticking in the doorframe, then stumbling in, Tyler laughing softly.

The room smelled like all hotel rooms, of disinfectant and air freshener, overlaid with the dust and leather scents of Tyler.

He hadn't left any lights on, and the room was dark as soon as the door closed. Jess glimpsed, before darkness was complete, one bed between nightstands and a dresser with a TV on it, typical hotel room furniture, the bathroom vanity on the other side of the room, clothes strewn about, a big duffel bag open on a stand.

Tyler grunted when he connected with a piece of furniture. Jessica lost hold of him, her hands burning as he fell away from her. She heard him hit the floor.

Jess fumbled for a wall switch, finally finding one on the other side of the room, and the bathroom flooded with glaring light, a square spilling to the bedroom floor.

In this light she saw Tyler flat on his face in the small space beside the bed, his head turned to the side. His eyes were closed, his body unmoving.

CHAPTER 3

———

TYLER GROANED WHEN SOMEONE SHOOK him. "Five minutes," he mumbled. "I swear."

"Tyler?"

He blinked, the smooth, soothing voice cutting through his haze of pain. It wasn't his lug of a brother Grant shaking his shoulder and trying to get him up. It was a beautiful woman with dusky eyes and curls of ink across her skin, her hair falling forward to brush him.

"You okay?" she asked anxiously.

I am now.

Tyler tried to roll over, to move, and he let out a sound of pain, remembering how he'd got here in this sorry state. His own stupid fault. He really didn't want to go to an emergency room—they'd patch him up and give him a ton of meds that would keep him passed out for a day. All he needed was some sleep, and he'd be fine.

"Come on." The beautiful woman—Jess—had her hands under his shoulders. "Let's get you cleaned up."

Tyler hauled himself up without leaning too

hard on her, his legs strong enough to carry his messed-up body. He found his arm around her again, her soft curves against his side, her fragrant hair near his nose.

They staggered into the lit bathroom, past the vanity to the room with the tub and toilet. Jess ducked out from under Tyler, sitting him down on the closed toilet lid. She grabbed a washcloth and quickly ran it under hot water, then rummaged for the cotton swabs and cotton balls in the makeup remover kit that came with every room.

"I have first-aid stuff," Tyler said. "In the closet."

He started to stand, but Jess pushed him back down with an admonishing hand. "Sit there," she growled. "I'm not picking you up off the floor again."

Tyler's amusement bubbled high, along with a vigor he'd not felt in a long time. "Sure thing, sweetheart."

"And stop calling me sweetheart."

Jess threw the words at him as she turned away and rummaged in the closet on the other side of the vanity. Tyler watched her through the open door, admiring the way her shorts bared everything from thigh to ankle.

Did she have sexy legs or what? Firm from her job on her feet but with nice curves, the way legs were meant to be. He noticed she favored her left one a little, and he hoped this ex of hers hadn't hurt her. Or Elijah. Tyler might have to gather his brothers, return to the bar, and have a little talk with Elijah and friends.

Jessica returned with a large case marked with a red cross. "This isn't a first-aid kit," she said in amazement. "It's a suitcase."

Tyler shrugged, which hurt. "We're stunt riders. We fall down."

Jess set the kit on the vanity counter and opened it. Her eyes widened at the rows of bandages, bottles of disinfectant and alcohol, gauze, scissors, medical tape, a splint, slings, syringes, a scalpel.

"Holy shit," she said in shock.

"We haven't ever used all that stuff." Tyler felt the need to point this out. "We're careful and we train. But you never know."

"I need one of these things for my kid," Jess said. "He wants to be a biker when he grows up. Right now he's into BMX trying to do stunts—even though he knows he's not supposed to."

Tyler heard the exasperation, pride, and worry all mixed up. Jess's face softened in a big way as she talked about her son. The wariness fled, and love shone in her eyes. It made her stunning.

"You said Dominic was nine," Tyler said. "When I was nine, I was making my mother crazy too. Except with horses instead of bikes. I can't believe she's survived this long without having heart failure."

"Oh, thanks." Jessica started wiping the dirt, blood, and pieces of parking lot out of his face with the damp cloth. "Are you trying to make me feel better? I have to worry about him all my life, you're saying?"

"You're a mom. Moms worry," Tyler said while she added some disinfectant from the first-aid kit and touched the washcloth to his cheek. It stung but her touch felt good.

"They sure do," she said. "So you have four

brothers?"

"Yep. No sisters."

"Five sons?" Jess shook her head. "The poor woman."

"Yeah, she drew the short straw. Five shitheads who can't keep out of trouble. Bet your kid's an angel compared to us."

"I'm starting to think so."

Jess wouldn't meet his gaze as she bent close to him, but the heat of the cloth put a flush on her face.

This woman was gorgeous. So why was Tyler going on about his family? When he swept women off their feet and into his bed, he used a whole host of sweet talking and compliments, going beyond stupid pickup lines to charm and flattery. He'd learned most of his skills from Grant, who'd been a master.

There he went again, bringing his asshole brothers into his thoughts. They were off talking business and calling their wives, saying gooey sweet nothings over the phone. Tyler had decided to ditch them tonight, hang out in a Dallas bar and see what was going on in the big city. He'd chosen one away from the rodeo area, tired of cowboys, seeing a claim on the online map that Brent's Bar had great beer. The beer had been only okay, and nothing in its ad had mentioned Elijah.

Or, maybe his map app hadn't steered him wrong. Jess, the most alluring woman he'd seen in a long time, was here in his hotel room, and he hadn't had to do any sweet talking at all. No, he just had to have ten guys throw him around, and wham—beautiful woman in his bathroom, leaning over him while she gently touched his face.

Her position put the lines of her tatts at his eye level. Tyler tried not to follow them into the gap her shirt made as Jess bent to him, but it was impossible to look away. He could shut his eyes, not take advantage of the situation, but—who the hell was he kidding?

Tyler looked. The tatts on her left shoulder snaked down inside the shirt, all the way to the soft curve of her breast.

The washcloth froze. Jess's hand had gone rigid, and reluctantly, Tyler dragged his eyes from her chest to her face.

Jess was staring at him, her lips parted, her breath quickening. Her flushed cheeks burned redder as he met her gaze.

"I can't help it." Tyler shrugged. "I'm a red-blooded male, and you have great ink. Are you an artist?"

"No. Wanted to be." The sadness in her voice caught at him.

"Why didn't you, then?" he asked.

She straightened up, as though more upset by the question than his checking out her breasts. "I didn't think I'd make enough to support Dominic. Besides …" Jess trailed off and shook her head as though stopping herself from saying more. "I don't have any real talent for it. I make enough tending bar, plus like I said, they have health insurance."

"Sorry. None of my business."

Listen to him, apologizing. Tyler never apologized to women. He took them out, showered them with attention, had brief but intense affairs with them, and then sent them on their way. None of it got too personal. Sexy—hell, yes—but not personal. There was a difference.

Jess went back to cleaning his wounds. "It's all right. Why are you a stunt rider?"

"I got dragged into it by my brothers," Tyler answered readily. "Story of my life. Well, okay, maybe not *dragged* exactly. When I was younger, I copied them because I thought they were cool. Now I do it because I love horses and will do anything to keep from sitting in a cubicle in a cold office building. I like being outside. You know, *living*."

And what the hell was he going on about that for? Here he was, a banged-up mess, bleating about what he loved. This was one hell of a first date.

But maybe he was talking like an idiot because it *wasn't* a date. Tyler wasn't winking at a cute girl in a bar, buying her a drink to convince her to go out with him. No impressing her by taking her to a fancy restaurant then back to an upscale hotel in Austin or a cozy B&B for the weekend. Just an anonymous hotel in Dallas, a white bathroom, and cuts and bruises all over his body.

"I get that," Jess said, longing in her voice. "About being outside. I love watching Dominic at his BMX meets. Worry like hell the whole time, but it's great being there with him outdoors. I couldn't make it working in a windowless cubicle either. Not that a bar ..." She shut her mouth quickly again—she didn't like talking about herself, Tyler noted. "Take off your shirt."

Tyler's fingers went immediately to his buttons. "Yes, ma'am," he said with enthusiasm. "Ow." His shoulder wrenched and he had to slow down.

"Shit, this is embarrassing."

Jess looked like she wanted to laugh. She reached for the buttons, undoing the top one gently but competently.

Tyler relaxed, letting her fingers move to the next one. "So much better," he murmured.

Jess glanced at him, her eyes close to his. Her cheeks went crimson, the flush moving all the way down her neck to embrace the tatts at her collar. She pulled away, starting to rise, but Tyler caught her hand.

No. Stay.

He couldn't say the words out loud. She might refuse, go, and for some reason Tyler didn't want her gone. He wanted her here with an intensity he hadn't felt in a long time. The crappy hotel room transformed into splendor with her in it, a different place tonight.

Jess's dark eyes moved to him, something in them he couldn't decipher, but she stayed put. She didn't reach to help him unbutton his shirt though.

Jess held the dripping cloth aside while Tyler tore at the buttons and stripped off the shirt, then the T-shirt he wore beneath.

He looked down at himself. "Shit."

His sides were turning purple where thick-soled motorcycle boots had connected with his flesh.

"That's it." Jessica folded her arms, splattering the floor with droplets of water. "Emergency room."

"Hold on." Tyler poked at the bruises, which were tender but not dangerously so. "Like I said, sweetie, I've been hurt worse than this. Someday I'll tell you about the time my horse Buster kicked the shit out of me. And then laughed."

Jess's eyes narrowed. "Horses don't laugh."

"Beg to differ. He was snorting and laughing and looking smug. If I ever introduce you, you'll understand."

"You still have him?"

She sounded surprised. And interested. Good. Not *I'm out of here, you crazy asshole.*

"'Course we still have him. He's our best showman. He knows it, the shit. He's amazing in the ring. You'll see him tomorrow."

"I don't know if I can like him knowing he did that to you."

"Aw, I'm touched." Tyler was astonished, actually. Most women rolled their eyes with boredom when he went on about horses. Even women who followed the rodeo, the buckle bunnies, only wanted him for his body. After a certain point, they didn't want Tyler to *talk.*

Jess knelt down, touching the cloth to Tyler's ribs. It felt good, and he couldn't help letting out a breath of relief.

Jess mistook him—she pulled the cloth away. "You all right? Did that hurt?"

"No." Tyler clasped her wrist, guiding the cloth back to his side.

Her arm was small under his fingers, but strong, soft, all woman. Jess stilled, her eyes flicking up to meet his. Neither of them moved.

She was breathtaking. Jess had waded into the bikers tonight to try to stop them from beating Tyler to death. She'd come after him to make sure he was all right, helped him up when he'd fallen.

Tyler had thought her an angel, but now he realized she was one damned remarkable woman.

He closed the brief space between them and kissed her.

Jess didn't pull away, smack him, curse at him, or call him names. Not that women did that when Tyler kissed them, but those women weren't Jess.

Just as she had when he'd kissed her behind the bar, Jess returned the pressure of his lips, her kiss shaky. The cut on his lip stung, but faded as the kiss went on.

She was sweet, with a hint of spice that made Tyler want more. Her eyes were open, her gaze casting downward as Tyler eased back, as though she studied his lips.

Tyler's heart surged with need, the sensation wiping out every coherent thought in his head. He laced his fingers behind her neck and pulled her close for another kiss.

Again, she responded by fitting her lips to his, her faint exhalation sending her cinnamon breath into his mouth. The slow flame in Tyler's heart flared to spread through his blood, erasing any hesitation.

He tugged her closer, thrilling to feel Jess respond. She didn't touch him except for where her hand and the washcloth pressed his ribs, and with her mouth.

Jess kissed tentatively, exploring, her lips moving with his as he coaxed them open. Her tongue flicked inside his mouth, the spark of it making him jump. She made a low noise in her throat, a faint sound of surrender.

Perfect. She was delicious, full of heat and sexiness. Her answering kiss cut through Tyler's pain and flared to life a need he hadn't experienced before. Sure, the buckle bunnies chased him, and

Tyler obliged to satisfy his libido, but he'd not felt this flash of yearning before, this *awakening*.

It leapt tenfold when Jess brought her other hand up to touch his side—softly, being careful of his bruises. The press of her fingers sent the last of Tyler's aches fleeing.

His heart swelled and bumped. It was going to happen. He'd have this beautiful woman, his avenging angel, next to his skin, and he'd be able to trace the enticing tatt all the way to its end.

Only if she wanted it too. Tyler liked women, but he wasn't a dickhead. It had to be mutual, or else what was the point?

He pulled out of the kiss, keeping his hand on her neck, his fingers soft—she could get away any time she wanted.

Tyler asked the question in silence, his breath coming fast. *Stay with me?*

The answering look in Jessica's eyes stumped him. He saw hunger, need, emptiness, longing. Also interest for *him*. Not because Tyler was a stunt-riding cowboy, but because he was himself, a man who kept a horse and cared for him even after that horse had hurt him.

Tyler touched her cheek. Jess started, as though she'd forgotten where she was for a moment. Then she closed her hand around his, guided herself back to his lips, and kissed him deeply.

Her response electrified him. Tyler put his hands on her waist and drew her up and onto his lap.

A glaring white bathroom wasn't exactly conducive, but Tyler was past caring. Jess was light yet strong, her arms going around him to hang on. Her fingers bit into his shoulders as she pulled herself closer to him. Jess's knees came around him, her body hugging his as she kissed him desperately.

This had to go somewhere. Tyler braced his feet in the tiny space and rose, lifting Jess with him. The wonderful woman didn't try to push from him— she wrapped herself more tightly around him and let him carry her, a step at a time to the bedroom.

Tyler didn't head for the bed right away. It was fun to kiss her standing up, her legs wrapped around his, her breasts against his chest. He spun slowly in place with her, leaning back on a blank space of wall to enjoy the kissing.

He never actually got to kiss very much. The women who chased Tyler were more interested in him from the waist down, eager to see if his large cowboy boots meant he was as big as they wanted him to be. From the excited squeals, he was—or at least they weren't going to admit any disappointment.

Jess didn't seem to be interested in the measurement of his cock at all. She slanted her mouth over his, opening his lips, tasting him. She rolled her tongue across his with leisurely enjoyment, then darted it playfully to light the sparks.

She responded to Tyler's every nuance, as though she loved kissing, and especially kissing him. It was damned flattering and stoked a fire Tyler hadn't let burn in eons. Jess had seen him get the crap kicked out of him, but she'd not looked at him in derision. She'd picked him up and brought him home out of pity.

'Lot to be said for pity,' Tyler decided, as Jessica's hands skimmed his bare flesh, taking all the hurt away.

CHAPTER 4

————

WHAT AM I DOING? THE question came knocking through Jess's haze of pleasure and wanting. In a hotel room, alone with a perfect stranger, and no one in the world knew where she was.

A gentle stranger whose touch was tender, something Jess had never experienced before. She had her arms and legs around Tyler's body, clinging to him while he held her. His blue eyes were closed, his lashes resting against his tanned skin as he kissed her as though they could kiss all night.

He'd thrown off his pain and showed a strength that astonished her when he'd stood and carried her from the bathroom. In spite of that, he held her lightly, and he'd sent her a look of inquiry—*Yes? or no?*

Giving her a choice. Not, *We're doing this whether you like it or not.*

The novelty of a man asking Jess instead of demanding what he thought his due made her fling herself at Tyler and kiss him like a crazed woman.

Then she settled down to enjoy him. Tyler smelled of male and the freshness of the night. He tasted like fire. That was the only way Jess could describe it—sparks and flame, warmth and need. Jess soaked him in to bolster herself against the nights to come.

Tyler tilted away from her to break their kiss, his head bumping the wall. He looked at Jess with eyes that were half closed, glittering midnight blue.

Those eyes held another question. *We gonna do this?*

Jessica's heart thumped. She should run, go home, hug Dominic, forget.

But for the first time in a long time—years—a man wanted her. Looked at her and saw not defects but Jess as she was, as she used to be. Made her feel like a woman again, not a drudge, not an ass to pinch when she served a beer.

A glance at the nightstand clock had showed her it was a little past midnight. Jess had been scheduled to work until two, closing time for extended-license bars, but Buddy had already shut the bar down. Which meant she had a sitter for Dominic for another couple of hours. Her meds weren't on the schedule until Monday, so no need to rush home for that.

This was stolen time, a moment in between, one she might never have again. A magical time that existed only here, outside her life.

Tyler was nothing like the men in Jess's world. His eyes were clear, his body hard, the tight curls on his chest black like the hair on his head. He showed no weakness, no haziness of the perpetually drunk or stoned. He was alert, quick. Resilient. He smelled of soap and his own spice—and he could *kiss*. As though he enjoyed every second of it. No rushing.

They were alone in the night in this un-time. Jess might never have a chance at this kind of joy again.

She gave him the faintest nod.

Need flared in Tyler's eyes before he pulled her to him and kissed her again.

This kiss was different. Not questioning and exploring, but determined. Not demanding though. Giving.

Tyler unwound her legs from him and set her on the floor, kissing her with more intensity. Jess slid her arms around his waist, finding his skin smooth and hot. His muscles were solid, curving under her fingers, firm and unyielding.

He worked his hands beneath Jessica's shirt and started to push it upward. He broke the kiss to lift it off over her head, the black T-shirt landing in the darkness of the floor.

Tyler traced the tatt on her left shoulder, the one she'd started after Dominic was born, and she'd learned that motherhood meant her life would never be the same again. The sleeve on her right arm she'd gotten throughout high school, the bright colors and packed flower design defining who she'd been then. The flowing one on her left arm was about her life now. Tyler ran his fingers over every curlicue, spiraling down to her breast, ending where the ink disappeared under her bra.

"It's a work of art," he said. "Special, like you."

Jess could let compliments like that melt her— make her *feel* special.

For answer, Jess kissed him, silencing his honeyed words.

Tyler's hands went to her back—no more questions. He skillfully opened the hooks of her bra and slid the straps from her shoulders, palms brushing her skin.

His eyes softened as he studied her, the bra falling into the shadows. His thumb followed the curl of the tatt to where it encircled her nipple.

"You are some sweet," he said, his voice a low rumble.

More flattery. Jess was already half naked with him—why did he continue to sweet-talk her? Not that she minded. Tyler was taking his time, appreciating her, a strange sensation. The men Jess had been with had taken it as read that she was supposed to please *them*. Why bother to compliment her?

Hands at her waistband made her take a sharp breath. The experience of being undressed was new. Jess silenced her inner thoughts as Tyler unbuttoned her shorts—she kissed him slowly as he did so, enjoying every second.

Tyler's lips were smooth and skilled, powerful like the rest of him. He returned the kiss as he unzipped the shorts and eased them down her hips. His hands were callused, the rough touch on her backside as he loosened her underwear making her shiver.

Jess's undies weren't sexy—practical cotton briefs were better for work, and who was going to see them? Tyler didn't seem to mind, or care, as he slid them down after the shorts and tossed them away.

Jess needed to catch up. She quickly popped his belt buckle apart and pulled on the button of his jeans.

Tyler caught her fumbling hands. "Easy. We don't have to rush."

Slow down and savor it, he meant. They'd have this time, then nothing more. Why hurry to put it behind them?

Jess nodded and stepped back. Tyler finished unbuttoning and unzipping his jeans himself, and then her tall, dark, and sexy cowboy was in her arms.

They remained silent, body to body, for some time, looking at each other while Jess trembled.

When Tyler skimmed his hands down Jess's sides, she thought she'd fall straight to the floor. Tyler bent to her, his lips going to her parted ones, the power of him easing from his mouth to fill her body.

Jess found herself moving backward, only a few steps in the small space, to the bed. Jess lost her balance—walking backward was not high on her skills list—but Tyler caught her around the waist and guided her down.

He came with her, no hesitation, no standing back to gloat or ogle her. Not that Jess would have minded a few minutes to ogle *him*. Tyler was tight and excellently made, her hands delighting in him.

More hot kisses as they landed on the mattress together and went down into the soft—no, the lumpy and hard—bed.

Tyler's brows drew together as he kissed her. Backlit by the bathroom light, his silhouette was a fine shape, a whole man ready to love her.

Jess was on her back, his warm weight coming over her, the firmness of his cock touching her.

She felt no worry, no guilt, no fear. None of those things existed here. In this hour, Jess was a real woman with a fantasy man, one who looked upon her as a woman with no defects, nothing wrong with her. Jess wasn't an object of pity to him or someone to be manipulated.

In that moment, she was only Jess.

Reality intruded slightly when Tyler rose from her, the bathroom light now outlining the long cock that stood straight out from his body. He retrieved a condom from the duffle bag near the closet door, ripped it from the package, and rolled it on. He did so without hurry, a man confident he had no *need* to hurry.

The cool touch of the condom wasn't as good as Tyler bare, but the gesture to protect her made Jess's excitement and gratitude surge.

She embraced her fantasy man as he came down to her, opening to him and drawing his fire inside her.

---

*F*UCKING HELL.

Tyler's aches fled as he slid into Jessica, her arms coming around him. She wasn't a meek, reluctant woman—she pressed her fingers into his buttocks and pulled him deep inside. She wasn't demanding or triumphant either. Jess welcomed him in, succumbing to pleasure.

Her hot, tight, slick opening sent Tyler's own pleasure skyrocketing. He wanted to stay in her forever, to hell with the world. Nothing was as good as this.

Tyler knew how to give pleasure in return. He pulled almost all the way out and then thrust back into her, liking the little groan she let out as he slid home.

She was smooth as silk, slippery but tight. Not someone who gave herself often. Tyler's heart hammered—Jess had chosen him and he couldn't help being very happy about that.

Her tatts didn't mar her, they decorated her. The one on her left shoulder flowed like flowering vines down to her nipple. Tyler wasn't in a good position to kiss and suckle her, but he'd be sure to savor her later.

For now, being buried inside her was the best thing he'd experienced in a long time. Years. Condom notwithstanding. Not that Tyler had abstained for that long—his reputation was well known. But this was different.

This was Jess.

Jess's dark eyes glittered in the half light, her face relaxing from the rigidity it had worn in the bar. There, she'd been on her own against a bunch of bikers. She hadn't been afraid, just careful.

Now she abandoned her cares. Surrendered.

Tyler thrust slowly into her, pausing only to kiss her. "You're beautiful," he said softly. He didn't know if she liked being talked to in bed, but he couldn't help it. "You're like sunshine."

Sounded stupid, but again, Tyler couldn't help it. "Sweet as honey." He licked across her lips.

Jess's smile turned his heart inside out. She was laughing at him, but who cared?

Tyler drew out and thrust in again, the rhythm taking over and erasing any more dumb-ass words. Jess held on to him, lifting to him as he slid in and out, her hips moving with his.

Tyler had wanted to be here the minute she'd given him her assessing look in the bar. Jess had asked what she could get him, and he'd wanted to say, *You*. He would have regretted it forever if he hadn't done everything he could to be with her tonight.

She was still the angel who'd picked him up when he'd fallen. Only now she was lying beneath him, her dark hair spread across his pillow, her eyes languid as she loved him. Jess's hips rocked in time with his, her body locked to him, the pull of her wiping out every thought in his head.

He only knew her beauty, and her squeezing tightness around his cock, her eyes on his, the welcoming glory of her body.

It hadn't been like this in forever. Never would again. Tyler knew that with all his heart even as his body flushed, his heart pounded, and he let out a yell as his seed sprang from him.

Jess cried out with him, the sound loosening something deep inside Tyler, a part of him he'd buried in a place he'd never wanted to open again. Jess was going crazy beneath him, her legs rising to lock around him, dragging him farther into her as she unashamedly shouted her coming.

Then nothing mattered but her lips, her touch, and this amazing bliss.

TYLER COULDN'T STOP TOUCHING HER. He lay on his side next to Jess, her body fitting into the curve of his arm. He'd gotten rid of the condom but brought another to the nightstand, just in case. He wasn't sated by a long way, already hard again.

For now, he traced her tatts and did what he'd

dreamed of—closed his mouth over the velvet of her nipple and suckled.

Jess ran unhurried hands through his hair as he tasted her, relaxed and unconcerned. Her little smile when he raised his head did something wild to his heart.

He wanted to see her again. This night wouldn't be enough. No way in hell.

Tyler would drive her home. He felt well enough to do that now. Find out where she lived and get her phone number, travel up here as often as he could to see her.

"Tyler," Jess whispered.

Her brows had drawn together, her face tensing again. Damn it, she was going to tell him it was time to go. That this wonderful night was over.

Tyler touched her lips to silence her, and then slid his hand between her legs, connecting with the place that made her body go slack. He watched with satisfaction as he moved his fingers, and Jess's chest rose in a sharp breath of pleasure.

He knew exactly how to make her feel good. Tyler let his fingers work their magic, coaxing her to give in to desire. Jess groaned as she lay back and let him.

Tyler continued to touch her, taking his time, stroking the glorious heat of her until she cried out and half sat up. Her head went back, hair trailing across her shoulders, as she rose to his hand, jerking against his palm as though she could never get enough.

When she collapsed to the bed and reached for him, her eyes wide with desperation, Tyler was ready, the condom conveniently near. He rolled onto her and slid inside, wanting her warmth, the two of them holding each other as they came together once more.

It was a long time before they fell to the bed, panting, laughing. Tyler drew Jess close and kissed her parted lips, clinging to the precious moments before oblivion took them both.

———

JESS WOKE WITH A GASP. Her cowboy was still wrapped around her, his arm heavy across her abdomen. Outside the room, a man and woman laughed together, passing on the balcony, the sound cut off by the slam of a distant door.

Real life rushed back at her with the slap of a crumbling wave. Jess was flat on her back, naked, on a strange bed in a hotel room next to a man she'd just met.

How long had she been asleep? She needed to get up and out of there, back to the bar, find her motorcycle and go home to Dominic before Mrs. Alvarez, the sitter, grew furious with her. The woman had a life and couldn't stay with Dominic all night.

Tyler let out a slow breath, and for a moment, afterglow threaded through Jess's panic. The core of warmth inside her was nothing like she'd ever experienced. Tyler had made her feel wanted, treasured. Though she knew damn well what this was—a one-night stand and nothing more.

But what a stand …

She had to go. She'd head to the hotel's front office and call a cab or one of those services that had people in the area pick you up and drive you where you needed to go.

Jess tried to ease herself out from under Tyler's arm, but she might as well have tried to lift the whole bed. His strength hadn't diminished with sleep, and he wasn't waking up either.

Worn out from his battle in the bar plus his stunt show before that, Tyler was sleeping the sleep of the just. Dominic slept like that, knowing he was safe, no worries in the world.

In the end, Jessica had to shove Tyler's arm hard and roll out from under him. She swung her legs over the side of the bed and stood up, trying to pull the clock around at the same time so she could read it.

Her weak leg chose that moment to collapse, folding up under her to send her to the floor.

Jess landed in a naked tangle next to the bed, a cry of frustration and pain escaping her lips. She lay there, like a bug on her back, mortified and unable to move.

CHAPTER 5

———

A GROAN SOUNDED ABOVE JESS, THE sound of someone waking up and not wanting to. The bed creaked and Tyler's head appeared over the edge.

He blinked sleepily at her with gorgeous blue eyes. Tyler dressed and cleaned up had been handsome enough—Tyler half asleep with his hair tousled from lovemaking was devastating.

Jess waited for him to burst into laughter or impatiently tell her to get up. He only stared blearily a moment before the bed rocked and Tyler's strong legs were next to her, his hands landing on her shoulders.

"You okay?"

"Yeah, I just …" Jess tried to get her legs under her, but they failed her again.

Tyler lifted her before she could stop him. Jess landed against his chest, his arms supporting her, his strength incredible. He was covered with bruises, which she could see in the bathroom light's unforgiving glow, but he didn't seem to notice. His expression held concern for her—no disgust, no amusement.

"I'm fine," Jess said breathlessly. "I need to go home. My son … his babysitter …"

She tried to step away, but her left leg, always a problem, wasn't cooperating. Tyler caught her again as she started to fall.

So this was what support felt like. Someone to catch her when she was off balance, to set her on her feet again, hold her until she was all right. Jess wished she could extend the metaphor to the rest of her life.

"Don't worry, sweetheart," Tyler said in his sexy rumble. "I'll get you home."

Jess drew a slow breath, trying to calm down. The more she panicked, the worse her pain and balance would be. "I guess you'd better call that cab," she said.

"Nah, I'll drive you. *If* we can find our clothes." Tyler grinned, the slow, easygoing smile of a man not worried about much.

"You can't drive," Jess said, some of her energy returning. "I had to bring you here, remember?"

"Yeah, but I feel so much better." The grin spread wider.

Jessica's entire body flushed. She stood unclothed against a man she'd met only a few hours ago, but she wasn't blushing about that. What made her shy was his allusion to the sex they'd just had—their no-holds-barred, passion-filled sex. She'd gone at it with gusto, Jess who always kept herself in reserve. Her reaction to Tyler had sent her inhibitions flying away on the wind, and she went hot at the memory of her complete abandon. Women must follow this man around, panting for even a small piece of him.

In fact, it was weird he didn't have a date tonight—one not her, that is. He hadn't gone into the biker bar looking to pick up a woman. If he'd wanted a hook-up, he could have gone to one of Dallas's popular cowboy bars, or a dance club where women wore as little as possible and hoped to catch the eye of a rich, handsome man.

Strange that Tyler had chosen that bar at all. But maybe he'd been looking for a little peace and quiet somewhere no one knew him. Jess remembered the emptiness in his eyes when he'd pulled her into his arms behind the bar. The flash had been incongruous, and made her curious.

She tried again to pry herself from Tyler's grasp. Nope, she wasn't going anywhere as long as he had his arms around her. Jess wished she didn't like the idea so much.

"Don't worry about me," she said. "A cab will be fine."

Tyler pressed a kiss to the top of Jess's head. "Sorry, but you're stuck with me, darlin'. I'm gonna make sure you get home okay. I'm a gentleman like that."

It didn't matter, Jess told herself. He'd drive her back to the bar, and that would be it. The sudden flood of sadness the thought brought almost made her fall again.

"Only if you're sure you're all right," Jess said, attempting to sound severe. "If you pass out while you're driving, I'm going to be mad at you."

Tyler's laughter wrapped around her like a blanket. "Honey, you'd be amazed at what I can do when I'm half passed out."

An agreeable shiver ran through her, but she kept her voice no-nonsense. "Just so you're not *all the way* passed out."

Tyler continued to laugh. "You'll know when I'm awake because I won't be snoring. My brothers say I snore like a buzz saw."

"No, you don't," Jess answered, surprised. Then her face scalded.

"Aw." Tyler pulled her back to him, kissed her soundly on the lips, and finally released her. "I'm liking you more and more. Sure you don't want to stay?"

Jess did. To remain in this bubble of happiness would be the best thing she'd ever done for herself. When she walked out the door, this magical time would vanish into dust, leaving her with only the memories.

"I can't," she made herself say. "Dominic … His sitter won't stay past two-thirty." Jess glanced at the clock and saw in dismay that it was already five after two. "Shit, I have to go."

Again Tyler caught her as she started to stumble. Jess had stepped away too quickly and lost her balance, weakness squeezing her leg. Damn it, not *now*.

"Easy." Tyler's voice was gentle, holding a caring she'd never heard directed toward her. He held her firmly but didn't confine her, and kissed her hair again. "You call your sitter," he said in his calm and quiet tone. "Tell her you're on your way, and we'll go. Or *him* if you have a boy babysitter."

Jess blinked back unshed tears. "Mrs. Alvarez. She's definitely a woman and likes to be called *Mrs.*"

Tyler's big smile split his face. "Then let's find your phone, and call your Mrs. Alvarez. Tell her hi from me."

———————

IT TOOK A WHILE FOR Jess and Tyler to sort
out shirts, underwear, socks, jeans. Tyler laughed
every time they found something halfway across
the room, and after a while, Jess did too. It was nice
to laugh about nothing.

Jess swallowed her laughter when she finally
found her cell phone and called home.

"Are you all right?" Mrs. Alvarez asked in worry.
Mrs. Alvarez—Carmina was her first name—had
been born and raised in Mexico City, emigrating
with her now-deceased husband when they'd first
married. She'd learned English as a little girl, and
spoke with no trace of accent. She was fluent in
French too.

"Fine," Jess said. She decided not to tell her *hi*
from Tyler, as he'd suggested. He was just being
funny. "A little problem at the bar, that's all. How's
Dominic?"

"He's asleep." Mrs. Alvarez sounded skeptical
about Jess's excuse, but her tone said she was letting
it slide. "How long will you be?"

"Half an hour?" Jess guessed. "It shouldn't take
longer than that."

"Don't worry." Mrs. Alvarez was brisk but kind.
"I'll stay. Good-bye."

She hung up, not one for long farewells.

Tyler was sliding into his jeans by the time Jess
turned around. Jess had dressed as quickly as possible, but Tyler took his time, a striptease in reverse.
He slowly zipped up the jeans, buttoned the fly
with calm precision, slid the belt through the

buckle, then leaned down to lift a T-shirt from his open suitcase. He gave that a few shakes before pulling it over his head and easing it down his torso.

The unhurried seduction halted when the T-shirt got stuck. Tyler struggled with the cloth folded up under his arms, grunting in pain when he touched his bruises.

Jess went to Tyler, grasped the shirt, and tugged it down, smoothing the cloth over his waist.

"Thank you, sweetheart," Tyler said. The heat of his glance tempted Jess to call Mrs. Alvarez back and ask her to stay with Dominic all night.

She wanted it so much she made herself turn her back on Tyler and head out the door.

The night had cooled, the chill raising goose bumps on Jess's bared arms and legs. She hurried, reaching the stairs before Tyler came outside and closed the door.

He caught up to her quickly, not seeming to mind that she'd bolted ahead, and descended the stairs behind her. Tyler also didn't seem to mind that she went down slowly, holding the handrail so she wouldn't fall. No impatience from him, no shoves, no sounds of frustration.

Tyler steadied her as they turned the corner at the landing, his hand warming her cold arm. Only when they were halfway down the bottom set of steps did he stop and say, "Shit."

Jess rocked on her feet and held more tightly to the railing as she paused to look for what had Tyler worried.

Three large men strode across the parking lot, heading for the stairs. Jess's heart missed a beat before she realized they weren't Elijah and his gang. Not bikers at all, but cowboys, complete with hats. Two had silhouettes and a way of walking so like Tyler's that Jess blinked. The other man moved differently, but was no less formidable.

"Damn it, who let them out of their cages?" Tyler muttered. "Don't worry, sweetheart. Just ignore them."

He didn't have to explain that the three men were his brothers. Two could have been clones of him, and the third had the same quiet confidence as the others.

The three came on toward the hotel, and they all met at the bottom of the stairs. Jess halted on the last step, something in her wanting the height advantage.

The man in the lead was the one who didn't look like the other two. He had lighter hair and his eyes were hazel, while the others had Tyler's blue eyes. The first man also wore a hard look Jess recognized, one that said he'd fought for his survival. Anything he had now he'd gained only after a long struggle. Jess saw in his expression that he instantly recognized that in her too.

The other two men had dark hair like Tyler's and shared his athletic handsomeness. One of them had scars on his face, shadows in the darkness.

While the first man studied Jess in suspicion, the brother directly behind him flashed her an interested look and swept the black cowboy hat from his head. "Hey there, gorgeous."

Tyler was next to Jess in an instant. "She's with me," he said with a growl she hadn't heard from him before.

"Oh, yeah?" The man looked straight at Jessica.

"I'm Grant, the better-looking Campbell."

"Go call your wife, Grant," Tyler said, the rumble a warning.

Grant paid no attention. "Carter, move. You're scaring her." He stuck out his hand. "Ignore my seriously rude siblings. I'm the nice one. And you are …?"

Jess, bewildered, accepted the offered hand. Grant squeezed hers in friendship, interested not because she was a woman in shorts with a tight T-shirt, but because she was with Tyler.

"Hey," she said and cleared her throat. "Jessica McFadden." She hadn't told Tyler her last name yet.

"Hey, yourself." Grant let her go. "This here's Carter." He jerked his thumb at the hard-faced man. "Adam's being strong and silent behind me, and I guess you already met Tyler. If Tyler upsets you, you just tell me. I know how to handle my baby brother."

"Fuck off," Tyler said in a deceptively mild voice. He put a hand on Jess's shoulder. "Jess and I were just going. Leave her alone or I'll tell … Mom."

Jess assumed Tyler was joking, but the threat appeared to have teeth. Grant lifted his hands, and Carter took a step back, giving them room to go around him.

The third man, the one with the scars—Adam— laughed. "Poor woman, meeting four Campbells at once. *My* wife would sympathize. You have a good night, sweetheart."

His voice was as deep and handsome as Tyler's. *Another charmer,* Jess told herself. Men came in several categories—the bullies and the charmers were what she saw most often at the bar. Each got their own way; they simply used different techniques. Tyler was most definitely in the charm category, along with Adam and Grant. She wasn't sure about Carter yet.

Tyler put his hand on the small of Jess's back and steered her past his giant brothers. Jess wasn't small, but she felt insubstantial against these four cowboys.

Only Carter hadn't spoken. Jess recalled Tyler explaining that their mother had adopted him, saving him from a life on the streets. Jess believed it. It wasn't just hair and eye color and different bone structure that set him apart from the brothers—his eyes held the darkness that came from harrowing experience. He watched Jess as though he knew exactly what she was. He thought she'd seduced Tyler, she realized, probably for dire purposes.

Maybe she *had* seduced him. It was hard to remember who kissed whom first.

No, Jess remembered exactly. She holding the washcloth to his side, Tyler leaning to her, touching his lips to hers. She'd met his kiss with one of her own, no resisting, no problem at all.

Carter didn't smile as Tyler guided her past him. Adam and Grant, on the other hand, kept up their interest, giving their younger brother knowing looks.

Tyler quickened his pace and took Jess out into the darkness of the parking lot.

"Sorry about that," he said once they were out of earshot. "My brothers can be dickheads. Why they're out traipsing around at two in the morning, I don't know. Then again, their wives are probably partying it up at home without them."

He unlocked his truck and ushered Jess into the passenger side, and then walked around and climbed to the driver's seat with perfect ease.

Not quite perfect. Tyler winced and let out a soft grunt as he adjusted the seat and again when he pulled the door closed.

"You sure you're all right?" Jess asked in concern.

Tyler nodded. "Yeah, just a little sore. I rode all day, got beat up, then spent a hell of a time in bed with a pretty lady."

Tyler sent her a dazzling look as he started up the truck, and then he reached over and took her hand.

A river of fire flashed through Jess, his touch flaring the memories of what they'd just done. It was going to take her a very long time to get over him, to forget, to get on with day-to-day life.

Jess glanced back at the hotel as Tyler turned out of the lot. She didn't see his brothers anywhere, but she could swear she felt them watching them go.

"You threatened to tell your mom on them?" she asked to force her mind from the picture of Tyler lying over her in the darkness. "Is she that scary?"

"Yep," Tyler answered as he accelerated down the street. "She raised five boys on her own, and let me tell you, we could get into some trouble. She's a glutton for punishment, I guess. We're all big and mean—at least those three are. Ross can be nice when he wants. But one small woman rules us all. If I tell Mom Adam and Grant were giving a woman I like hell, she'll come down on their asses. Worse, she'll tell their wives, and then my bros are so screwed." Tyler laughed gleefully, looking exasperated and fond at the same time.

Jessica had learned what love truly was when Dominic had come along. She could hear the same kind of love in Tyler's voice, see it in his face. Her heart squeezed.

"It sounds nice," she said, hearing the envy in her voice. "A big family." She'd never had much of one.

"Sometimes," Tyler said. "Sometimes it's a serious pain in the ass. Where am I taking you, darlin'? Back for your bike? Or straight home?"

"The bar for my bike." Jess answered without hesitation. She didn't trust Elijah not to return and mess with it if she left it too long. Then he'd offer to fix it for her, for a price.

"Got it."

Tyler didn't ask for directions but drove unerringly along to the correct exits, and then down back streets to the quieter area where the bar was located.

The road to Brent's Bar was mostly deserted this late except for a wandering homeless guy or two. They were the only ones conspicuously around, that is. There'd be more people deep in the shadows, either doing business or simply waiting for the next thing to happen. Jess felt pretty safe here while the bar was open, but there was a reason she had found a house for herself and Dominic far from this neighborhood.

The bar was shut down and dark by now, but Jess's motorcycle was there. Buddy had pulled it to the back door and hidden it in shadows under a tarp, not obvious to roaming thieves. She'd have to thank him for doing that.

Tyler pulled the truck close to the back door as Jess requested. Her heart thumped as he halted the pickup and set the brake.

This was it—time for good-bye.

Tyler rested his hands on the steering wheel and said nothing, didn't even look at her. Coldness flooding her body, Jess popped the door handle and started to push open the door.

A hand on her arm stopped her. Tyler was leaning to her now, his eyes glinting in the darkness.

"Stay put. I'm taking you all the way home."

"I can't leave my bike," Jess said quickly.

"This truck is plenty big enough to carry it." He glanced around at the dark parking lot, not moving. "I don't like the thought of you riding home alone."

"Like I do every night of my life?" Jess tried a laugh. "I'm fine."

Tyler shook his head. "Not with your friend Elijah on the loose. I don't want him taking his anger at me out on you."

"Elijah is always like that," Jess said, hoping she sounded offhand. "I'm used to him."

Tyler's eyes went tight, his expression hardening into determination. "That's it. I'm taking you home."

He slid out of the truck with agility before she could say anything else, moving to the back to let down the tailgate. Jess jumped out, intercepting Tyler before he reached the bike.

"You can't be picking up a motorcycle after you've been hurt," she said in a rush.

"Who say's I'm picking it up?" Tyler's words were easy. He removed the tarp over the bike, released the kickstand, and wheeled her beloved motorcycle to the back of the truck. Once there, he reached inside the bed and hit a few controls, and a lift lowered from the truck's bed.

Jess caught the handlebars of the bike to help guide it—she needed to do *something*—but it was Tyler who competently pushed the motorcycle onto the narrow platform and then let the lift raise it into the truck.

"We have to haul equipment sometimes," he explained as he settled the bike and retracted the lift. "Carter's and Grant's ideas can get complicated. Me, I just ride."

The satisfaction with which he said the final words gave her another pang of envy. How wonderful it must be to work at something you loved, to make a living at it. Not simply taking whatever job was available to make ends meet and hope it lasted.

Tyler strapped down the bike and closed and locked the tailgate. He escorted Jess to the passenger door and helped her inside again, as though he wouldn't dream of leaving her to climb in alone.

Charmer, she reminded herself.

Didn't mean she couldn't enjoy being charmed though. Tyler's hand on her elbow was nice; he boosted her in without Jess having to struggle at all.

Tyler returned to the driver's seat once he'd shut her door, and put the truck in gear. "Okay," he said without hurry. "Where to?"

CHAPTER 6

———

TYLER LIKED THAT JESS DIRECTED him well away from this crappy neighborhood and north into more agreeable parts of the city.

He didn't much understand why people lived in Dallas, with its endless traffic, mess of freeways and toll roads, and building after building—offices, stores, apartment complexes, restaurants—row after row of them that ultimately all looked the same.

He did understand about having to live where the jobs were and blessed his fortune that he was born on a ranch and loved it. Tyler knew people from cities who were sure they'd die living in a small town—*I mean, what do you* do? He wondered if Jess would be like them, bored out of her mind and running the first chance she got.

And why did Tyler think he'd even have the opportunity to find out?

Jess lived in a house, it turned out, a small one-story home in a respectable-enough neighborhood, front yards enclosed by chain-link fences so kids could play without running into the street.

"This is me," Jess said, pointing.

Tyler pulled to a halt in front of a mailbox that

read *427*. A light was on over the porch as well as in a front room. The house looked inviting—plants in the front yard, small strip of grass mowed—not unhappy, Tyler was pleased to see.

Jess was out of the truck before he could turn off the ignition. A woman used to finding her own way, not waiting for a man to do things for her like open the door of a vehicle and escort her down. Which meant there probably wasn't a man in her life. No one in his way.

Before he could analyze why that situation made him triumphant, he went to the back and maneuvered her motorcycle to the ground. It was a nice one, a black Harley with a small seat, well cared for, decorated with swirls of silver paint that looked like Jess's tattoos. The bike went well with her.

"Thanks," Jess said as Tyler wheeled the motorcycle into her carport, parking it against the wall in front of a small, dark blue Toyota sedan. A large pickup sat in the driveway, probably belonging to the sitter—Mrs. Alvarez.

Jess cast a nervous glance at the front door, as though expecting Mrs. Alvarez to come storming out and demand to know what she was doing. "Good night," she finished quickly.

Tyler caught her hand. The carport was deep in shadow, and Tyler turned Jess to face him.

"You sure you're okay?" he asked in a quiet voice.

"I should be asking you that." Jess gave a nervous laugh that ended with a shiver.

"I mean at work. Is Elijah going to give you shit?"

Jessica shrugged. "Like I said, I'm used to him. Everyone is. He won't be happy that Buddy called the cops, but he understands. He and his boys get out of hand sometimes."

"Which makes me not want you going back there even more." Tyler scowled.

Jess pulled away, her smile dying. "Oh, really? That's nice for you—with your family and fancy truck and a show you can give away tickets to. Looking for a job is hard. Not everyone rushes to hire someone like me, so I make the best of what I have. Working somewhere else won't keep Elijah away from me anyway. Brent's wasn't *his* local bar until I started working there. But I know how to handle him. I don't need a knight in shining armor to lock me away in his castle for my own good. I don't want to be locked away, all right? In any case, what does it matter to you? I'll never see you again."

Tyler stilled while she raged, her eyes flashing and her fists clenching. Now she was an avenging angel, protecting herself, her family, her home.

He let her anger wash over him, the frustration and pride of a woman defending her choices. Tyler waited until she ran down, not tiring of watching her beautiful face.

"You'll see me tomorrow if you come to the show," he reminded her.

Jess planted her hands on her hips. "Not the point."

"I know." Tyler fished his leather card case from his back pocket and extracted a pale rectangle from it. "This is *me*," he said. "I mean my ranch. With the phone number. If you need me—anytime for anything—to clean out your carport or fix your plumbing or just to talk—you call that number. They'll find me."

Jess stared at the card, though it was too dark to read it. Tyler expected her to throw it away and storm into the house, but she closed her fingers around it. "You can fix plumbing?" she asked, her voice faint, as though her anger had drained her strength.

"No, but I know how to call someone about it. I just finished rebuilding my apartment—I know contractors all over central Texas." He finished with a note of pride.

Jess let out a long breath. "You're a shit."

Tyler reached up to tip his non-existent hat. "So they tell me—"

His words were cut off by her kiss. Jess's body landed against his, her mouth crushing his in an abrupt but heartfelt and vastly sexy kiss.

Tyler gathered her closer, gripping her hips as she dug her fingers into his shirt.

The kiss went on, Tyler tasting the passion they'd shared, the goodness of her. The warm breeze of a Texas summer night wafted around them, bringing with it the scent of dust, wilted grass, and old-growth trees.

He would have wrapped his arms around her, drawing the kiss out even more, but the sound of the front door opening made Jessica jerk back, bumping his lips as she broke the kiss. She stared at Tyler in wide-eyed panic a moment before pushing away from him.

"Good night," she gabbled and rushed from the carport along the sidewalk to the front door.

Tyler watched her long legs in the brief shorts, her hips moving as she ran in a somewhat shuffling gait. An indomitable woman, doing what it took to survive and protect her son. Another emotion added itself to Tyler's feelings for her—admiration.

"Good night," he said softly as she disappeared into the house and slammed the door.

Trying to ignore the hollow feeling in his heart, Tyler kissed his fingers to the front window then made himself walk back to his truck, climb in, and drive away. His thoughts were troubled, his body hating him as he maneuvered through the uncaring traffic to the empty hotel room at the road's end.

———

MRS. ALVAREZ PICKED UP THE remote and switched off the television as Jess entered behind her. Jess leaned on the door she'd banged closed to get her balance, not to mention catch her breath.

Mrs. Alvarez turned around to look at her. She was a tall woman, pleasantly ample. Large and strong, Mrs. Alvarez had the best posture Jess had ever seen.

"Who was that man?" Mrs. Alvarez asked in her quiet voice. She had the uncanny knack of knowing everything that went on in Jessica's life. "Why did he have to drive you home?"

"Fight at the bar." Jess pushed from the door and limped into the kitchen. She was hungry, and Mrs. Alvarez usually left something for her to warm up.

"Chilaquiles in the fridge," Mrs. Alvarez said as she followed Jess. "Warm them up for fifteen minutes in the oven at three hundred and fifty. Don't use the microwave—they'll dry out. Elijah again?"

"Who else?"

"That man should be in prison," Mrs. Alvarez said with certitude. She was right, but Elijah was careful, keeping a good lawyer on retainer and making sure evidence of his crimes didn't lead back to him. "What did he do tonight?"

"Picked on a cowboy," Jess said. "Except this cowboy is a stuntman. He held out for a long time against them and recovered fast."

Jess busied herself taking the casserole of layered chicken, tortilla strips, cheese, and sauce out of the refrigerator and putting it in the cold oven, cranking it to three-fifty. She never bothered with preheating.

Hoping Mrs. Alvarez would drop the subject, Jess set the timer and left the kitchen for the short hall and Dominic's room at the end. The house she rented had three bedrooms—two good-sized ones and one little bigger than a walk-in closet, which was what it had become.

She didn't want to wake Dominic, but she was eager to see him, to ensure he was all right. She trusted Mrs. Alvarez, but that wasn't the same as seeing her son breathing, well, and happy.

She opened the door quietly, her entire body going slack with relief to behold the lump under the blankets, the dark head on the pillow.

Jess crept to the bed, intending to kiss Dominic and retreat, but he rolled over and looked at her, wide awake.

"What stuntman?" he demanded. "Did you meet him?"

Of course, Dominic would have heard every word and picked up on the one thing that interested him.

Mrs. Alvarez arrived at the doorway. "Is that who drove you home?"

"What is this, an interrogation?" Jess was exhausted, even after her nap in Tyler's bed. How wonderful that deep sleep in his arms had been!

Both Dominic and Mrs. Alvarez gazed at her expectantly, and Jess lifted her hands in surrender. "Fine, fine. His name is Tyler Campbell. He's a cowboy with a stunt show going on at the Mesquite rodeo grounds. He was stupid enough to go into Elijah's bar, he drove me home because I helped him, and he gave me tickets to his show tomorrow."

She pulled the tickets from her back pocket, pleased they were still there—they hadn't gotten lost when she and Tyler had flung off their clothes.

Jess held up the tickets, the name of the Mesquite fairgrounds stamped on them, and realized they were expensive seats, entitling her to sit arena-side. She also realized Tyler had given her three.

Mrs. Alvarez plucked one from Jess's hand. "I'll take that. I'd love to see his show."

She gave Jess a sharp look as Dominic reached for the remaining tickets, Mrs. Alvarez too perceptive for Jess's comfort.

She was also protective, wanting to keep Jess safe from men like Dominic's father. She didn't trust Jess's judgment, which, Jess had to admit, hadn't always been the best. But that was the past, Cade was out of her life, and Jess didn't need anyone else cluttering it up.

She repeated that to herself as the oven timer went off. Mrs. Alvarez took the tickets back from Dominic, and Jess kissed him good night before she scuttled to the kitchen to get her dinner.

For all her nosiness, Mrs. Alvarez was a damned good cook, Jess thought as she bit into the cheesy and spicy chicken mixture. *Fine.* They'd all go to the show tomorrow. No getting out of it now.

Jess only hoped she wouldn't do anything that betrayed how special Tyler had made her feel, and how she would be hugging that to herself for the rest of her life.

———

SHE WASN'T GOING TO SHOW up. Tyler glanced at the box for the hundredth time, seeing the three seats for which he'd given Jess the tickets empty. Three seats so she could bring her kid and any significant other she had. He'd handed them to her in the bar before he'd decided he wanted Jess all to himself.

He'd already deduced she had no one else in her life, but he hadn't come straight out and asked. Tyler wasn't sure how he'd react if she entered holding her son's hand on one side, some asshole's on the other. She'd glance at Tyler, knowing they'd spent a secret night of passion, maybe even send him a covert smile. But that night would be all they'd ever have, and Tyler would burn with jealousy.

Moot point, he told himself in irritation. She wasn't coming.

The Mesquite rodeo arena was indoors, so the bright sunshine and Texas heat wasn't as big a factor while they rode. The rodeo had been running for several days—the Campbells' stunt show today was a warm-up before the finals of the roping and bull riding events. Right now, a drill team of horseback riders with flags were showing off for the crowd, while Tyler waited in a side ring for their show to start.

The tickets Tyler had given Jess covered the whole day, with the schedule listed on the back. Tyler knew Jess hadn't come earlier though, because he'd kept his eye on the box all day long, and hadn't seen her.

The horses, far calmer than he, waited in the corral. Buster and Bobby, a bay and a brown with white socks, stood together in the center of the ring, reins loose on their saddles. Occasionally they'd glance around, or touch noses, or let out a snort, not worried about a thing. Buster and Bobby were pros.

"If your head's not in the game, don't go into the ring." Adam's voice rumbled behind him. Tyler turned to find his oldest brother a few feet away, giving him a hard look.

He understood what Adam meant. Though Tyler and his brothers trained until they could ride this show in their collective sleep, the unexpected could always happen. A rider not paying attention was a hazard not only to himself but his fellow riders and the horses.

Adam bore scars on his face and down his neck from a bad accident involving a movie stunt gone wrong, which had nearly ended his career. Adam knew better than most how one simple screw-up could be disastrous.

"I'm fine," Tyler said.

Adam looked him up and down, knowing Tyler was full of shit.

Adam, Grant, and Carter had been shut in their rooms by the time Tyler had returned to the hotel last night. Surprisingly, none of them had banged on his door to cross-examine him, and none had said anything about Jess this morning. Grant had given Tyler a knowing look when Tyler met them at the arena after breakfast, but so far, they hadn't said a word.

They weren't being nice, Tyler knew, or discreet, or respectful. They were saving up for later.

"Seriously, Tyler. Head in the show, or don't ride," Adam repeated. "We can do this with just Carter."

They always had a backup plan in case one of them got hurt or sick at the last minute. The show must go on.

Tyler took another look at the ringside box near the middle of the arena. The seats remained empty and forlorn.

Jess wasn't coming. Tyler would not see her again, and he'd go on living as he had before. Nothing had changed.

Tyler squared his shoulders, gave Adam a nod to indicate he was all right. Adam shot him a skeptical look but finally departed for his designated gate.

The drill team went through their last maneuvers to much applause, and the ring cleared, a tractor whizzing through to rake over the churned-up dirt. Then the announcer excitedly proclaimed that the best Wild West show in Texas was about to begin.

No one came to claim the seats in the box. Tyler checked his equipment one more time—making sure Buster hadn't let out his held breath to loosen the cinch—and prepared for his entrance. He mounted Buster and walked him out of the corral, leading Bobby, wondering why his mouth was as dry as the dust that coated the arena floor.

———

JESS FINALLY FOUND THE BOX in front—
actually, Dominic found it by bringing up a
schematic of the arena complex on Jess's phone.
The stunt show had already begun by the time
they entered—she'd heard the announcer's voice
soar, the thump of music in speakers, the roar of
the crowd.

It had taken them forever to get going this morning—Mrs. Alvarez had had a flat on her way over to
the house and had to wait for a friend to come and
help her fix it. She'd never call for a tow truck or a
road service to help her. That wasn't her way. And
anyway, that likely would have taken longer. Jess
changed her mind six times about what to wear,
finally settling on simple jeans and a short-sleeved
top. She also dragged her feet because she wasn't
sure she should go. Only Dominic's insistence got
her out of the house at all.

What would Tyler do when he saw her there?
Give her a polite nod? Ignore her completely? Jess
had made it clear she wasn't searching for anyone
to take care of her, but he'd looked offended when
she'd said it. She wouldn't mind being friends
with Tyler, but she didn't think he was a man who
wanted to be best friends with a woman. She had
a feeling that with Tyler it would be all or nothing.
She'd told him it would be nothing, so why would
he be happy to see her?

Her throat was tight as she and Dominic, with
Mrs. Alvarez behind them, pushed their way down
toward the ring, and finally dropped into the seats

by the rail. Two men on horseback were rushing around the ring, riding counter to each other, barely missing each other as they passed.

The box was raised from the arena floor enough that they could look over the ring's rail and positioned so they could see every corner. Jess's heart skipped a beat as one of the cowboys rode past, inches from her, the horse's hooves thudding in the dirt. But she realized at once the rider wasn't Tyler.

The announcer confirmed it, blaring over the pulsing music, "Let's give a big Texas welcome to Adam Campbell!"

The crowd cheered as Adam stood in his stirrups and waved, his black duster coat and bandana around his neck flowing as he galloped toward the center of the ring. The moment he passed the center point he threw himself off his horse—then caught himself by the saddle horn before he reached the ground. He hung on to the horse's side for several strides, feet straight out in front of him, before he flowed back up into the saddle.

"Cool!" Dominic cried. "Mom, did you see that?"

Adam continued around the ring while the announcer listed a long string of movies Adam had performed in, to Dominic's delight. He and Jess had seen most of them.

"Sorry ladies, he's taken," the announcer felt the need to say. "Now let's give a big Texas welcome to his brother Grant!"

Grant Campbell suddenly swung around in his saddle until he was riding backwards, waving both hands at the audience. Dominic snapped a picture with Jess's phone as Grant rode by. Grant saw Jess, recognized her, and saluted her before he was gone.

Grant somehow flipped himself around to face forward again, and then he and Adam rode in complicated patterns around each other, while the announcer reeled off Grant's riding awards and the movies and television shows *he'd* been in.

Grant and Adam did a few tricks, vaulting onto and off their horses, jumping from one horse to the other at the same time, or standing up on the saddles before dropping back down. It was breathtaking and scary, but they landed each time without slipping, their movements seemingly effortless.

The crowd and Dominic loved it, but Jess impatiently scanned the gates at either end of the ring. Was Tyler out there somewhere? Would he even be in the show today, considering how hurt he'd gotten last night?

It shouldn't matter, she told herself. Jess had come today to let Dominic have some fun. That was all. Mrs. Alvarez was enjoying it too, clapping and poking Jessica from time to time to say, "How did they do that? Oh, honey, this is fun!"

The music's rollicking beat abruptly took on a darker tone, and the announcer said worriedly, "Uh-oh, boys, looks like trouble heading your way."

The gates at both ends of the arena opened. Through one came a single cowboy, riding low in the saddle, his bandana up to his eyeballs and his black hat pulled down. He crossed his hands and thrust them under his coat to draw out two pistols, which he aimed at Adam and Grant.

Adam and Grant instantly broke apart from where they rode together, each racing to opposite ends of the ring. The new cowboy chased Adam, but Jess could see as he went by, close enough for her to touch, that he wasn't Tyler. It was Carter, with his flash of hazel eyes in a hard face, looking meaner than any real Wild West villain probably ever did.

Dominic loved him, snapping pics as Carter rode by. Jess strained to see who, if anyone, would come through the other gate.

Carter raced past the open gate, not even glancing at it. The instant he was clear, two more horses burst in, running close together, with a lone rider balancing on top of them, one foot on each saddle. His bandana covered his face, and his hat was black, and his long duster coat rippled behind him.

The new cowboy twirled two six-guns that sparkled under the arena lights. Without missing a beat, he rode both his horses at his older brothers, ready to shoot them out of their saddles.

CHAPTER 7

———

JESS KNEW THE MAN WAS Tyler, knew it without a doubt. He had the agile awareness Jess had seen in him at the bar, in tune with every molecule of air around him.

She remembered how he'd dropped and rolled when the fight had started, eluding his attackers, beating a few down so swiftly they were on the ground before they realized they'd been hit.

Tyler rode straight at his brothers, moving with both horses as though he never noticed their uneven rhythm. Grant pulled out his prop gun and shot at Tyler, the boom of the pistol making Jess jump.

Tyler dropped between the two horses instantly, but instead of falling he, as Adam had, grabbed the saddle of one horse and hung off its side. The second horse shielded him from his brothers' shots, Tyler sandwiched between the beasts, the horses running in step without crushing him.

But any second, Tyler could fall and be trampled, or the horses could run into each other, breaking his bones. Jess found her hand going to her mouth, her worry escalating. He'd been hurt last night …

Tyler brought his feet down, using the contact with the ground to send him up into the saddle of the darker horse. Somehow, his pistols had become holstered, because he slid them out again, riding hard at Adam, shooting.

Adam ducked and dodged while the crowd oohed. The gunfight looked very real, except miraculously, no bullets touched the horses or the brothers, and the horses didn't try to bolt.

The announcer kept up a running commentary about Carter and Tyler, the "bad guys" though he called them the "Sutherland Boys." He told the audience all about the horrible deeds they'd done, the homesteads they'd burned, the women they'd stolen, the men they'd robbed and killed. All part of the show, but Tyler and especially Carter looked the part. Tyler shook his fist or shot his gun every time the announcer revealed some of his villainy, to the delight of the crowd.

Dominic ate it up. "Which one did you meet, Mom? Which one's Tyler?" Jess pointed him out, and Dominic said, "Cool!" and clicked photos of him.

The four men rode around one another, dodging bullets and each other by jumping off horses and springing back on, exchanging mounts, or grabbing the second horse Tyler had brought in and doing acrobatics on it. The horses were amazingly docile but kept up their pace with spirit.

While all the brothers seemed to defy gravity, Tyler had a lightness that went beyond that. He'd cartwheel over a horse on one hand, land precisely on his feet, and be out of the way of another running horse in the next instant.

Jess bit back a scream as Tyler dove off a horse, right in front of Grant's oncoming mount. He rolled away from the horse's hooves a second before he would have been trampled. Instead of lying there, catching his breath, Tyler sprang to his feet, vaulted onto the back of Adam's horse as it skimmed past, and started fighting Adam in the saddle.

Music escalated as the show wound to its climax, a thumping beat that caught Jess and pulsed under her skin. Adam managed to push Tyler off his horse, Tyler landing in time to catch the saddle of one of his own horses and land on its back. The prop guns blazed, smoke filling the air. Carter at last was down, lying forward, limp, on his horse's neck as the animal raced around the ring.

The two "good guys" closed in on Tyler. Jess held her breath as Tyler wove in and out between them, ducked behind his own horse, jumping onto his second horse, and finally rising to balance on both horses at once again. Tyler's feet were steady as his horses ran at Adam and Grant.

It was his last stand. Adam and Grant rode straight for Tyler, a bizarre game of chicken on horseback. Just before they met, Tyler's horses split apart under him. Jessica gasped as Tyler went down, but at the last minute, he pulled himself up onto one horse, resting easily in the saddle.

This allowed Grant to shoot him point blank. Tyler threw up his arms as blood burst out of his back and smeared itself on his chest. Jess found herself on her feet, a cry escaping her throat. The blood looked all too real. She squeezed the rail until her knuckles ached.

Tyler collapsed, throwing his arms out dramatically as he fell backward onto his horse's rump. He lay there, staring up at the arena's ceiling as the horse went around. Finally, Tyler slid all the way off the horse and landed in an unmoving heap on the arena floor.

Grant blew smoke from his pistol, twirled it on his thumb, and thrust it into his holster, raising his fist at the crowd as they cheered.

"And that was the end of the Sutherland Boys," the announcer said in triumph.

Jess did not like how still Tyler lay in the dirt. The cooling system sent a breeze wafting down that stirred the dust and tails of Tyler's coat. She remembered how he'd lain in the parking lot while Elijah's men beat and kicked him, remembered her fear for his life. Elijah had kicked him pretty hard— if Tyler had been bleeding internally since then …

Grant glanced Tyler's way, his grin vanishing in a frown of concern. He rode to Tyler and dismounted. Jess watched, her hand frozen on the rail, her breath aching in her lungs. Dominic had quieted, and the crowd wound down to mutters.

Adam wheeled his horse and trotted toward Tyler and Grant. Carter continued to play dead, lolling on his horse, which wove this way and that.

Grant touched Tyler's shoulder, and Adam bent from the saddle to watch.

Quicker than thought, Tyler rocked forward on his hands and pushed off the ground to flip to his feet. He spun and delivered Grant a roundhouse punch on the jaw.

Grant's head snapped back, and he threw up his arms and went down. Carter suddenly came to life, rode at Adam and shot him out of the saddle. Adam landed hard to a collective *"Oh"* of the crowd.

"Whoa there!" The announcer yelled. "I told you those Sutherland Boys were mean ones. Someone needs to stop them!"

The someones turned out to be small children on ponies. They raced in from the far gate, about a dozen boys and girls, who surrounded Carter and Tyler, their adorable ponies hemming them in. The audience laughed and cheered.

Carter and Tyler ended up on their knees, surrendering to the kids. Adam and Grant rose and made their way over, encouraging the crowd to applaud their rescuers.

"A big hand for the courageous Dallas Pony Riders!" While the arena went crazy, the announcer continued that the Dallas Pony Riders was a charitable organization for underprivileged kids, supported by large donations from the Circle C Ranch in Riverbend, Texas.

The kids waved and rode out again. The brothers lined up in the middle of the ring and took their bows to screams and whoops—the happy screams were mostly female ones. Jess didn't blame the ladies for going crazy for the four hot cowboys as they bowed with lithe ease. If they could move like that on horseback, the ladies must be speculating, what would they be like in bed?

Jess knew, at least in Tyler's case, and the knowledge was a nugget of warmth in her heart.

The brothers broke apart, each catching a horse. They swung aboard and rode around the ring once more, doing various acrobatics along the way.

Tyler headed for Jess. Jessica couldn't move, pinned in place by blue eyes over his bandana as

Tyler homed in on her. The dark horse he rode strode smoothly, as though it hadn't been galloping constantly for the better part of an hour.

Tyler turned the horse at the last minute and halted against the rail. His dusty jeans and boots were at Jess's eye level, his foot firmly in the stirrup.

Staying in character, Tyler pushed back his black hat with the tip of his pistol, and said, "Ma'am."

Jess tried to answer but nothing would come out of her dry mouth. She stood there like a fool while Dominic raised her phone and snapped a picture of Tyler, the fake blood still wet on his shirt.

Tyler shifted his gaze to Dominic, tugged down his bandana to reveal his handsome face, and winked at him. Tyler's bruises had faded, only a purpling around his jaw and left eye to say he'd been hurt the night before.

Tyler took off his hat, flipped it down his arm, and set it gently on Dominic's head. Jess dimly felt Mrs. Alvarez come up beside her, saw the interested crowd craning to look. Jess's world narrowed to Tyler smiling at her son then turning to wink at *her*.

His grin widened as Jess flushed. Without a word, Tyler swung his horse around and raced after his brothers, who were disappearing out of the gate, Carter leading the extra horse. Tyler waved behind him to more cheering, then he rode out the gate and was gone.

The music eased down to a distant thumping, and the crowd, released, started to drift away, either leaving for the day or taking a break before the next event. Jess remained at the rail, frozen in place from the dazzling smile Tyler had sent her.

He hadn't worn the look of a man bored with a woman because he'd gotten what he wanted, or annoyed that she'd pushed him away. He looked more like … Well, Jess wasn't sure what. She also wasn't certain what to do now.

Before she could suggest they go home, Dominic said, "Can I meet him? Come on, Mom, please?"

Mrs. Alvarez was clearing their seats, picking up the miniature motorcycles Dominic insisted on carrying around with him and Jess's purse. Jess expected her to gently but firmly quash Dominic's hopes, but Mrs. Alvarez said briskly, "I don't see why not. You need to be careful around the horses—both of you."

Jess stopped herself saying, "Yes, ma'am." Dominic nodded, holding Tyler's big hat on his head as though fearing someone would take it from him.

Jess rescued her phone and let Mrs. Alvarez shepherd them out of the box and into the flow of people leaving the stands.

They made their way to the end of the indoor arena where Tyler had ridden out of the gate, and went outside, but Jess didn't know where he would go after that. The corrals and stables for the horses and cattle were separate from the arena, and she imagined no one would let people randomly walk among the animals.

The problem was solved when she spied Tyler lounging at a temporary fence that separated the arena from the parking area for horse trailers and RVs. Whether he waited for her specifically, Jess couldn't tell. He was signing autographs and posing for pictures with kids and excited young women.

One woman insisted her friend take a picture of

her kissing Tyler's cheek. Tyler agreed, the knock-out smile he gave both women tearing a hole in Jessica's heart.

Why do I care? Jess wondered, irritated with herself. *We're not dating, engaged, married, or in any kind of relationship at all. We were two people passing in the night.*

Even so, something burned in her chest as the woman's friend turned to Jess as she approached and said, "Hey, will you take a picture of both of us with him?"

Tyler's face reddened, but the showman in him didn't fade. Jess awkwardly took the woman's phone while the two ladies rose on tiptoe on either side of Tyler, their lips on his cheeks. Tyler's face went redder still, but he draped his arms around their shoulders and flashed a smile for the camera.

Jess clicked the photo then another for good measure. She calmly handed the phone back to the woman, nodding when both ladies thanked her.

If Jess had slightly jerked the phone on both pictures, and they came out blurry, that couldn't be helped. Her hand shook like that sometimes.

The ladies strolled away, moving slowly, as though hoping Tyler would call them back. But they couldn't compete with Dominic, who ran straight to Tyler, questions tumbling from his lips.

"Can I take a picture with you? How do you fall off like that and not get hurt? Do you want your hat back?" The last was said with a falter.

Tyler bent down to Dominic's height. "The hat's yours, son. Come over here and let your mom take a picture of us."

Jess's hand shook again as she raised her phone,

but this time, she did her best to still it. Tyler crouched next to her son and they both beamed at the camera. Dominic had never looked so happy.

Tyler straightened up when the photo was done. He focused his blue eyes on Jess, not flicking his gaze away in spite of Mrs. Alvarez hovering behind her.

"Our next show isn't until tonight," he said. "We're going to grab lunch once the horses are taken care of. Want to come?"

They were magic words to Dominic. Dominic didn't answer, but he squeezed his fists tight and mouthed, *Please, Mom?*

"Go to lunch where?" Mrs. Alvarez asked. "Dominic's not going to a cowboy dive or a run-down greasy spoon."

Tyler's nod was respectful. "No, ma'am. It's a local barbecue place. Lanny D's. We always go there when we're in Dallas."

"Oh, Mom, I love Lanny D's!" Dominic had been there once, for a friend's birthday party.

"That sounds all right," Mrs. Alvarez said. "We'll meet you there."

Jess and Tyler exchanged glances, Tyler's eyes holding amusement.

"All right then," he said. "Meet you in an hour. You're Mrs. Alvarez, I take it?"

"I am indeed." Mrs. Alvarez bent Tyler a severe look. "We will see you *later.*"

Tyler's lips twitched, but he only nodded and held out his hand to shake Dominic's. Jessica then ushered the excited Dominic, who was keeping the hat steady, after Mrs. Alvarez, turning back toward Tyler.

She realized, as she sent him a good-bye smile, that Dominic and Mrs. Alvarez had done all the talking during their encounter. Jess and Tyler hadn't exchanged a word.

———

TYLER WAS THE LAST TO reach the restaurant. Buster had decided to be a pain in the ass, kicking up a fuss—literally—to being tied, groomed, fed, watered, whatever. He was such a fucking prima donna. On every trip one brother was given the responsibility of Buster, and this time, Tyler had drawn the short straw.

Then Tyler had to get rid of his shirt stained with blood that came out of the packs Adam had taped to his back and chest before the show—a remote held by one of their assistants outside the ring triggered the bursts of blood at the appropriate moments. Now Tyler rushed to the horse trailer they used as a dressing room and dug around for a clean button-down shirt, changing his dust-coated jeans as well.

By the time Tyler made it to Lanny D's, the place was packed. It was Sunday, the day families went to church, to the rodeo, and to lunch at Lanny D's. Tyler scanned the restaurant, hoping the crowd hadn't made his brothers give up and go elsewhere. He let out a breath of relief when he saw Adam's dark head over the mob, and next to him, Jessica.

They were sitting at a table against the far wall, so Tyler had to pick his way over, dodging kids, waitresses, and customers coming and going. Mrs. Alvarez, the dark-haired woman of about fifty, sat close on Jess's right, while Adam squashed in on her left. Dominic sat between Grant and Carter across the table, Dominic's mouth moving as he talked animatedly.

Tyler ducked around a waiter with a heavily laden tray and reached the table, to find there was no room for him. Six chairs surrounded two smaller tables pulled together, with only a tiny space between those tables' ends and the crammed-full ones on either side. Tyler's daydream of snuggling up close to Jess crumbled and died.

His brothers had obviously become friends with her already. He could tell by Jess's easy smile at whatever Adam was saying, and by the way Grant listened with interest to Dominic's chatter. Carter's shoulders were relaxed, his suspicious tension of last night gone. Mrs. Alvarez had joined the conversation with Grant and Dominic, her look that of a woman enjoying a chat.

Tyler had to stand at the corner of the table for five minutes before anyone noticed him. No good shouting at them—he couldn't hear a damn thing over this noise.

Mrs. Alvarez finally spied Tyler and called, "Someone get Mr. Campbell a seat!"

Jess rose about an inch then sank down, sending Tyler a rueful look. She couldn't budge. Grant started up, but Mrs. Alvarez had already taken charge.

"Are you using that chair?" she yelled to the people at the next table, a mix of women and men in a huddle so they could hear each other. Mrs. Alvarez pointed to an empty seat on their far side.

One of the guys waved. "No, go ahead." Tyler couldn't actually hear his words, but that's what the man's mouth said.

Tyler grabbed the chair with a nod of thanks. He turned it around, fitting it at the corner next to Grant. Mrs. Alvarez wasn't about to move and let Tyler sit next to Jess, and by the looks of things, neither was Adam.

The brothers glanced at Tyler indulgently as they'd done when he and Ross had been the littlest Campbells, stuck at the baby table during holiday dinners. Tyler was twenty-seven now and still his brothers could make him feel like an afterthought. The only reason they didn't treat Ross, even younger than Tyler, like that was because Ross was usually armed.

They'd already ordered, of course. Tyler didn't need a menu since he ate the same thing every time he came here, but he had to wait until the server happened by to refill everyone's iced teas before asking for something to eat and drink. Normally he'd smile flirtatiously at the waitress so she'd hurry back, but today, not only didn't he want to do something like that in front of Jess, their server wasn't a woman but a burly young man with a sour look on his face.

Once the server had shuffled away, Tyler strained to hear the conversations around him. Whatever Adam and Jess were talking about, Carter putting a word in every once in a while, was lost in the roar. Grant had his head turned to listen to Dominic, which left Tyler with the dragon, Mrs. Alvarez.

"Carter says his wife is about to have a baby," Mrs. Alvarez said loudly. "His second. He has a little girl already, right? Grant and Adam are new fathers, they say." Tyler nodded. Adam's son and

Grant's little girl were already in danger of being the most spoiled rotten pair in River County, but they'd be rivaled by Carter's baby when it came. Faith, Carter's daughter, doted on the cousins like a mother hen. Faith was crazy excited about Carter's upcoming kid, looking forward to having a brother or sister of her own.

"What about you?" Mrs. Alvarez demanded. "Do you have any children? Are you married?"

The woman didn't pull any punches. She eyed Tyler with sharp assessment as Tyler answered.

"Never married. No kids."

"Why not?" Mrs. Alvarez's dark eyes were shrewd. She'd seen plenty of the world, those eyes said.

Tyler shrugged, struggling a little more with the truth. "Right one never came along?"

Mrs. Alvarez looked him up and down. Tyler could follow her thoughts—here was a healthy man, young but not too young, with a well-off family and a job, if you could call jumping onto horses and falling off them a job. The business was lucrative, anyway, and Tyler got his cut. So why was he single? Tyler should have married a girl from the next ranch and settled down by now.

It was more complicated than that, but Tyler wasn't about to yell his life story to Mrs. Alvarez over the crowd at Lanny D's.

"Girlfriend?" the dragon went on.

"Not at the moment," Tyler admitted. This was certainly true. Tyler's relationships never lasted long. A few months was his record.

Mrs. Alvarez firmed her mouth as though she could read his thoughts. Tyler couldn't blame her for being suspicious. In a way, he was glad she was so protective of Jessica.

Tyler wanted to ask Mrs. Alvarez all about Jess, picking her brain about Jess's life, but the noise level in the restaurant only increased. Finally it became impossible to talk at all, and Mrs. Alvarez went back to watching Dominic.

Adam had no problem leaning down to speak into Jess's ear—whatever he said had her laughing. Tyler hoped Adam wasn't telling her hilarious and embarrassing stories about him.

The food came for everyone else, and Tyler had to watch while they ate. Jess shot him a glance and pointed to her fries, offering to share, but Tyler shook his head.

Much more fun if he'd been sitting beside her while she fed the fries to him. He imagined her fingers at his lips, wiping off the clinging salt. He'd kiss her fingertips, maybe nipping one.

The vision made the noisy barbecue house abruptly fall away, until only Tyler and Jess existed. Together, alone, she looking at him in the sultry way she'd done when they'd finished making love the first time. She'd watch him nip her finger, then she'd take his hand and slide it down the front of her shirt while she leaned to him and kissed his lips, tasting of salt and Jess …

A kid shrieked behind him, slicing through Tyler's thoughts. The boy was in a highchair not far away, bouncing, laughing, screeching—another person having fun while Tyler ate his heart out.

Jess lifted a fry and took a dainty bite. Tyler grabbed his iced tea and gulped it down to halt his hardening cock. He longed for a beer, but the brothers had a rule that they always went into the ring sober. Their trick riding depended on balance and timing—if one thing was off, they'd be heading to the ER, or worse.

The waiter jostled Tyler's arm as he dumped Tyler's barbecued beef sandwich in front of him. Tea sloshed into Tyler's face, and he started to cough, grabbing a napkin to mop up.

Jess flashed him a look. Her face was pink, her mouth bunched up as though trying politely to hold in her amusement, but the next second, she gave up and let out a laugh.

She was lovely when she laughed. Tyler couldn't hear her over the chaos but her face lit up and her dark eyes sparkled. Gone was any tension in her face, any tightness.

Again, the restaurant fell away, and he and Jess were the only two people in the world. She'd laugh at him as she pulled him closer. Tyler would lift her shirt and lean down to lick the path of her tatts. He swore he felt Jess's fingertips on his face, her breath on his skin, her heartbeat under his lips.

Something clattered then smashed. Tyler jerked out of his daze and realized the others had finished their meal. The waiter had been grabbing up the dirty plates and dropped one.

While other servers came out of the woodwork and helped him clean up, Adam and Carter gallantly assisting, Tyler bolted his sandwich, trying not to choke on it. He wiped his mouth on the last bite, and the waiter snatched the plate out from under him. The guy hadn't been this attentive when Tyler had sat down.

Now everyone was leaving. Time to get back to the arena and prep for the evening show.

Tyler was cut off from Jess as they pushed their way out of the restaurant. He'd never realized his brothers were so damned big, but they blocked his way every direction he turned. They didn't do it on purpose—they were just natural obstacles.

Not until he burst into the sunny parking lot was Tyler able to sidestep around Carter and reach Jess.

"Can I talk to you a minute?" he asked.

CHAPTER 8

JESS AT LEAST TURNED BACK to Tyler, flushing a little as she waited for him. Tyler knew he
was about to embarrass her, but there was no use
hoping for a fortuitous moment or a second alone
with her—Tyler knew that wouldn't happen with
his luck.

Dominic headed for them. Mrs. Alvarez, with
canny perception, caught his hand. "Let's go see
the Campbells' truck."

Dominic pivoted and trotted readily away with
her, following Adam. This finally left Tyler alone
with Jess—that is, alone with half of Dallas who'd
decided to come to Lanny D's today.

"Your ticket will let you into the second show,"
Tyler said, stammering over the words. *Smooth.
Real smooth.*

He knew as soon as Jess dropped her gaze that
she wasn't staying, and something churned in his
gut. "Dominic has school tomorrow," she said.
"Summer is over—it starts this week. He can't be
out too late."

"Yeah." Tyler couldn't tell a mom to blow off her
son getting a good night's sleep before school. Car-

ter had all kinds of rules for Faith that he wouldn't let anyone break.

Tyler cleared his throat and adjusted his hat—a backup for the backup he'd given Dominic. "Maybe after the show, you and I could—"

Jess was already shaking her head. "Mrs. Alvarez doesn't babysit on Sundays. She came with us today for the fun of it, not to work."

"Okay, then." How pushy could Tyler let himself be? A hell of a lot more than this, he decided, if it meant not saying farewell to Jessica forever. "I could stop by after the show, just to say good-bye. Tonight's our last night in Dallas."

Her eyes flickered, pain flaring before she hid it from him. "Dominic would be too excited to sleep if you came over. Like I said, he has school tomorrow."

Damn it, why was Tyler trying so hard? Jess obviously wanted him to walk away, so why wasn't he walking away?

Because she was worth the fight. Worth anything he had to do.

"You still have the card I gave you, right?" When Jess nodded, Tyler drew on his courage. "I wasn't kidding when I said you could call. You call anytime. Next weekend, I don't have any shows. Riverbend is only four hours away. Easy for me to drive up here—"

"I have to work." Not a lie, but again, Jess was grabbing at an excuse.

Tyler's stomach turned over again, and he knew it wasn't because of the barbecued beef he'd eaten too rapidly. "So tell me when you're not working, and I'll come. Anyway, you need to get yourself out of that dive. It won't do Dominic any good if you get hurt there."

Oops. Tyler, who had the right line for every woman on every occasion, had just managed to say exactly the wrong thing. Jess's head came up, defiance sparkling in her eyes.

"I told you, it's fine," she snapped. "It's the best I can do for now. And it's none of your business."

Tyler raised his hands and took a step back. "Okay. Excuse me for caring."

Jess's face was dark red. "Thank you for the tickets. It was fun. Dominic! Let's go."

She was going to walk away. Out of his life. Gone, like she'd never been there. The emptiness that kicked through him not only hurt but scared him to death.

Tyler caught her arm. At first Jess resisted, then she relaxed and let him pull her close to him. "Promise you'll call me. If you need help, if you need *anything*. Please, Jess."

Tyler Campbell never pleaded, not with women. He loved them and walked away. But, this was different.

Jess's chest lifted in a sharp breath. Tyler stilled until Jess gave him a barely perceptible nod.

Tyler exhaled in some relief. Now he should release her, suck it up, and walk away.

Instead, he laced his hand behind her head and pulled her to him for one hard kiss. Jess started beneath him, then she did what she'd done last night—gave into the feeling and kissed him readily in return.

Her mouth was heat, spice, the sweetness of Jess. Tyler slowed the kiss, savoring her as long as he could, while Jess held on to him as though the crowds that swept by didn't exist. Hot wind swirled around them, the sun pounded down, and the blast of voices pushed at them.

None of it mattered. Jess was his for the moment, still under his touch, her kiss the best thing that had happened to him in a long time.

When Tyler finally eased away, he and Jess simply looked at each other, too much between them for words.

And yet, there wasn't enough. Tyler would never have enough of Jess McFadden.

Jess slid from his embrace, gave him a look that held tears, and walked away, hurrying to join Dominic and Mrs. Alvarez. Tyler watched her go, her legs in form-hugging jeans something he'd dream about in the lonely nights.

But this wasn't over. Tyler had pissed her off, pushing her too hard—he would learn how to talk to her. He wouldn't give up, not by a long way, until he saw Jess again, and made her give him a chance to coax her into his life.

MONDAY MORNING AFTER A SHOW meant letting the horses who'd performed rest—light exercise, nothing more. The brothers didn't get to rest though, Tyler thought grumpily. Ranch work went on, plus they had their post-show meeting.

They gathered at the dining room table, the only place big enough for all Campbell brothers to sit with their notebooks and charts, plus food and drink. Adam and Carter were in full swing by mid-morning, discussing what had gone right and gone wrong in the show, Grant joking around as usual. Tyler doodled on the piece of paper in front of him and thought about Jess.

He'd had plenty of show fucks in his life. Once that weekend was over, Tyler would retain fond memories of the fun, but he moved on. He focused on horses and helped run the ranch. He didn't draw loops that reminded him of Jess's tatts and daydream about her like a teenager.

But as he kept telling himself, Jess was different. She wasn't like the women who followed the rodeos, looking for a cowboy and another notch on her bedpost.

Jess's surrender had been honest, an opening up that had startled him. She hadn't held back, giving all of herself. He could still feel her beneath him, relive every thrust, every touch of her hands, every taste of her. She'd been incredible.

Then when he'd suggested they continue what they'd started, Jess had closed up and shut him out. No woman had ever done that to Tyler. He and his show lay would either part in mutual agreement, or Tyler eased himself out, letting the woman down as gently as he could.

He should take the hint, walk away, never look back. Dallas was a big city—too damned big in his opinion. He'd never seen Jess before when he'd gone up there, and if he didn't seek her out, he probably never would again. Cities swallowed people, made them anonymous.

Tyler drew another curl, like the one that encircled her nipple.

"And we'll finish by blowing up Tyler's head,"

Grant said. "Or maybe his balls."

Tyler blinked. He realized he'd been drawing on their show schedule for the next year, blotting out all of September. "What?"

His brothers were staring at him. Grant waved a big hand in front of Tyler's face. "Oh, good, he's still in there."

"I think he's still in Dallas," Adam said. "With a pretty bartender."

"She's nice," Carter said, which was high praise from the taciturn man. "But trouble," he went on. "Lots of baggage. Watch yourself."

"What's wrong, Tyler?" Grant said as Tyler scowled. "She give you the boot?"

"I barely know the woman," Tyler growled. "I just thought her kid would like the show."

Grant shook his head. "Yeah, that's why you took her to your hotel room, I get it. To convince her to bring Dominic to the show."

"So she *did* give him the shove," Adam said with sympathy.

Grant suddenly became serious. "Don't take no for an answer, little brother," he said. "Go back next weekend and try again. You gotta let a woman know you want her."

They all watched Tyler, Carter with caution, Adam with some understanding.

"Like you did with Christina?" Tyler said to Grant. "Yeah, you two had a relationship we all want to model."

"I know," Grant said without offense. "This is how I learned. Take it from me. Be up front with what you want—don't let Jess walk away because of a misunderstanding."

"There wasn't a misunderstanding," Tyler snapped. "You have to have a conversation for a misunderstanding. I couldn't get next to her at the damned restaurant to say two words to her."

"Meaning the night before you didn't have a conversation either?" Grant asked, eyes twinkling. "What were you doing all that time in your room?"

"Not saying two words," Adam said, then let out his deep laughter. Carter unbent to chuckle with him.

Tyler's brothers' amusement and knowing looks irritated the hell out of him. They did this all the time, teased Tyler about his women. He remembered the day they'd started, about five years ago now, and he'd actually been grateful that they'd quit tiptoeing around him.

But now it was about Jess, and it pissed him off.

"You know what?" Tyler pushed aside his doodles and got to his feet. "Screw you guys. When you want to talk about work, come and find me."

He stalked out. Grant said, *Ooo,* and Adam chortled.

Whatever. Assholes. It was like being in high school again. Worse. Now his brothers had suffered through life and weren't just being ignorant and young.

Tyler slammed out of the house. From the front porch, the view over the ranch, with hills that ran to the horizon under the blue sky, almost soothed him. Almost. He looked over at the barn, which was teeming with ranch hands and horses. Circle C was a working ranch, which meant they never stopped working.

Horses filled every stall in the barn and the mare

pens outside it. One of the corrals held a couple horses, old friends, one a mare who'd just foaled. The foal, a little filly, was adorable with her wobbly long legs and tiny face. She didn't like her mother to be too far from her, but she was wide-eyed and curious. Dominic would love her.

Damn it.

Even the arch of sky, soft air, far cooler than the August pall in Dallas, failed to ease him. Tyler marched along the porch that stretched the full length of the house and in again through the kitchen door. He'd grab a cold drink and head to the office or maybe help turn out the horses due for corral time.

The kitchen wasn't deserted. Grace Malory—no, Grace Sullivan—her belly protruding with Carter's coming baby, puttered between refrigerator, stove, and counter, cooking something that smelled awesome. Savory and spicy, just what Tyler liked. His mouth watered.

Grace turned as Tyler stormed in, her smile a bit tired but welcoming. "Try this," she said without greeting.

She shoved a spoonful of something meaty and flavorful into his mouth. Tyler chewed, tasting beef and sauce, with spices that made his eyes water.

"Damn, that's good," he said when he could speak. "You should have married Carter a long time ago."

"So it's not too much? Too spicy? Does it need more oregano?"

Tyler had only a vague idea of what oregano was so he shook his head. "It's perfect. I'll eat that."

He started for the stove, where a pot of whatever

it was he'd tasted bubbled. Grace stepped in front of him before he could get far—she could move fast for a pregnant woman.

"Don't even think about it." She glared. "It's the enchilada filling for dinner. I'd like to have enough to actually put into the enchiladas."

"Fine, fine." Tyler surrendered. Grace was one hell of a cook, had been ready to go pro at one time, and was once more putting together plans to open a restaurant here in Riverbend. But woe to anyone who got in her way. "I'll just grab a glass of water." Tyler fetched a glass from the cupboard and filled up from the RO faucet on the sink. Unfiltered Texas water was best left for washing dishes.

"So, are you going to see her again?"

Tyler nearly choked. Grace stood next to him, spoon in her hand and a steely look in her eye.

Tyler had known Grace Malory all his life—they'd been in the same grade in school. She had dark hair and green eyes and the Malory good looks, but Tyler had never had a chance with her. Her heart had always belonged to Carter.

Any of Tyler's suggestions that he and Grace go out once they were in high school had been met with a polite rebuff. Tyler had finally stepped aside, telling himself the good girl thing wasn't for him.

Carter had sure lucked out though. Grace was pretty, sweet, *and* she could cook.

She also had a will of iron. Tyler wasn't getting out of here without answering the question.

He shrugged. "It was a one-time thing, honey. You know how it is with me."

Grace's frown deepened. "Don't *honey* me. Carter told me all about Jessica. You've never brought any of your conquests—not to mention her son and her son's babysitter—to a family lunch. Who is she, and are you going to see her again?"

Tyler loved his family, especially his sisters-in-law, but shit, their prying could drive a man crazy.

"She doesn't want to see me again," he growled, and was again startled at how empty that made him feel. "My brothers probably scared her off. You should be asking *them* about her."

He made to storm out, but Grace got in his way. He couldn't exactly shove aside the woman carrying his niece or nephew—they'd decided to have it be a surprise—so he stopped, waiting for her to let him pass.

"Don't get all grouchy," Grace said. "Carter says she's *nice*. But also that she has a lot of troubles. It's likely she doesn't want you caught in them. So, what are you going to do?"

Tyler made himself not snarl. "I thought maybe I'd leave her alone and mind my own business."

That was definitely *not* what he would do, but his family didn't need to be in on every detail. He'd already discussed things with a friend of Carter's and put a few plans in motion.

Grace gave him a sisterly look. "We worry about you, Tyler. That's all."

Of course they did. Had since he'd been eighteen and nearly gone off the deep end at Lindsey's death, out of his mind with grief and guilt. His whole family had clubbed together to look after him, fearing the worst.

Tyler had wanted to tell them they had nothing to worry about—he wasn't self-destructive. That would be too easy. He also knew that a life for a life was no answer. He had to suck it up.

Except he hadn't been able to tell his brothers and mom that because he couldn't talk about it. Literally. When he tried, his lips would stiffen until they wouldn't move, and his tongue had lain like lead in his mouth.

Tyler knew his family cared, and way in the back of his mind, he appreciated it. The front of his mind had mostly gotten drunk.

He'd gone on, day by day, getting involved in the ranch and the running of it. Horses were used in therapy by some psychologists, and Tyler could attest that hanging around the animals worked. Horses didn't judge you—well, except for Buster—and they didn't ask you twenty times a day if you were all right. They accepted you as you were and didn't fret about existential stuff.

Tyler had slowly regained his equilibrium. He'd started dating again a few years later, and the family had held their breaths. He knew they'd hoped he'd find a woman, settle down with her, and forget.

Didn't work like that. Tyler hadn't wanted to get close to anyone, not anytime soon. The wound still smarted. He never wanted to face that grief again.

And now, Jess …

Jess was special. Grace understood that without even meeting her.

Special because she wanted nothing to do with Tyler at all? Or maybe because, from what he saw in her eyes, she understood pain?

No—Tyler had gone out with lots of women who played hard to get, and plenty of people understood pain. There was an unfortunate amount of it in the world. Neither one was the reason Tyler had fixed on Jess.

Maybe it was because she'd been soft under his body, her kisses igniting him. Or maybe the way she'd run her hand down his back, pulling him against her, her eyes darkening in passion. Or the honesty of her release, the utter joy of feeling every second of it.

There was something real about Jess. She didn't layer on a ton of makeup to hide the tiniest wrinkle, or slide into clothes way too tight and pretend to be the life of the party. Jess hadn't had a goal that night. She'd just been living her life. Tyler had been living his, as weird as it was, and they'd ... connected.

Grace's worried look had relaxed, and Tyler blinked himself back to the present.

"Call her," Grace said. "I dare you. You might be surprised."

Such sage advice. Tyler realized two things—one, he agreed with Grace, and two, he didn't have Jess's phone number.

But he knew where she lived and knew where she worked. That was something.

Tyler caught a startled Grace by the shoulders and gave her a firm kiss on the cheek. "You're a sweetheart, Grace. You should have held out for me instead of Carter. I'm so much better looking."

He knew damn well Carter had entered the kitchen, stopping just inside the door. Grace glanced at her husband and took on a look of radiant happiness.

"That's what *you* think," she said to Tyler.

"Tyler, quit kissing my wife and go do something useful." Carter headed for Grace, ready to barrel Tyler out of the way.

Tyler gave him the finger as he moved past Grace to the back door. He turned to give Carter a parting shot, but the words died when he saw Carter reach Grace.

He watched from the doorway as Carter rested his hands on Grace's belly and sank into her. Things were awkward with Grace's rotundness, but that only changed the picture from lovers to a family.

Tyler left them to it, a hollowness in his heart. He was glad that Carter, a seriously damaged man, had found so much happiness. But their joy reminded Tyler of his own loneliness.

Up until this weekend, he'd been able to banish that loneliness. Now, it reared its ugly head and bit him like Buster.

JESS TRIED TO GET BACK to normal, and quickly realized "normal" pretty much sucked. Her first night back at the bar, Elijah and his boys didn't show up at all. Neither did Tyler.

Jess spent that night staring at the stool where Tyler had sat and first caught her eye, not liking how empty it looked. She imagined he was at home now with his brothers, or maybe at his local bar, flirting with the ladies there.

Jess's heart burned at the thought, and she turned away to scrub out glasses with unneeded viciousness.

Dominic went to school and Jess picked him up afterward. He was excited about the first week but grew restive as the days went on, wanting to ride his bike as often as he could. Mrs. Alvarez arrived every day after Dominic got home, and Jess went to work. Over and over again.

Jess treasured her time with Dominic, but the rest of her life was hard. She was never caught up with money—something always went wrong as soon as she had an extra dollar or two.

She knew Tyler had a point about her working here, but Jess's point was valid as well. It wasn't easy to simply march out and demand any job she wanted. She was a good bartender, but not all bars were equal. Some paid crap. Some wouldn't even consider hiring her, because of her occasional shakiness. Not every bar or restaurant had good insurance, and Jess needed that, both for herself and Dominic.

This bar's owner provided decent health coverage that didn't take too much out of her paycheck, and she made tips. If Jess changed jobs, it would mean starting all over again, and she'd either be denied coverage altogether or her premiums would be through the roof.

Jess went through the motions, working night after night among dangerous men who kept their hands off her only because they'd have to answer to Elijah or her ex. She served drinks, kept her head down, and went home to Dominic.

One day, maybe, she'd save enough, and she and Dominic would get a place of their own. Then she could stop.

Dominic might be an old man by that time, married with kids and grandkids, and probably taking care of *her*. But whatever. At least, no matter what else happened in her life, she had Dominic.

As the days went by, Jess's gaze strayed more

and more to the barstool in the corner, her heart squeezing whenever she saw another man sitting there. Tyler had touched her life, whether she liked it or not. He wouldn't be leaving her thoughts anytime soon, and that was the way of it.

—————

TWO WEEKS LATER, JESS HAD one of her very bad days—her pain levels were high, and she'd been off balance and dropping things, her left hand weakening as it sometimes did. She told Buddy at the bar what was happening so the waitresses could take the drinks without Jess having to lift them. She had workarounds for everything, but it was frustrating to be so slow and clumsy.

Of course, Elijah had to show up tonight. He hadn't been around for two solid weeks. Jess had half hoped he'd moved on, or been arrested, or decided to emigrate to whatever country would let him in.

That would be too good to be true. Unfortunately, his permanent absence would cause her some problems, especially when it came to paying for necessities. The man had her right where he wanted her.

Elijah sidled up to the bar, giving Jess a nod as she automatically poured out his favorite draft beer.

"How you been?" he mumbled in his gravelly voice, broken from too many years of smoke and alcohol. "Doing okay?"

"Fine," Jess responded, pushing the beer to him. If her shaky hand made a bit of foam slosh onto his reaching fingers, oh well.

"You look good." Elijah's light blue eyes moved up and down her as he wiped his hand on his jeans. His gaze settled on the curve of her bosom that showed over her low-cut top. "How's the kid?"

"He's fine." Jess answered more stiffly this time. She didn't like Elijah talking about Dominic, or even saying his name.

"He's a good kid." Elijah took a sip of beer, and Jess shot him a sharp look. Elijah never took much interest in her son.

A group of guys crowded against the other side of the bar—the unassuming biker who'd been nursing a beer there picked it up in annoyance and moved to the pool tables. Jess left Elijah to draw more beers. Her training in complicated drinks was wasted here.

When things quieted down, Jess turned to see that Elijah had moved to the barstool where Tyler had sat. Elijah with his craggy face and grizzled hair, prematurely gray, was a far cry from Tyler's lazy handsomeness.

Jess's heart skipped as she thought of Tyler bracing himself over her, his face softening with passion as he slid inside her. She'd never had better—she never would again.

Did Elijah's smirk mean he'd deliberately taken Tyler's place? Or was he just being his usual shit self?

"We need to talk, Jess," he said casually.

With Elijah, nothing was casual. "What about?"

"Lots of things. You getting any better?"

"No," Jess said in a hard voice. "*Chronic* means no."

"That's too bad. I'd hate to cut you off from what

you need."

Damn it. Elijah always said crap like that when he wanted a favor.

"I'd find a way to get by," Jess said without confidence. Insurance helped, but it didn't pay everything. No one without money was allowed to have anything wrong with them, it seemed.

"Sure, you would," Elijah said. He gave her what passed for a smile. "If you're wondering where I've been, sweetheart, I've been to see Cade."

Jess stopped, her heart thudding. Cade Emmons. Her ex-husband.

His image rose in her mind—trim, handsome, with a goatee beard and dark hair that curled back naturally from his forehead. When she'd first met Cade, Jess had been bowled over by how good-looking he was, how take-charge. He didn't have the muscular bulk of Elijah and other bikers, but he had strength and a forbidding air that had attracted her in her innocence. Jess had been just eighteen, with a dad more interested in his new family in Houston than in her, and a mom who worked too hard to pay attention. Jess had been reaching for someone who would tell her what to do in a bewildering world, and Cade had been there.

She'd realized her mistake too late. By the time Jess had discovered that Cade was a womanizing, brutal bully, her mother had moved to Wyoming with a new husband, and Jess was left on her own to take care of a child and figure out life.

Though they'd already been divorced when he'd gone to prison, with a restraining order on Cade, Jess had only felt a modicum of safety once

Cade was behind bars. The prison was in El Paso, a day's drive, but that was not far enough, Jess always thought. She wondered if she could convince the prison system to transfer him to Alaska or some other satisfyingly remote place.

"Oh?" Jess said, as Elijah waited for a response. "Did you have a good trip?"

"Don't try to be funny." Elijah rested his tattooed fingers on the bar. "He's looking forward to seeing you again."

Tendrils of cold brushed Jess's spine. "He's serving a ten-year stretch for being a violent criminal," she said, more to reassure herself than anything else. "And he keeps getting into fights, from what I hear."

"Not lately." Elijah looked triumphant. "The parole board reviewed his case again, and finally decided in his favor. They're letting him out next week. And you, Jess, are going with me to pick him up."

CHAPTER 9

———

JESSICA WASN'T SURE HOW SHE got out of
the bar, but she dropped the cloth she'd picked
up and fled, dodging and patrons and tables until
she was outside in the parking lot, pacing in the
night's heat.

Elijah strolled out after her, taking his time. He
leaned against a motorcycle parked there, not his
own, and lit a cigarette. Jess saw another biker
who'd also come out for a smoke halfway across
the lot but she didn't much care if Elijah's friends
heard her.

Elijah's cigarette end glowed orange. Jess faced
him, rage cutting through her fear.

"This wasn't the deal. The deal is, I don't have to
see Cade ever again. And in return—"

"In return you do me favors. This is one. Me and
his lawyer convinced the parole board that you
wanted your husband back, especially so his son
could see his daddy. You come with me to pick
him up, to keep up the picture that you want him
back. Got it?"

Parole boards in Texas didn't always meet in person—they reviewed the files and made decisions

in a short meeting over the phone. No dramatic parole hearing scenes where she could plead for them to not let Cade out. They'd met several times, denying him parole each time, and Jess had assumed he had no hope.

"You lied, you mean." Jessica slammed her arms over her chest, deliberately not coughing at the stream of smoke Elijah blew into her face. "Forget it. Cade is dangerous, and he's not coming near me or Dominic. Ever. You *promised*."

"He's my best friend." Elijah's voice hardened. "You're the bitch who ruined his life. I take care of you because *Cade* asked me to, not because it's what you want. There's nothing wrong with him. Don't piss him off, and he's a perfect gentleman most of the time."

"Right, tell that to the guy he put into a coma for six months. Cade's a pussycat. But I've seen cats fight. They're vicious, like Cade. I'm not doing it, Elijah. I'll even tell the board you lied, if you keep pushing me."

Elijah rose, took a long inhale of the cigarette, and flicked it away.

"No, you won't." He planted himself in front of Jess. "It's your fault he's in prison anyway. He never would have busted up that bar if you hadn't walked out on him."

Jess's eyes widened. "Seriously? Cade couldn't reach me to beat up so he beat up someone else, and that's *my* fault?"

Cade had tried that argument before, but Jess had more self-possession than to believe Cade's attack on other bikers was her responsibility. He'd been involved in a high-dollar drug deal with another gang and had done something with the money—put it who the hell knew where instead of sharing out. The bikers wanted their cut, and Cade had decided not to give it to them. He'd even met them to teach them a lesson when they demanded he pay up, and he'd been busted when the fight had turned lethal.

His own damn fault for cheating them—for dealing meth in the first place, the idiot.

The fight had been Cade's choice. As had resisting arrest so hard. It had taken five cops to wrestle him down.

"Yes," Elijah said without blinking. "You got him thrown in prison, and you are going to play along that you want him out again."

"Does he think I'm going to take him back?" Jess demanded. "The answer is no. He's not coming near me, or Dominic."

"He's calmed down a lot," Elijah said. "Five years will do that to a man. He knows he doesn't have a chance at winning you back, but he just wants to see you again. I didn't tell you he was up for parole before, because he didn't want to give you a chance to run off before he could talk to you. And see his son."

"He tried to throw Dominic across a room because he was crying," Jess snapped. "He was four years old! It's why I took Dominic and left."

"And Cade's real sorry about that." When Elijah tried to soften his voice to a reasonable tone it was even scarier than when he yelled. "You'll see."

"No," Jess said firmly. "If I go to El Paso, it will be to tell everyone I can all the things he did to me and tried to do to me. He even beat the shit out of *you* for losing a deal for him. He never told you where he stashed all that money before he was arrested, did he? What kind of a best friend is that?"

Elijah shrugged. "I deserved it when he got mad at me. I let him down. And it's his business what he did with the money he made." He started to reach for Jess but dropped his hand at the last second. "I know you hate him and won't do anything for his sake, but you'll do it for your son's sake. And for your own."

Jess took a step toward him. "If you even threaten Dominic, I'll have the cops on you so fast you won't know what hit you."

Elijah's cajoling vanished, and he became the nasty, dangerous man he was. "Don't even think about threatening *me*. I'll cut you off. You need me, and my money—"

"—Which you shove down my throat every chance you get."

"Shut up, bitch. I get sick of your yapping. I'm taking care of you for him, and your damned son. I can pull that plug any time."

He could. While Cade legally had to pay child support even from prison, what Elijah did was extra and she needed it, and he made her know it.

Jess shuddered to think what Cade and Elijah would do if they paired up again. It wouldn't be having a few beers while they swapped stories about the last five years. The two of them were evil incarnate. Elijah, if anything, had his wings clipped without Cade.

Jess could not let Cade near Dominic. No matter what.

Elijah must have seen the determination in her

eyes, because he put heavy hands on her shoulders, biting through her thin T-shirt.

"You'll do this, Jess. You owe him. And don't try to get out of it—I'll tie you up and drag you out there if I have to. Dominic will come with us, and stay with me until you greet Cade like a wife happy to see her husband."

Jess flooded with chill fear. Elijah would do it. He'd hold Dominic hostage for Jess's good behavior. If she resisted anymore tonight, he might storm to her house right now and take Dominic, or plant himself inside it until they left for El Paso.

She'd fight him, but there was no telling what Elijah would do before she could stop him. He was always armed, and he had buddies in the police force. He might not shoot Dominic, because he'd have to answer to Cade, but he wouldn't hesitate to shoot Mrs. Alvarez or Jess herself.

And who knew how Cade really felt about Dominic? He'd never tried to see him or communicate with him—or even to send a message to him through Elijah. Not that Jess wanted him to, but if Cade truly cared for his son, he'd have shown that somehow. So, Elijah might not hesitate to hurt Dominic in order to impel Jess's cooperation.

Shit, shit, shit.

"Fine," Jess said, tight-lipped. "But you don't need Dominic. I'll go." She mentally crossed her fingers as she spoke, having no intention of going anywhere near Cade's prison.

"We'll take him with us, just in case," Elijah said, his smile snakelike. "He'll have fun. It will be a road trip."

Jess's shivers returned, but she kept her voice

strong. "I can't pull him out of school. I'll have to set things up with Mrs. Alvarez—she'll take care of him while we're gone."

Elijah shoved his face toward hers, exhaling stale-smoke breath. "No, Jess. Dominic's coming with us so you don't do something stupid. I'll give you time to pack and tell his teachers he'll be out. They're letting Cade go Tuesday. I'll come and get you Monday morning."

This was Thursday. Three days for planning. Crap on a crutch.

"Fine," she repeated, her voice stony but resigned. "I'll be ready, and we'll get it over with. And hey, they might change their minds and not let him out. No telling what trouble Cade can get into by Tuesday."

"Don't count on it," Elijah returned.

Jess scowled at him. "My break's over. Don't get me fired on top of everything else."

Elijah studied her, as though gauging her honesty, then stepped away, giving her a satisfied nod. He might not believe she wanted to cooperate, but from his look, he believed he'd cowed her.

Jess tried to act exasperated and fearful, just as she would if she'd truly decided to obey him.

The card Tyler had given her burned through the wallet in her pocket. Elijah hadn't mentioned Tyler or the fight. No one had talked about him at all in the last couple weeks except for a few times when the guys who'd been there congratulated themselves on schooling a wise-ass cowboy.

Then they forgot about him. No one had seen Jess leave with Tyler, except Buddy, and he wouldn't say a word. He didn't like Elijah, and besides, he had no way of knowing she'd stayed with Tyler, slept with him, had lunch with his family …

Jess stepped past Elijah and walked toward the bar, pretending she only wanted to get on with work. The biker who'd come out for a smoke was already at the door and held it open for her. So polite. Too bad his politeness, like Elijah's claim that he took care of her, was all a sham.

———

ON SUNDAY AFTERNOON, JESS, DOMINIC, and Mrs. Alvarez got into Jessica's car. Mrs. Alvarez offered to drive, and Jess let her—Mrs. Alvarez often drove when they all went out together, considering it one of her duties as Dominic's caretaker. They headed out of the neighborhood to Dominic's favorite pizza parlor; at least, that's what Dominic yelled to the neighbors as they pulled out.

Jessica's motorcycle looked forlorn in the carport as they backed out, breaking her heart. If all went well, she'd see it again, she tried to reassure herself. But Dominic was more important. Always would be.

A small bag and backpack rested in Jess's trunk, which she'd put there late the night before. Jess knew Elijah had someone watching her house—the girlfriend of one of his guys—but if she saw Jess packing and loading her car, she wouldn't think much about it. Jess and Dominic and luggage couldn't go all the way to El Paso on Elijah's bike, so she'd already won the fight that she'd drive.

Jess had asked Buddy for the time off, starting Sunday, so she'd have time to pack and clean up her house. Buddy agreed, but told Jess it would be time off without pay. Jess said she understood.

Jess had called the lawyer she'd used to get the restraining order on Cade, asking him why she hadn't been informed of Cade's parole. The lawyer explained, in his clinical way, that the board was only required to tell the victim and his family as well as the lawyers at Cade's trial. Jess hadn't been involved in any way in his court case or been the victim in this particular crime, so informing her was optional.

It would have been nice, she'd snapped, but the lawyer had remained cool. No one had told him either, but from what he'd been able to find out, Cade had been a model prisoner lately, and when the parole board had interviewed him, he'd come across as repentant and ready to walk the straight and narrow path. He'd bamboozled them, Jess thought silently. Cade was always good at that—he'd certainly bamboozled her.

Now as Mrs. Alvarez took the car carefully down the road, Jess used her phone to look up the directions to Riverbend, Texas.

She didn't worry that Elijah or any of his gang would hack into her phone and figure out where she was going. Elijah was strictly low tech. Computers only messed you up, he said. Even his cell phone was painfully simple.

The pizza place was near the I-35. Mrs. Alvarez parked in its full lot—the restaurant was popular— and they went inside to order. Dominic played his favorite video games on the machines across the room. As far as he knew, they were going back home after this, and heading to El Paso with Elijah tomorrow. He didn't want to go, but he'd understood they had no choice.

Mrs. Alvarez remained at the restaurant when they left. She was meeting friends there, and they would take her home.

Jess had asked Mrs. Alvarez to come to Riverbend with them, fearing what Elijah would do when he realized Jess was gone. Mrs. Alvarez had argued her down. If she disappeared, her friends would scour the state for her, and inadvertently lead the bikers to Jess.

Those same friends would protect her, Mrs. Alvarez assured Jess, if Elijah tried to interrogate her. Middle-aged women were far more formidable than anyone thought.

Jess had a lump in her throat as she gave Mrs. Alvarez a brief hug and kiss on the cheek, telling her to have fun with her friends. Mrs. Alvarez had tears in her eyes, but only gave Jess a quick hug in return and a cheerful wave as Jess steered Dominic out of the restaurant.

Jess's heart thumped as she started up the car. Her hands were so slick with sweat they slipped off the steering wheel as she was backing up. She had to jam on the brakes and start again.

The car had a full tank of gas, as Jess had filled it up Saturday before work. She'd insisted Dominic use the bathroom at the pizza place, and she had too, so there would be no emergency stops too close to Dallas.

Her chest was tight, her breathing shallow as she eased onto the 35. She saw no bikers around her, not even the girlfriend who kept an eye on her house.

Jess headed south. By the time she was on the outskirts of town, her head was spinning. She prayed she wouldn't have to pull over and quietly pass out.

But this was the tricky part. If Elijah caught her within the city limits, Jess could claim she was doing last-minute shopping. Once she left town, it would be clear she was running.

The demarcation between Dallas and the countryside was fairly sharp. Within twenty minutes of leaving the city, they were in farmland, the ribbon of freeway cutting a swath through it.

No one followed her. Jess glued her gaze to the rearview mirror, so much so that she nearly ran into the back of a slow-moving pickup before she swerved to avoid it. But so far, she saw no familiar bikes with Elijah and his men hunkered over them.

Dominic looked up from the game he was playing, noticed where they were, and then stared at her.

"Um, Mom? Where are we going?"

"For a drive," Jess said. "To visit friends."

Dominic's eyes narrowed. Jess didn't think low-tech Elijah would bug her car, but he could have thought of something simple like leaving a cell phone on under her seat. She'd checked for that and found nothing, but she might have missed something. In her paranoid state, she wasn't taking any chances.

"Sure," Dominic said. He took in Jess's nervousness, glanced behind them, then sank down in his seat. "Will you tell me when we get there?"

"Of course," Jess said brightly. "It won't be long."

Dominic gave her a sideways glance and returned

to his game. Her son might be only nine, but he was no fool—he'd had to grow up far too fast. He knew something was up but he took his cue from her and said nothing more.

"I love you, Dominic," Jess said.

"Yeah," Dominic said. "Love you too, Mom." The unspoken *Whatever* was loud and clear, which only bolstered her courage. Dominic wasn't afraid.

They made it through Waco and continued southward. Jess didn't relax though. When she failed to return home this evening, the woman watching her house would alert Elijah. Jess figured she had about a four hours' start, at which time she could be in Riverbend.

She hadn't thought much about what she'd do once she got there. Tyler might want nothing to do with her—he might not even be in town. He and his brothers could be traveling with their stunt show.

Didn't matter. Jess would find a place to stay and start over. Riverbend was a name, a haven that called to her. Whether Tyler Campbell would be happy to see her in it or not made no difference.

There was no sign showing a turnoff to Riverbend. All the better. Jess knew which highways went there, and the GPS voice that had spoken from her phone since Waco led her on.

"In twenty miles, turn south on state highway 29," the voice droned.

Otherwise, all was quiet. Dominic had shut off his device, grown bored with looking out the window—not much to see from the interstate—and dozed off.

Jess took the turnoff, following directions for

the next thirty miles, bearing left, then right, then making a sharp turn to the next highway. Texas road systems could never be straightforward. Dominic woke up as the narrow road started up and down hills.

Farmland eased away and trees thickened on the hills. There were the inevitable mesquites, which grew like weeds everywhere, but also live oaks and ash trees, their limbs full of summer green. Open spaces studded with wildflowers unfolded around them. Jess was used to seeing bluebonnets on the sides of highways in spring, but out here they obviously had flowers for every season.

Jess had never been to Hill Country, only viewing it in photos or hearing about it from friends. She hadn't realized how beautiful it would be. A little ache began in her heart.

As she drove on, instead of growing less nervous, her worry increased. She hadn't seen any sign of Elijah or his men, but as the miles dropped behind her, doubt crept in.

What the hell was she doing? She'd fled with one bag of clothing for her and one for Dominic. She'd pulled cash out of her bank account over the last couple of days, ostensibly for the El Paso trip, because she didn't want to use her credit card— the only one she had—once she left Dallas, in case Elijah managed to have his cop friends trace her through it.

So, she had about five hundred dollars to her name, and a son to raise, and now she couldn't go home. Elijah would scour the state for her. Would this town of Riverbend be hidden enough from him? Would the people of the town help her? Or

betray her? Small towns in Texas could be cliqu-
ish—outsiders weren't always embraced, unless
they had connections to a family there.

Jess had met the Campbell brothers, and had glorious sex with Tyler. Was that a connection?

She gripped the steering wheel. To hell with it.
She could do this. Jess had started over once before,
when Cade had gone to prison, and she'd finally
been free of him. She'd simply start over again.

She'd find a job in Riverbend or somewhere
beyond it. Open a new bank account, find a place
to live. Jess hadn't had that much in the bank anyway. Mrs. Alvarez would give the people Jess rented
from her notice, so no one would come after her
for back rent and utility payments. The car was paid
for, as was her bike. Nothing more would connect
her to Dallas. She'd still have to worry about her
necessary prescriptions, but one enormous hurdle
at a time. She'd taken some this morning, as usual,
and had enough left for another week, packed
carefully in her suitcase.

Mrs. Alvarez said she'd talk to Dominic's school
as well. Getting Dominic transferred down to Riverbend would be the tricky part—Elijah might
figure out he could trace them through Dominic's
school records. Schools were pretty protective of
their kids, but Elijah wasn't above using violence
to get what he wanted. Jess would just have to trust
Mrs. Alvarez and her posse of middle-aged women
to keep Dominic's location safe.

She bit back a laugh that ended up a sob. Mrs.
Alvarez was a wonderful woman, and Jess hoped
this wasn't good-bye forever.

"Turn right on farm road 1223, and proceed five

miles to your destination."

Jessica turned right. In a few minutes, the sign *Welcome to Riverbend! Home of the Friendliest People in Texas* loomed before her. After that was a curve in the road, a dip that hid whatever was on the other side. High banks of green grass seemed to embrace her.

When they came out of the dip—nothing. Rolling ranch land, waving grass, wildflowers, emptiness under a blue, blue sky.

And yet, it gripped Jess and wouldn't let go. *Welcome to Riverbend*, the sign had said.

It might as well have said, *Welcome Home.*

CHAPTER 10

———

"WHAT DO WE DO NOW?" Dominic asked.

They stood at the town's gas station, Jess filling her car, the slightly worn midnight blue Toyota blending in with the other cars and pickups. So normal. She felt a twinge of deep regret when she saw a woman drive through on a sweet Harley. Well, maybe Mrs. Alvarez would learn to ride it if she couldn't send it safely to Jess.

Jess laughed and then almost cried again, picturing Mrs. Alvarez and her friends on motorcycles, heading off to battle.

Dominic's question brought Jess out of her musings. This was the first concern he'd voiced, and even now, he trusted her to tell him how things were going to go.

"We talk to people and see what happens." Jess had already paid for the gas, but an eager, raw-boned young man who worked for the station headed over to her.

"Hi there," he chirped. "You visiting? Can I help you find anything? Hey, Mrs. Ward is starting on her apple pies again. You have a bite of those, and you'll think you died and went to heaven."

Dominic gave Jess a hopeful look. He'd be hungry—it had been five hours since the pizza.

Even so, the sun was still high in the early September sky, the warmth seeping into Jess's bones.

"Is there a motel nearby?" Jess asked the young man. "Oh, and do you know where this place is?" She took out the card Tyler had given her.

Circle C Ranch. It sounded like something out of the Old West, yet so inviting.

"Oh, sure. The Campbells," the young man said after one swift peek at the card. "You go back down this road and hang a left. Along there for about—oh, maybe a couple miles—and then there's a little road off to the right. Might be a sign there, but not always. It blows down, or people steal it—isn't that crazy? Anyway, turn there and you'll see the gate about half a mile after that. You looking to buy a horse?" The kid cast a doubtful glance over Jess in her sleeveless top and jeans shorts, messy hair and no makeup. She must not look the horsey type.

"No, I …" Crap. Jess had no idea what to tell him. "We're just visiting," she finished.

The young man narrowed his eyes, obviously trying to figure out who she'd be visiting at Circle C and why, but he kept up his friendliness. He was curious, not hostile.

"Well, tell Mrs. C.—all the Mrs. C.'s—" He broke off and chuckled. "Tell them Hank said hi. And that the apple pies are wanting some eating."

"Thank you," Jess said sincerely. "Will do."

"All right then. You take care. And you need any more directions, you just come on back here and ask."

Hank loped away with a wave as Jess got into the car. Dominic sank into his seat as she started it up.

"Is he a hick?" he asked as they rolled out of the gas station.

"Dominic!" Jess hastily made sure no one was within hearing distance. "Don't call people hicks. It's not nice. We might have to live here."

Dominic gave her a puzzled look. "Don't get mad. I just want to know. I've never met a hick before."

"Well, don't say it again, all right? I don't need people angry at us the first ten minutes we're in town."

"Okay, okay. Calm down."

"I'll explain everything when we have time," Jess said. "Promise."

"I know why we left Dallas," Dominic answered. "I can hear you when I'm in my room, you know, and Mrs. Alvarez can't whisper to save her life. I didn't want to go to El Paso anyway."

Jess started, then realized she shouldn't be surprised. Dominic was sharp. "You can't tell anyone where we are, do you understand? Not even your closest friends. I'm sorry, honey, but it's too dangerous. You especially can't tell Elijah."

"I said I get it." Dominic scowled. "Like I'd be texting Elijah anyway. He's a creep-toid."

A good word for him.

"Now, help me find the turnoff," Jess said as she took the left Hank had indicated.

Dominic scanned the side of the road. Jess did as well—there were no other cars behind her, and she could slow down to search.

"There it is," Dominic said excitedly.

He pointed at a low white sign, nearly hidden in the brush. Boards had been painted white with a black logo—a C inside a circle—with an arrow pointing to Jess's right.

She pressed hard on the brakes and turned quickly onto the tiny road the arrow indicated. She signaled out of habit, but no one was behind her to see—or ahead of her for that matter.

The road was paved but very narrow. Only one vehicle at a time would fit. Trees obscured the view at first, the lane like a tunnel with green branches lacing overhead.

The trees parted abruptly, and Jess drove under a wrought-iron arch with *Circle C Ranch* spelled out with square iron letters across the top.

The road took them to the crest of a rise. From there Jess could see, to her right, several corrals, an open ring and a covered one, and beyond those, rows of stables. To the left was a wide swath of green with a half dozen horses dotting it, heads down, grazing.

At the top of another rise, where the drive ended in a long arc, was a low, rambling one-story house. Made of brick, it stretched across the green ground as though embracing it. To the left of the house was a huge garage with what must be a guest house built over it.

Jess's dashboard clock read six in the evening, but the ranch wasn't quiet. Men roved about, leading horses, carrying bales of hay, shoveling, raking, one driving some kind of low-slung tractor through the covered ring.

Two men rode horses in the open ring, which was close to the drive. Jess pulled the car to a halt beside it, her heart pounding.

The riders wore plain T-shirts and jeans, both men in cowboy hats, one straw, one black. The horses were loping slowly around each other, the riders watching every step. Jess turned off the engine and very carefully got out of the car, entranced by the graceful dance.

The man in the straw hat—Carter—snapped a command.

Instantly both cowboys rolled from their saddles to the rump of the opposite horse. They executed the move smoothly, the horses never missing a step.

"Cool!" Dominic said excitedly from beside Jess. "Tyler! Hey!"

The man in the black hat snapped his head around. He stared straight at Jess, and then his hat tumbled from his head and hit the dirt.

Tyler followed the hat down a second later. He landed on his butt then sprawled onto his back, spread-eagled, as dust rose gently around him.

———

SON OF A BITCH.

Tyler was on his feet faster than Carter could leap down to help him.

Didn't it figure. The lady of his dreams had materialized out of nowhere, and so Tyler fell flat on his ass in front of her.

Tyler slapped the dust off his jeans, aware they had holes in them, as did his worn-out T-shirt. His hat was on the ground, wind tossing his hair.

In contrast, Jess looked perfect. Her jeans shorts set off her long, curved legs; the sleeveless top hugged her chest and showed off the gorgeous tatts on her arms. Her dark hair was tousled, making Tyler want to run his fingers through it and tousle it more.

His horse, a new gray called Diehard, jogged gently around the ring, stirrups flapping, probably wondering if Tyler's move would be part of the show.

"Tyler!" Dominic waved as though worried Tyler wouldn't see him. "Remember us? Mom wants to live here now. That *is* what we're doing here, right, Mom?"

"Dominic." Jess's already flushed face went redder still.

Carter sent Tyler a hard glance. Whether he disapproved or was telling Tyler not to upset Jess, he couldn't tell. Carter could be difficult to read.

Without a word, Carter walked away to catch the horses, giving Tyler relative privacy to screw up with Jess again.

She stepped hesitantly to the rail, Dominic with her. Tyler remained rooted in the center of the ring, unable to move his feet to walk to her.

Jess took a breath, which moved her breasts under the white top. "You were right—I needed to leave where I was for a better place. Can you recommend somewhere I can stay while I look for a job? A motel or B&B or—"

"Yes, you can stay right here."

Jess blinked, her face going scarlet. "I'm not here to take advantage of you. I want to start over, and Riverbend sounds like a good town to do it in. Just point me to a motel, and you'll never have to see me."

Dominic stared at her in bafflement. "Why don't

you want to see him, Mom? I thought you liked him."

Jessica couldn't possibly blush any more, although the redness in her face crept down her neck to her chest. "Dominic," she said in agonized tones.

"Y'all are staying here." Tyler's feet came unstuck, and he strode to the rail, stepping up to swing over it. He landed lightly next to her, no falling on his ass this time, though it was a close thing. "It's a big house, lots of room. Or—tell you what. You and Dominic take my apartment over the garage, and I'll stay in the house a while." When Jess opened her mouth to protest, Tyler shook his head. "You'll have more privacy, and won't have to put up with my brothers. I just finished remodeling the bathroom—it's real nice. Stay as long as you want."

Dominic grabbed Jess's hand. "Come on, Mom. *Please?* Elijah will never find us here. *We* barely found it."

"Elijah?" Tyler asked sharply.

His awkwardness fled. Carter's friend, whom Tyler had paid to sit in the Dallas bar every night and make sure Jess was all right, had reported that Elijah had been absent for a couple weeks but had reappeared this past Thursday. Elijah and Jess had argued about something in the parking lot—Noah hadn't been able to hear exactly what—but Jess had held her own, and Elijah had left again. Jess had come in and done her Friday and Saturday shifts as usual, but Elijah hadn't returned.

So what had happened to make Jess run?

"Dominic, you need to learn to keep things to yourself," Jess said in a tone Tyler sometimes heard his own mother use. There must be a "mom" class that taught that sternness of voice.

Dominic rolled his eyes with nine-year-old astuteness. "It's the truth, and Tyler and his brothers are good guys. I can tell the difference. I'm not stupid."

"No, but you're mouthy." Jess's anger broke through her distress, making her eyes sparkle and her head lift.

"Hey, Dominic." Tyler pointed at a small figure emerging from the house. "That's Faith, Carter's daughter. Go tell her I told her to show you her horses. Your mom and I need to talk."

Dominic studied Faith, who'd halted on the bottom step of the porch to shield her eyes and peer at them. He sighed. "Okay, I'll go talk to a *girl*." He sounded doubtful. "Don't blow it, Mom. I don't want to sleep in the car."

Jess watched in exasperation as Dominic marched toward the house, squaring his shoulders as though bravely facing an ordeal.

Faith came off the step to greet him. Tyler couldn't hear what they said, but he knew Faith was being her usual sunny self. She gestured for Dominic to follow her to the barn.

Dominic glanced over his shoulder at Jess, his look saying he was being self-sacrificing. Faith came back to Dominic, caught his hand, and led him on.

Tyler turned away from the scene and walked past Jess to her car. The keys hung in the ignition, so Tyler slid into the driver's seat and started it.

"Get in," he said to her through the open window. "You bring any bags?"

"In the trunk." Jess yanked open the passenger

door and climbed inside. "I'll pay you rent."

Tyler put the car in gear and shook his head. "We'll fight about *that* later."

He drove to the house and around it to the garage. The driveway ended in a wide slab of concrete in front of the garage doors, surrounded by graded dirt to accommodate the many vehicles that sometimes parked here. For now the concrete held Carter's truck and Tyler's, Grace's new pickup, and Tyler's mom's SUV. Adam and Grant, who had homes of their own, usually parked by the office at the end of the barn when they came to train, though the brothers had already departed for the evening.

Tyler had been renovating the rooms over the garage—which a hundred years ago had been a carriage house—for about a year. He was almost done, his apartment becoming luxurious. He figured that if he was going to be a grown man living with his mom, he should do it in style.

He parked Jess's car behind his pickup, turned off the engine, and hauled himself out. He pressed the button on her key fob to open the trunk and lifted out a small roller bag and a backpack before she could reach him.

"Is this it?" he asked as Jess arrived at his side. As usual, she hadn't waited for him to open her door.

"All I had time for. You can't overpack when you're going for stealth."

"That's all right." Tyler hefted both bags, finding them light. "We actually have stores in Riverbend, or we can head to Austin if you want something special."

"No, no. For now I'll stay right here. I don't need

much."

Tyler didn't miss the ugly fear in her eyes, which made something grim in him tighten.

He shut the trunk. "Upstairs," he said, gesturing to the outside staircase, its spindles painted a fresh white. "Then you are going to tell me everything."

"Will Dominic be all right?" Jess cast a glance at the barn. "He's not used to horses. Neither am I."

"Faith is," Tyler answered. "And Carter watches Faith like an overprotective hawk. Plus we have plenty of guys—and gals—working in that barn who will make sure he's okay. Now, up the stairs, sweetheart. Or do I have to plant my hand on your ass all the way?"

Jess's answering look, in which he read that she was picturing the last time he had his hands on her ass, sent fire through his veins. He shouldn't think about things like that.

"Don't try it, cowboy," Jess said. "I'm used to fending off bikers. You don't stand a chance."

Her answer fueled Tyler's need to wrap himself around her and keep her safe. Elijah and his bikers should be taught a lesson, and Tyler knew plenty of guys who'd be happy to help him do it.

He said nothing, only followed her up the stairs, letting his gaze rest on the firm ass in question. "Go on in," he said once they reached the top.

Jess opened the unlocked door and stepped into the light and airy living room. The apartment was almost done—Tyler had to finish the floor in the front closet, but he wasn't ashamed to have Jess see it.

Tyler set the bags on the sofa. "Let me give you the grand tour." He spread his arms. "This is the living room. Over there is the kitchen." He indicated the small but all-new kitchen beyond the granite-topped breakfast bar. "In here is the bedroom." He walked through a doorway into the spacious, sunny room with a large bed. "Bathroom in there."

Through another door was a bathroom almost as big as the bedroom. He'd put in a large soaking bathtub as well as a shower stall with plenty of space in between for drying off. Tyler worked all day in dust and horse shit—he wanted to smell a little better than that when he went out for the evening.

"And that was the tour." Tyler remained in the middle of the bedroom, dropping his hands to his sides.

Jess left for the living room but not self-consciously—she was just looking around.

"It's nice." She sounded surprised as she took in the cream-colored sofa with bright cushions, the stainless steel appliances, the plantation shutters, the framed posters for their stunt shows on the walls.

"What did you expect?" Tyler moved past her to the kitchen and the refrigerator.

Jess shrugged. "I don't know. Plaid furniture. Brands burned into the fake wooden paneling."

"Well, I *was* going to do that," Tyler said, straight-faced. "But my sisters-in-law come up here and give me all kinds of advice." He let his voice rise to a falsetto. "Tyler, you need more pillows on the sofa. Tyler, you need a nice rug in here and matching towels in the bathroom. Don't forget the little soaps—everyone loves the little soaps."

Jess turned in place to take it all in. "Your sisters-in-law have good taste."

"They fit right in with my pushy family. Want a beer?"

She hesitated as though fighting an automatic *No*, then spread her hands. "Sure, what the hell?"

Tyler stocked several different kinds of beer, never knowing what his guests would like. He chose a blond ale for Jess and picked up his favorite amber. Texas boys were supposed to drink only commercial American brands but Tyler had fallen in love with craft beer, which had a huge range of choices and tastes. A local brewery had started up in White Fork, and the brewer had opened Tyler's eyes to a new world.

Tyler pried off the bottle caps and carried Jess's beer to her as she took a seat on the sofa next to her bags. The bags crowded Tyler out, but that was his own fault. He was the idiot who'd put them there in the first place.

Jess studied the label and gingerly tasted the beer, her expression changing to delight. "Perfect. Crisp, not sharp."

"You like craft beer?"

"I'm a bartender," Jess reminded him. "A trained and experienced one. I've tasted plenty of local brews, good and bad. Most of my customers like what's on tap though, no matter what it is. By the pitcher." She took another sip. "Blond ale, not too fruity. Nice. I don't like IPAs though. Don't know why. I just don't."

"Me either." Why did Tyler's heartbeat speed at that tiny connection? He held up his bottle, and Jess clicked it with hers.

"Come on, now," Tyler said, once they'd drunk in silence a moment. "We're alone. You can chill out and enjoy your beer—and tell me every last thing that happened."

CHAPTER 11

———

JESS WASN'T AS RELAXED AS she pretended
to be—though this was damned good beer.
Tyler sat on a chair with charcoal-colored uphol-
stery that contrasted the sofa's cream. He leaned
forward, his beer bottle resting between his big
hands, his blue eyes focused on her.

She could lie and say she'd decided to move
Dominic far from Elijah's influence—which was
part of the truth—but Tyler wasn't imperceptive.
Her conversation with his brothers at Lanny D's
showed her that the Campbells were smart and
resourceful, and savvy businessmen. Tyler hadn't
been able to join in, but Jess had learned a lot about
his family and his background that day.

She let out a breath and spilled all of it—from
Elijah announcing he wanted her to be there when
Cade was released to leaving the pizza parlor and
heading for Riverbend.

By the time Jess finished, she was shaking with
shock and release. She set down the bottle and
rubbed her cold arms. "I wasn't coming here to
impose myself on you," she made herself say, "Or
tell you that you have to take care of me because

we—" She broke off, her face heating.

"Had mind-blowing sex?" Tyler finished without a blush. "I wasn't kidding when I gave you the card. I said to call me, about anything. If you'd have let me know what was going on, I could have rescued you with more pizzazz." He spoke lightly, but Jess heard the anger in his voice.

"And had Elijah coming after you?" Jess shivered. "No way. He has a lot of friends, and all of them carry weapons. I have no intention of bringing shit like that down on you. I just want somewhere to start over, and Riverbend sounded nice." She trailed off, longing in her heart.

It was so quiet here. The noises coming through the front door Tyler hadn't shut were birdsong and the wind in the trees. Distantly, she heard voices of men working and the occasional neigh of a horse.

Horses. Jess started to get to her feet. "I should check on Dominic."

"Dominic's fine, but okay." Tyler unfolded himself, setting his beer bottle next to hers. "Elijah threatening you and Dominic like that is actionable, Jess. Why didn't you call the cops?"

Jess shuddered. She was tired, only a few sips of beer had loosened her tongue, and she was in danger of flinging herself, sobbing, at Tyler. She wanted to relax, tell herself they were safe, but there was no guarantee, never would be. Elijah was too powerful.

"What good would it do?" she asked. "Elijah has plenty of people on his payroll—cops, dispatchers, assistant D.A.s … Plus, it's my word against his. No witnesses."

Tyler frowned. "None at all?"

"No—we were out in the parking lot when

Elijah said he'd take Dominic hostage so I'd go with him. There was one biker out there having a smoke, but I don't think he heard. Even if he did, he'd never back me up. He'd take Elijah's side."

Tyler shrugged, his cheeks going faintly pink. "You never know. But what I want you to do right now is stop worrying." He put his hands on Jess's shoulders.

Elijah had done the same thing when he'd argued with her in the parking lot. But while Elijah's touch had been heavy, oppressing, Tyler's was kind and lent her strength.

"Don't," Jess said rapidly. "If you try to comfort me, I'll fall apart. I have to keep it together. Dominic…"

"Is in the safest place he's ever going to be." Tyler's voice was quiet, gravel deep. "So are you."

No. Jess wasn't, not by a long way. There was plenty she needed to take care of still.

Tyler's tug on her couldn't be resisted. He didn't force her against him so much as coax her. Jess found herself leaning on his broad chest, his arms around her.

He rubbed her back, his palm drawing warmth down her spine. The caress wasn't sexual—this was the embrace of a friend. Jess so rarely had either that his touch, non-threatening, melted her against him. She could believe, for the space of this moment, that she was safe.

Tyler pulled her a little closer. They stood in silence while Texas heat flowed in the door and around them, the tiniest hint of evening coolness on the breeze.

Shouting abruptly filtered to them from the stables, and Jess came instantly alert. *Dominic.*

"It's all right," Tyler said, his voice retaining the soothing rumble. "We'll go find him."

He released Jess, brushing one finger over her cheek. "Come on," he said with his unfailing energy. "Let's see what everyone's yelling about."

———

DOGS. TWO STRAYS GRACE AND Faith had been taking care of had gotten into the barn, and a few of the newer horses hadn't liked them. The dogs, yellow-brown and of indeterminate breed, were friendly enough, but not all horses were good with them.

Dominic was safe and sound outside one of the corrals with Faith, the two of them watching while the ranch hands rounded up the dogs and calmed the horses.

About that time, Grace emerged from the kitchen door and rang the huge cowbell dangling from the porch ceiling, summoning the family to dinner.

Jess looked spooked when Tyler gestured her to the house, Jess saying she and Dominic could order a pizza or something—they hadn't come here for a free meal. Tyler rolled his eyes, took her by the arm, and marched her to the main house.

Grace had set places for Jess and Dominic, and Tyler made damn certain this time that he got to sit next to her. He held out Jess's chair for her and plopped himself down beside her before anyone could suggest otherwise. Carter, without a word, took a place across the table.

Adam and Grant had gone to their own homes for dinner, for which Tyler was thankful. He loved it when the whole clan was together, but tonight, he wanted Jess more or less to himself.

Dominic sat next to Carter. Carter welcomed him, Faith taking the chair on the other side of her father. Grace chose the foot of the table, and Tyler's mom glided in at the last minute and took her place at the head.

His mom, Olivia Campbell, was a warmhearted woman with a lot of strength. She'd kept the family together and the ranch going after Tyler's dad had died in an accident so long ago. Her softly cut gray hair and turquoise bracelets didn't seem daunting, but looks were deceiving.

"I'm so glad to meet you, Jessica." Olivia leaned down the table to clasp Jess's hand. "I've heard all about you. Now, don't you worry about a thing. We always have room at our table for friends."

Jess flushed, no doubt wondering a) what his mom had heard, and b) whether Olivia considered a one-night stand to mean "friend."

"My nosy brothers told her about you," Tyler said to Jess. He made an X over his heart. "I didn't say a word."

Faith shot Tyler a grin. "Careful, Uncle Tyler. *Not* talking about a girl you want to like you can be insulting."

Tyler turned to her. "'Scuse me—I mean my nosy brothers and my nosy *niece*. Leave Jess alone. She's had a long day."

"Quit your moaning, Tyler," Olivia said good-naturedly. "And say grace for us."

Tyler feigned a resigned sigh. But he didn't mind clasping Jess's hand as everyone joined around the table, waiting for Tyler to start the brief prayer.

Tyler became so fixed on the feeling of Jess's cool, slim fingers twining his that he almost forgot to take Grace's hand on his other side.

Grace didn't though. She reached out and grabbed Tyler in a tight clasp, her fingers strong.

As Tyler drew a breath to start, he was interrupted by a sudden spurt of gravel flying up on the drive outside. Through the windows, he saw a police SUV spin to a halt in front of the house, wheels kicking up dust. No lights, no sirens, but Jess leapt to her feet, panic on her face. Dominic spun around to look out the front window, his eyes wide.

"What's wrong, Mom?" he asked fearfully. "Do we need to go?"

A single sheriff's deputy hopped out of the SUV and sprinted up the steps, banging in through the front door.

Tyler stood and took Jess's hand. "It's just Ross," he said as gently as he could. "Our baby brother. Sit down, sweetheart. It's okay."

Jess shivered under his touch, but she let out a breath and sank to her chair. She didn't let go of Tyler's hand. "Sorry," she said. "I'm just tired, I guess."

Olivia's wise look told Tyler she understood Jess's nerves. Nothing was secret in this family.

Ross charged through the large living room into the dining room. He was a younger version of Adam, blue eyes sparkling under his buzzed dark hair, his khaki deputy's uniform creased and clean, badge shining. "Am I too late? Did I miss out on one of Grace's kick-ass dinners?"

"Tyler's about to say grace," Olivia told him

without admonishment. "Sit down, so we can get on with it."

"Awesome." Ross plunked himself into the only empty chair, which was between Jess and their mom. He took Jess's hand, giving her a thorough once-over. "You're Jess, right? And Dominic? Pleased to meet you. I'm Ross, the law-abiding Campbell."

Ross's bright blue eyes held way too much interest. He, like Tyler, was single, plus he had that man-in-uniform thing going for him. He also had a big smile, packed a large gun, and carried handcuffs. Tyler didn't worry so much about his older brothers around Jess—they were happily married—but Ross ...

"Law-abiding *now*," Carter said in his deep rumble, the corners of his mouth twitching. "When he was fourteen, he stole a truck and tried to go to Mexico."

"I *borrowed* it." Ross explained to Jess. "I brought it back. I didn't realize how far away Mexico really was. I thought it was a few minutes down the road past San Antonio."

Tyler made a derisive noise. "Because you didn't look at a globe."

"I was fourteen and never been farther than San Antonio. I thought the Alamo being there meant it was right on the border."

Dominic laughed. "Really?"

"Really."

Tyler had never, ever been jealous of his little brother. Tyler had gone through his school days and afterward surrounded by friends and captivated women while Ross had been either cute and adorable, or awkward and nerdy. Now Ross shone, having emerged from his geeky teenaged shell into a strong, smart, capable and courageous man. Tyler was proud of him.

Did *not* mean Ross got to steal Jess out from under Tyler's nose.

Jess relaxed and smiled at Ross's banter, which made something inside Tyler loosen. It was good to see her unwind.

Carter wasn't wrong about her though. Jess had some baggage, and Tyler would have to help her sort through it. Fine with him. She'd carried her burdens long enough.

Tyler cleared his throat, took Jess's and Grace's hands again, and said the prayer, thanking God for their guests' safe arrival and the food his sister-in-law had slaved over all day. As soon as he finished, hands shot out toward the serving dishes, Tyler tonight grabbing food to offer to Jess first. Grace had cooked up a feast of fried chicken and roasted potatoes, a mess of vegetables, and biscuits that were about a mile high and came apart in layers of bready goodness.

As they started eating, talk turned to Jessica's plans. She asked about jobs in Riverbend, which made the rest of the family laugh. Riverbend wasn't a booming metropolis with tons of new employment opportunities every day. Most residents were carrying on family businesses or working remotely for companies in other cities or states, or they commuted to jobs in Austin or San Antonio. Austin had grown so much, and continued to grow, that driving to its outskirts to work was a quick trip these days.

Tyler knew without Jess saying a word that she didn't want to commute. She wanted to crawl into the hole of Riverbend and never come out.

"Christina manages the bar now," Faith said, breaking through the adults' pondering. "Jess is a bartender. Put it together."

"No," Jess said quickly. "Don't put Christina on the spot." She sent Faith a wink. "I am the best though. I can even make a Pink Lady without looking it up."

"Not much call for that in Riverbend," Ross said. "The drunks I take to jail are never there for drinking too many Pink Ladies."

"You never know," Jess said. "They're full of gin and applejack—a couple of Pink Ladies can land a large man on his butt. I've seen it happen."

Tyler broke into the hilarity. "If Elijah is looking for you, Jess, the first place he'll try is a bar."

Jess lost her smile. "I know, but it's what I know how to do. I trained, and I have lots of experience."

"I bet there's plenty you can do at the ranch," Tyler said stubbornly. "We always have something going on and can use the help. Plus there's AGCT Enterprises. Our organization that helps local businesses start up or get back on their feet. The office is in the middle of town—I bet they'd have something for you there."

"That means she'd have to work with Karen Marvin," Ross pointed out. "I thought you liked Jess."

Everyone laughed, including Carter, who let out a chuckle. They'd all come to like Karen, but there was no denying she could be one scary bitch.

"Or what about being a tattoo artist?" Tyler went

on. "You said you wanted to do that. You could be the first one in Riverbend."

"I wanted that when I was eighteen," Jess said impatiently. "Before I figured out I couldn't draw. And it's not like bikers don't go to tattoo parlors." She gave Tyler a stern look. "Working at the bar is fine with me. But only if there's a position open. I don't want to take away someone else's paycheck and tips."

Tyler made himself shrug under the scrutiny of his family. "We'll talk about it."

Jess might as well have flames coming out of her ears, but she turned away and took a bite of Grace's meal. The chicken was perfect—crisp and juicy—the biscuits amazing, or at least the rest of the family claimed. Tyler couldn't taste a bite.

By the time supper was over, the night had darkened. Tyler prepared to walk Jess and Dominic back to his apartment, but Olivia stopped him on the porch.

"Need you a sec, Tyler."

Jess had already descended to the drive with Dominic and took her son's hand. "Go on," she said. "I think I can find the way."

Her look said she thought it amusing he'd been intercepted by his mother, but the sparkle in her eyes sent flames through Tyler's blood.

He watched in regret as she walked away, but enjoyed the picture of her limber body in the brief shorts. Dominic, still keyed up, danced at the end of her hand.

Tyler kept his eye on them until Jess climbed the steps to his apartment and let herself and Dominic inside, the light going on to show her through the windows. Tyler watched until she disappeared into the back room then turned his steps to follow his mom around the house to her suite of rooms in the rear with its own private porch.

This was his mom's retreat, her sanctuary. Tyler didn't remember much about his parents' early years, but Grant and Adam told him that this particular wing of the house had been built first, where they'd all crowded in, their mom and dad madly in love and happy with their growing family. The main part of the house had been finished the year their dad had died. It was no surprise Olivia had remained in this suite and used it as her private refuge, to be alone with her memories.

Tyler leaned against the porch railing outside the suite's door, folding his arms and resting one foot behind him on a post as he faced his mother. "You know, I dreamed of walking my girl home tonight, showing her the stars. Not being held after class by my mom."

He kept his voice light, but Olivia only gazed at him unblinkingly.

"Tyler," she said in her straightforward way. "She isn't yours."

CHAPTER 12

———

TYLER KNEW WHAT HIS MOTHER meant, but he kept the banter in his voice. "I'm not stepping aside for Ross. He can't have everything just because he's the baby."

"Not my point."

Tyler gave up. He turned to gaze at the rolling hills behind the ranch, the sky dark blue with dusk.

"You mean I should let her live her own life," he said, and shook his head. "You didn't see those goons in the bar where she worked. This Elijah is bad news—and I'm not saying that because he kicked the shit out of me. I'll do anything to keep her from him. If her ex-husband is anything like him—she doesn't need him finding her either. I want her away from him. From both of them."

"Why?"

Tyler snapped around to see Olivia watching him with calm blue eyes. Folks in town said that the Campbells' father, Dale, had been a wild charmer, but he'd fallen hard for the quiet young woman with beautiful eyes, who'd graduated high school at the top of her class.

Olivia still had beautiful eyes, and age had only

made her wiser. She'd thrown herself into raising her boys and helping troubled teens—everyone speculated she did so to keep her mind off her grief at losing her husband.

But Tyler knew that this was just who she was. She'd loved his dad to distraction, but Olivia Campbell was her own woman.

"What do you mean *why*?" Tyler asked. "I'm worried about her. Just like you worry about the kids who come out here to work with horses and escape their pasts."

"Not the same, and you know it." Olivia gave him a severe look. "You can't smother her, Tyler. That's part of what she's trying to escape. We can offer her help and support, but ultimately, it's her decision. You have to let her make it."

"You mean stop being a high-handed dick?" Tyler usually wouldn't use rough language around his mother, but the subject was too touchy for restraint.

Olivia didn't flinch, used to working with teens who liked the F word. "Exactly. She's terrified, and with good reason. Let her calm down and settle in before you frighten her with your well-meaning intentions. And you didn't answer the question."

His mom's quiet look unnerved him. "Which question?" Tyler pointed at her. "See, this is why we're scared to talk to you. We always have to figure out what you mean."

"You know exactly what I mean. Why are you so concerned about *her*? A lot of people you meet have problems. Are you going to let them all move into your apartment and get them jobs at the ranch?"

"Why do you think?" Tyler jammed his arms across his chest. "She's hot."

His mom wasn't having that. "Your one-night stands are famous, Tyler. I've never yelled at you about them, because I understand grief and pulling away. It's a hard thing to feel, a hard thing to get past. I know you well enough to see that the way you look at this woman is different. And I like her. But you can't force it. If you try to grab on to her, she'll go. It's the old saying—if you hold a butterfly in your fist, you'll destroy it. You have to let it sit on your open hand and enjoy its beauty."

"For however long it lets me," Tyler answered, subdued.

"I'm afraid so, sweetie."

Tyler released a long breath. "You sure I'm not all worried about her because she's hot?"

Olivia gave him one of her warm, rare smiles. "I'm pretty sure. So are you."

Tyler knew she was right. "Shit." He folded his arms over his chest, tightening in on himself. "Don't tell my brothers."

His mother patted his arm. "They already know, dear."

———

JESS DIDN'T LIKE HOW ECSTATIC she was that Tyler came to the apartment to say good night, though her elation dimmed when he remained at the bottom of the stairs and waited for them to come out.

Dominic jumped happily down to Tyler, thanked him enthusiastically for letting them stay, then ran upstairs to enjoy the novelty of sleeping on a bed that came out of a sofa.

"Call the main house if you need anything," Tyler said to Jess, his expression guarded. He'd planted himself five feet from the bottom step Jess was on, his arms folded, shutting her out. "Hell, just yell out the window. Someone will come running."

Someone, he said. Not *I'll come running*. Something had happened since dinner to make him close up and stand back.

"Tyler, I'm really grateful," Jess said, coming off the step. "I'm sorry I've been cranky—I don't want you to think I'm blowing off what you're doing for us. No one's ever gone the extra mile for me. It's hard to know how to handle it."

Tyler shrugged, the movement tight. "Then you know the wrong people."

His blue eyes held caution, but behind that lingered the heat of a thousand suns, and Jess wanted to touch it. She'd get burned, Jess knew that, but it would be worth it to feel his warmth one more time.

Jess closed the distance between herself and Tyler before he had time to pull away. In the bed in the impersonal hotel room, she'd lost herself for a glorious time, nothing mattering but that moment. She'd give anything to experience that again.

Correction, to experience it again with *Tyler*. Jess rested her fingers on his chest, the thud of his heart beneath his shirt telling her his indifference was a sham. His withdrawal had nothing to do with how much he wanted her.

Tyler remained perfectly still as Jess rose on tiptoe and kissed his lips. Didn't reach for her, didn't unfold his arms. His lips didn't move either.

Jess was about to pull away, when his sudden responding kiss kept her riveted in place.

The kiss was slow, deliberate, Tyler's lips parting hers, the flash of his tongue in her mouth electrifying. He never reached for her, never unlaced his arms, only leaned down to let his mouth take hers. He was heat in the night, an anchor against the world.

Jess's fingers curled, clutching the fabric of his shirt. She rose to prolong the kiss, not wanting to let go, reluctant to retreat upstairs without him.

Wind brushed her, whispering in the grass beyond the path, ringing in the wind chimes above her. Slowly, very slowly, Tyler eased from the kiss.

He and Jess stared at each other in the dark, the breeze stirring Tyler's hair, his eyes unreadable. Tyler unclenched his arms, lifted his hand, and brushed a firm thumb across Jess's cheek.

The wind chimes jangled in the increasing breeze, and Tyler stepped away. "Good night, Jess."

Jessica swallowed. "Night."

She wanted to add … *Stay.* Just as he'd done in silence in his hotel room a few weeks ago, when the need in his eyes had been unmistakable.

But Dominic waited upstairs; Tyler's family, including his mom, was in the house, and she didn't know what they truly thought of her. The Campbells were friendly enough, but it was impressed into every Texan to be hospitable. Even when you didn't like a person, you still gave them what you could before sending them on their way. True acceptance took time and had to be earned. Sometimes it never came.

She and Tyler shared another look in the growing darkness. If they'd been the only two people in these hills, Jess would have stretched out her hand to him. And Tyler would have taken it.

Instead he repeated, "Night, Jess," and started to turn away.

Jess's heart ached as she watched him go, and when he abruptly turned back, her heart bumped so hard she could barely hear his words.

"Grace fixes a mess of breakfast every morning around seven," he said. "Plenty for everyone. If that's too early, she keeps something back for late risers. Just ask her. She's a sweetheart."

Another nod, Tyler's neutral stance returning, and he walked away.

"Tyler," Jess blurted.

He swung around so fast he was a blur in the rising moonlight. "What?"

Jess swallowed. "Would you mind calling Mrs. Alvarez for me? To tell her I'm all right? I don't want to call myself, in case …"

Tyler appeared to understand. "Sure." He took out his phone as he strolled back to her. Jess slid hers from her pocket and brought up Mrs. Alvarez's details so Tyler could copy her number. He stood too close when he did it, the powerfulness of him unnerving.

"Tell you what," Tyler said when he was finished. "I'll ask my mom to call. I have a feeling those two will get along fine."

"Fixing the lives of everyone around them?"

"Something like that." Tyler's grin flashed.

His smile tempted Jess to let her inhibitions take flight. Tyler was a man any woman would want to hug. Holding on to him, listening to his voice, his laughter, made everything bad go away.

Scared Jess to death. She never wanted to be dependent on anyone again, not emotionally, not financially. Standing on her own two feet was hard, yes, but she'd not become a victim once more because she longed for someone else to take care of her. Never again.

She sensed it wouldn't be like that with Tyler, but Jess wasn't sure that feeling was reality or only wishful thinking.

The good thing was, she'd be able to stay near Tyler, safe from the rest of the world, and find out.

Did not hurt at all that he was worth looking at while she got to know him. Jess let herself enjoy the view as Tyler turned and walked away to the house. His long, tall body and fine ass was a sight to see. Nope, didn't hurt at all.

———

JESS SLEPT WELL PAST THE communal breakfast. By the time she trudged into the kitchen at nine-thirty, Dominic at her side, Grace was the only one in the house.

Grace looked around from the stove when Jess entered from the dining room and beamed her and Dominic a wide smile.

"Good morning," she said. "I figured you'd want to sleep, so I made sure the mob didn't eat all the food. I have *migas* in this casserole—easy to heat, or traditional bacon and eggs if you want. Plenty of juice, and of course, coffee. You just let me know."

Grace looked like a beauty queen—one whose hot husband had knocked her up. She had dark hair and green eyes and a fine-boned face. Her body was swollen with her pregnancy, but the way she rested her hand on her abdomen made Jess's heart squeeze. She remembered the feeling with Dominic, a love and protectiveness she'd never lost.

Grace was kind too, from what Jess had seen, one of those women who were lovely all the way through. You couldn't hate them as much as you wanted to, because you knew they weren't hate-able. They were just *nice*.

"Thanks," Jess said. "I'll take the *migas*, if you don't mind. Mrs. Alvarez makes those."

"Hers are awesome," Dominic put in. "Mrs. Alvarez can seriously cook."

Grace gave him an amused look as she took a casserole dish out of the refrigerator and popped it into the oven. "Let's hope mine live up to it."

They did. The *migas*—eggs, fried tortilla strips, tomatoes and peppers, onions and cheese—were warm, flavorful, and satisfying.

Grace continued to cook while Jess and Dominic devoured the food. She chopped vegetables and sautéed things, dishing food into containers, which she stacked in the refrigerator. She waltzed back and forth with movements that went with her name.

"Perfect," Jess said, wiping her mouth when she finished.

"Thank you," Grace said brightly. "How'd I do?" she asked Dominic.

"Almost as good as Mrs. Alvarez's," Dominic said in all seriousness.

Grace's smile widened as though she understood this was high praise. "That's terrific. I'm going to open my own restaurant. I started to before, but then crap happened, and I had to give up. But it's my dream. It will be a pastry kitchen right here in town. I'm putting things on hold a few months for obvious reasons, but after that..." She brushed her abdomen again.

Jess didn't want to tell her that after her child was born, her priorities about everything would change—in a good way. But then, Grace had a look about her that said she would have the where-withal to do anything she wanted. Jess had seen Grace's husband, the hard-eyed Carter, gaze at her with loving admiration.

Jess instructed Dominic to carry his plate to the sink, which he did, rinsing it off without being told. She'd already sat him down this morning and explained that they weren't in a hotel—this was someone's house, and they couldn't expect maid service. They had to clean up after themselves, which was polite. Dominic had then explained back that he was nine, and he wasn't a barbarian.

As Jess had showered and dressed this morning, she'd decided she'd ask Tyler if she could stay on as a tenant, renewing the offer she'd made yester-day to pay rent. The apartment over the garage was nice, and it would be easier on her and Dominic to live there, at least for a while. Looking through the small town for an apartment or house rental would entail a credit check. Her credit was fine—she just didn't want one more record for Elijah or his bud-dies to find.

But first—"Any ideas on what kind of job I can do?" Jess asked. "Or do I go to the bar?"

Grace considered. "Be careful if you accept Tyler's offer to work here at the ranch. I was hired on as the cook, and look what happened." She indicated her thickening body.

Jess knew Grace teased but her heart beat faster. If Jess worked in the ranch's main office, with Tyler coming in and out, she'd never get anything done. She'd be fired within a week.

"I'm still the cook though," Grace said, serious again. "For the whole ranch, I mean, with a salary. I'm not the little woman shoved into the kitchen."

"You're not little," Dominic said in surprise.

He meant it as a compliment, Jess knew, but she darted a swift look at Grace and opened her mouth to apologize.

Grace grinned at Dominic and spread her arms. "I know. I'm *huge*." Her green eyes sparkled. "Want me to show you the town, Jess? I've cooked plenty this morning. If the menfolk can't find enough for their lunch, then tough. They can make it themselves."

"The menfolk?" Jess asked, wanting to laugh.

"A good name for them. Want to go?"

"I would, yes." Jess sprang up with an eagerness she hadn't felt in a long time. A new place, a fresh start. "I can help you with the dishes first."

Grace glanced at the sink where Jess's and Dominic's breakfast dishes lay among the pots and skillets she'd dirtied, and waved an indifferent hand.

"They'll be here when we get back. A rule in my kitchen is, if you complain, you do the work yourself."

"And you get paid for that?" Dominic asked in admiration. "Mom, I want to be a cook when I grow up."

"A celebrity chef," Grace said with enthusiasm.

She peeled off the full-length apron that had kept her cheerful pink shirt and stretch black shorts clean. "Then you can hire people to do all the dishes for you. Let's go."

She departed through the back door with a quickness a woman eight months gone shouldn't have. When Jess and Dominic caught up to her on the porch, Grace led them to the garage and the pickup parked in the driveway below Tyler's apartment. She opened its door without having to unlock it—must be nice to feel safe enough to leave a vehicle open.

"I can drive if you want," Jess offered.

"No, no. I want you looking out the window. I know where everything is." Grace caught Jess's glance at her abdomen. "Don't worry. I'm three weeks out and if anything happens, this is a small town. My doctor and the clinic are minutes away. I bet everyone in Riverbend knows how to deliver a baby anyway. They've either had to do it at home before the clinic was built or they've done it enough with horses and cows. But I refuse to lie on hay."

So chattering, Grace had them in the truck, Dominic in the cab's back seat, and started it up. She rolled down the windows as they moved out through the drive.

"Wave at Tyler," she said, pointing.

Tyler stood in the middle of the small ring where Jess had seen him yesterday. At the moment, he was holding the end of a very long rope while a horse at the other end galloped around him.

Dominic waved enthusiastically, as did Grace. "I'm kidnapping Jess," Grace called out the window to him. "Buh-bye."

Tyler raised his hand in acknowledgment, though he didn't speak. He turned to watch the truck all the way out of the ranch, never mind the horse kicking up its heels at the other end of the line. Jess knew Tyler watched because she looked back at him until the trees cut off her view.

"What was he doing?" Dominic asked.

"It's called a longe line," Grace said, her plump hands placed precisely at ten and two o'clock on the wheel. "They use it to exercise the horses they won't ride today, or to warm them up for other things, or to gentle new horses. The brothers are constantly training. It's a lot of work."

Dominic thought about this. "I'm thinking cook is better."

"I don't know," Grace said. "You fall in love with horses pretty fast. You might be a cowboy yet."

"Mmm," Dominic sounded skeptical. "Maybe."

As they passed under the gatepost, Jess was seized by sudden panic. Circle C was a safe place, a haven. Last night and this morning, she'd been sure nothing bad could happen to her as long as she was at the ranch. Now she was emerging into the real world with all its dangers.

Her mouth went dry, her pulse beating hard as Grace slowed to a halt at the end of the drive. Jess half expected to see a line of motorcycles strung across the grasslands waiting for her, Elijah in their lead.

What confronted her was an empty, two-lane road, its black asphalt faded by the Texas sun. One pickup raced by them, and Grace pulled onto the road behind it. Oblivious to Jess's tension, she kept up her conversation.

"The ranch is within Riverbend's town limits, but just barely. The rest of the metropolis is over the rise."

"We were at a gas station yesterday," Dominic told her.

"*The* gas station," Grace said. "Good, then you've seen most of Riverbend already. I'll show you the rest then we'll go to the diner. It's the heart of the town—or maybe its stomach."

Jess's hands began to unclench as Grace drove on. She saw no sign of Elijah and his men, very few bikers at all. This was ranch country—most of the vehicles were pickups and SUVs built for hauling loads of hay or pulling trailers.

Dallas, for all its big-city might, was surrounded by farms and ranch land, so Jess was used to horse trailers and trucks full of hay bales. Absent in Riverbend were slick cars and businessmen in suits, high rises, coffee houses on every corner, and chain restaurants, strip malls, and big retail stores.

"This is downtown," Grace said as she passed the gas station and drove around a square with a large courthouse in the middle. "The shops in this area are all owned by locals—Carter and his brothers help small businesses set up here instead of letting in the chains. AGCT has been running a year and so far has been very successful." She didn't bother to keep the pride from her voice.

"Where's the school?" Dominic asked.

"Not in Riverbend. The elementary school is in White Fork, and the high school is in between the two towns. I went to both, as did the Campbells. They're kind of famous. *Not* for their good grades."

Grace chuckled.

"Mom won't let me get bad grades," Dominic said darkly.

"That's smart of her," Grace said.

Jessica didn't like that the school was in another town, which meant she'd have to send Dominic off on a bus. Either that or drive him there and back, and worry about him all day. Then again, maybe she could get a job at the school. She could work in the office or maybe be a cafeteria lady. She bit back a laugh picturing herself in an apron with a plastic hair net, but then she sobered. She'd do it if it meant a paycheck and the ability to watch over Dominic.

Grace showed Jess the shops along the square, the small area of old bungalows where Christina and Grant and their little girl now lived. Adam and Bailey had built a house down the road from the ranch. Ross had an apartment over the shops on the square near the sheriff's office where he worked.

"None of the Campbells ever wanted to move far from home. Isn't that sweet?" Grace headed the big truck toward the gas station and the diner beyond. "I have no room to talk. My family's ranch is down that road." She pointed to a turnoff beyond the square. "I moved a whole ten miles."

"You love it," Jess said with conviction. "It shows."

Grace shrugged. "I'd never live anywhere else. I like going to Austin to shop and have fun, but it's crazy. So much traffic, development everywhere, crime. Riverbend has its share of crimes, but nothing like the cities." Grace gave her a sideways glance. "Oh, but you know that. You're from Dallas.

No offense."

"I lived in a little town in north Texas when I was younger," Jess said. "It was a farm town, though I didn't live on a farm. My dad had a feed and equipment store. When he and my mom split up, she and I moved to Dallas. Easier for her to find work there. I was too young to have ties to leave behind, and my dad sold up and left. I don't see him much." As in never.

"Well, you'll make ties here. *If* you decide to stay, that is." Grace's cheeks went pink. "Not trying to push you."

Grace wanted Jess to say she'd come down here to be with Tyler, she realized. All the Campbells did. At the same time, they danced around the subject, as though fearing she hadn't and wondering if Tyler would be hurt by it.

They exited the square, and Grace took the road toward the Malory ranch, showing Jess and Dominic wide stretches of land and the winding road that made its way to the Colorado River. The huge bend in it, she explained, gave the town its name. Jess gazed over the river as Grace drove slowly past it, the sparkling water cutting through green banks thick with trees, reflecting the wide, Texas sky.

The quiet beauty tugged at something inside Jess. She'd love to come up here with Tyler, hold his hand and gaze at the place of peace. In her fantasy, they'd have brought a blanket to put on the ground, so they could enjoy more than just the view.

Grace then drove back toward town, passing the clinic which sat a little way outside it, where she'd be having her baby, she said, and then into Riverbend.

Grace pulled the pickup to a halt in a parking lot, the biggest one in town, that surrounded the diner. "Hungry?" she asked Dominic. They'd been driving around for a while, and it was nearing noon. "I know you had a big breakfast, but Mrs. Ward always has something good cooking."

"Pie?" Dominic perked up. "The guy at the gas station yesterday said she had pie."

"She does. The best in the world." Grace hopped out of the truck and helped Dominic down without seeming to, preserving his male ego.

She led the way into the diner, Jess following and darting her gaze everywhere. If this was the only restaurant in town, that meant everyone who lived in Riverbend went there, and they would all see Jess. They'd spread the word that there was a new girl in town, from Dallas, with her nine-year-old son, staying with the Campbells. Who knew what connections Elijah had in Hill Country and South Texas? Even a rival might alert him if only to gloat.

Jess was relieved to see no bikers in the restaurant, only cowboys and ranch workers, ordinary people having lunch, but she remained wary.

Grace waved to friends right and left as she steered Jess to a booth in the back. *A popular beauty queen,* Jess amended. She wondered what that must have been like.

A large woman who turned out to be Mrs. Ward herself took their order. She gave Jessica a hard look, reminding her of Mrs. Alvarez, but she was pleasant enough. Her gaze turned more approving when Jess ordered burgers for herself and Dominic, with the works—no asking for tiny salads or fat-free recommendations. Grace had a chicken sandwich and plenty of fries to go with it.

"Enjoying it now," she explained. "After the baby is born, everyone will bug me to lose weight."

"You look fine," Jess said in surprise.

Grace wrinkled her nose. "Aw, I like you. Dominic, your mom is wonderful."

As they waited for the meal and then ate—the juiciest, freshest burgers Jess had tasted in a long while, Grace told her about the Campbells. How they got started in the stunt business as teenagers, how Adam had run off to Hollywood at age eighteen to make big movies.

The other brothers had remained home, but were hired for commercials, TV shows, and movies made locally and in New Mexico, plus live performances. They took their stunt show on the road in the summer, and trained horses for themselves and others the rest of the time.

Each brother had his specialty in the business. Adam coordinated with movie studios and used his experience to direct the stunts, Carter focused on the money side, and Grant and Tyler trained horses and dealt with the people who hired them.

"Grant is the charmer; Tyler is the show-off," Grace said. "That's why Tyler does PR for both their businesses. Tyler can make stunt riding look easy—he's the one who convinces people to let the Campbells train their horses or the show people to hire them. Grant keeps them happy through the process. But the two of them aren't just sweet-talkers. They understand what they're doing."

Grace spoke with the conviction of one in the know. Jess believed her—she'd gathered something of Tyler's effervescence and Carter's hard-headed business sense. Adam had quit the movies, Grace said—for the most part—returning home after an accident involving a car stunt. That explained the burn scars on his face.

Good conversation, Jess asking interested questions about the family and the town, made the meal go by quickly. Dominic, having cleaned his plate, now wanted his reward of pie. Grace said she'd take him to the counter and show him how many kinds they had—Mrs. Ward would let him have a taste before he decided.

Jess watched them go, warming at the way Dominic reached for Grace's hand. Grace, a few years younger than Jess, had the air of someone who could take care of the world. Grace had told her all the Campbells' ages—Tyler was the same as Grace, twenty-seven, which put him two years younger than Jess. Something else to think about.

Jess's view of Grace and Dominic was cut off when a woman slid into the booth in Grace's seat. She was a businesswoman all over, from her slick suit to her neatly styled hair to her tasteful jewelry to her shrewd brown eyes. She was way out of place in this diner, yet the other customers, after one glance, didn't pay her undue attention.

The woman held out her hand across the table. "I'm Karen Marvin," she said briskly. "Jessica McFadden? Right? I run AGCT Enterprises. Welcome to Riverbend." Her look turned knowing as Jess shook her hand. "Can I give you a bit of advice, honey? Forget Tyler, and go for Ross."

CHAPTER 13

JESSICA BLINKED AT KAREN AND quickly withdrew her hand. "What? Did you really just say that?" *Forget Tyler?* How was that possible?

Karen nodded, not the least perturbed. "Ross is a sweetheart and doesn't have as many issues as Tyler. Tyler picks up women and discards them right and left, though I hear his breakups are usually amicable." She signaled to a passing busboy—the only one in the diner—and he hurried over with a glass of ice water. "I've been here a year," Karen went on after a sip and a polite thanks to the busboy. "And I've already seen Tyler in action. Ross, dear. Trust me."

Jess couldn't stop her indignation. "Tyler has been extremely good to me. Generous—above and beyond the call."

Karen's expression softened. "I know. He can be incredibly sweet. But ... issues." She wriggled her fingers. "He was supposed to marry his high-school sweetheart. But right after graduation, she died in a car accident. Tyler hasn't been the same since."

Jessica thumped back in her seat, shock opening

her mouth. "Shit." She sucked in a breath, her heart flooding with sorrow. "Oh, poor Tyler."

Karen nodded, leaning forward to speak in a quiet voice. "It was nearly ten years ago, but from what I hear it was very, very tough on him. There are all kinds of speculations about it—that the girl was cheating on him and coming home with a lover from San Antonio; that Tyler was yelling at her and she ran away crying and got into the accident. Only Tyler knows the real story, so you should hear it from him."

Jess remained frozen, her hands flat on the table. No wonder his family walked on eggshells around Tyler, no wonder they scrutinized Jess as closely as they did. Adam and Grant had pretty much grilled her at Lanny D's, though they'd been friendly and interested. Their mother had looked piercingly at Jess last night at supper, and Grace showed a burning curiosity.

They were hoping Tyler had found someone to care about again. That he'd recovered. And they also worried that Jess wouldn't reciprocate and would tear his heart to shreds.

"Thank you for telling me," Jess said, her voice a croak.

Karen gave her a sympathetic look. "It's the country way. Everyone knows, but no one talks about it. But you deserve to understand. And take my advice on which brother to go after."

"Country way?" Jess clung to the one amusing thing in the conversation.

"I'm a big city girl. I don't fit in, if you hadn't noticed." Karen glanced around with a faint smile, giving a wave to a group of tough-looking cowboys in the corner. "But I like it. It's so *homey*." She turned back to Jess and became brisk again.

"So, you'll be looking for a job. There isn't much in Riverbend, as Grace will have told you. I'll see if I can find you something to do at AGCT Enterprises, but I'm not sure you'd be happy there. What are your job skills?"

"I'm a bartender."

Karen's brows went up. "Then why did Tyler call me about employing you at AGCT? I own the bar, but Christina decides who we hire. I'm sure she can find you something there, even fill-in work."

So Tyler had called Karen, already making plans for Jess. She tamped down her irritation. "Tyler isn't thrilled with the idea of me bartending," she said. "The last place I worked was pretty dangerous."

Karen gave her a wise look. "Any bar has the potential to be. It's what happens when you mix alcohol and testosterone. Anyway, what does Tyler have to do with it? It's your job, your life."

"Exactly what I keep trying to tell him." Jess relaxed a fraction, pleased she'd met someone who understood.

Karen shook her head. "The Campbells are protective of anyone they take under their wing. Even me."

She could not be much older than Jess, but Karen had the sharp edges of a woman resolved to make it in a man's world, edges she'd have needed. But she spoke of Riverbend with affection. If a cold businesswoman could soften in this town, maybe Jess could too.

"Are you warning me off Tyler for your own

reasons?" Jess asked, putting a teasing note in her voice.

Karen looked puzzled. "Not at all. I have my eye on Ross. He's adorable. I was being generous. Although—lately I've been more taken with the Malory brothers, Kyle and Ray. Hmm, which man of rodeo goodness do I want?"

Jess laughed. "You're terrible."

"Realistic, honey. I need to make a choice before they're both snatched up. I once thought I could have fun with Grant, but his heart belonged to Christina. Oh, speaking of Malorys …"

Karen turned in her seat to blatantly stare at two men who'd walked in and now surrounded Grace at the counter.

They weren't quite as tall as the Campbells, but they were large of body, muscles hard. Their dark hair was the exact shade of Grace's, and the way they hovered over her in nearly identical positions showed the two were brothers.

"Kyle on the left," Karen said. "Ray on the right. Champion bull riders. You'd do all right with one of them too."

"As long as I leave you the other," Jess said.

Karen flashed her a gleaming smile. "Well, of course."

Grace pivoted and came back to the table with Dominic, the brothers following her like protective pit bulls.

"I picked out pie for everyone," Grace was saying. "Hey, Karen, how are you? Jess, these louts are my brothers, Ray and Kyle."

She flapped a hand at each one in turn. The Malory men were much alike, but Kyle was a bit younger than Ray, while Ray had a few more muscular pounds on him and more wisdom etched into his face.

Their eyes were green, like Grace's. Karen wasn't wrong that they were good-looking—if Jess hadn't seen Tyler first, she might be staring long and hard.

"Welcome to Riverbend," Kyle said, extending a hand to Jess. Everyone was polite here. "Hope you stay a good long while. You need anything, you just let us know." He squeezed Jess's hand before releasing it.

Ray's hand, big and callused, was right there as soon as Kyle's disappeared. "Anything at all," Ray said. "I'll be around to fix it for you."

"Such sweethearts." Karen beamed a smile at both brothers.

It tickled Jess to watch Ray and Kyle back up a nervous step. They knew a predatory woman when they saw one.

"Do you really ride bulls?" Dominic asked them.

"Yup," Kyle ruffled his hair, which Jess could warn him Dominic didn't like.

Dominic put up with it, looking enthralled with the two big men. "Why?" he asked in genuine curiosity.

Both Kyle and Ray burst out laughing, filling the diner with a deep, warm sound.

"The challenge, I guess," Kyle said. "It's fun."

"Money and fame," Karen put in, nodding at Ray.

Ray flushed. "More like we're crazy. But it's what we do."

"All right, you two, you've ogled her," Grace said. "Go have lunch." She gave Jess a sage look as Karen vacated her seat and Grace sat down. "They usually have lunch at home, but I foolishly told them I'd be here. I only asked if they wanted me to bring them any pie. But they figured out I was showing you around and had to barge in."

Kyle quickly raised his hands. "No, we didn't. The pie just sounded too good to wait for."

Karen linked one arm around Kyle's and the other around Ray's. "Since you boys are here, why don't I treat you to lunch? No strings … well, unless I think of some."

So saying, she herded the Malory brothers away. They gracefully and politely didn't flee, but looked a bit pale as they let Karen escort them to another table.

Grace didn't hide her mirth. "They were nosy, and they paid for it."

"Does everyone in town know I'm here?" Jess asked, the ever-gnawing worry lurking. "I'd hoped to fly under the radar."

"Of course everyone knows. You can't keep a secret in a small town. On the other hand, it stays in town. No one will talk about you to outsiders."

They wouldn't mean to, Jess knew. But someone might mention it to a friend in Dallas, who might know a biker, who might know Elijah or one of his cronies.

Jess shut down the thoughts. She was tired of fear. Dallas was a huge city, and Elijah didn't know every single person in it, as much as he pretended to. Maybe this time, Jess really could be free.

"More nosiness," Grace said at the same time a man crowded into the booth beside Jess.

Jess's body heated instantly, and Dominic's face lit

up. "Tyler!" he cried.

Tyler smelled good, like soap and shaving cream. He must have showered and changed—he was no longer covered with the dust the horse had stirred up in the ring.

Grace's eyes twinkled. "What are *you* doing here, Tyler? Come for pie?"

Tyler shrugged, his arm brushing Jess's. "It's lunch time. What do you think I'm doing here?"

"I left plenty of food in the fridge."

Tyler gave her an innocent look. "Which your husband and everyone who works at Circle C devoured while I was cleaning up. Thought I could go for a burger."

"And pie," Dominic said. "I'm having apple." He cut off with a squeak of delight as Mrs. Ward and another waitress set four huge slices of pie on the table.

"I figured you'd want some too," Mrs. Ward said as she slid the biggest piece in front of Tyler.

Dominic looked shocked. "He hasn't had his lunch yet."

Tyler lifted the fork the waitress had set down and plunged it through the mountain of whipped cream to the slab of pie underneath. "Pie for lunch. What a great idea." He winked at Dominic. "Don't tell your mom though."

Dominic grinned. He jabbed his fork into his pie the exact way Tyler had and tried to take as big a bite. The two of them made a game of what kind of *Mmmm* noises they could make as they tore apart their pieces and stuffed them into their mouths.

Tyler was funny, fun, and good with Dominic. Jess had feared he'd change in her eyes when she saw him again, in light of what Karen had told her about the death of his high-school girlfriend. But he didn't. He was the same charming, handsome, hot Tyler he'd been before she'd known about his tragedy.

The promising look Tyler slanted Jess as he curled cream into his mouth from his fork held nothing of grief. He was a man liking a woman, and wanting her.

He wasn't out for sympathy, Jess realized. He didn't want pity.

He wanted life. That was a dream she could share with him.

————

JESS INSISTED ON GOING TO the bar that night.

Tyler tried to talk her out of it, but apparently Karen had stuck her oar in and saw no reason why Jess shouldn't work at the bar if she wanted to. When they reached Circle C, his mother gave Tyler a look that reminded him of their conversation the night before.

You can't smother her, she'd said.

You mean don't be a high-handed dick? he'd replied, knowing she was right. Tyler sighed inwardly.

"All right, all right," he said. He'd at least convinced Jess to sit down on the porch out of the afternoon heat while they enjoyed fresh-brewed iced tea. Adam and Grant had come to train, and Tyler decided to let them do some work for a change while he took a break. "We'll put on our party clothes, and we'll go."

"I don't have any party clothes," Jess said, looking

dismayed. "I brought only bare essentials."

Tyler tried not to read too much innuendo into the phrase *bare essentials*. "Doesn't matter. This is Sam's bar in Riverbend. What you're wearing is party clothes."

Slim jeans shorts. A scoop-necked white top with short sleeves that showed off the tatts lacing down her arms. Her long legs ended in sandals perfect for the later summer weather.

She was frigging gorgeous, and all the iced tea in the world wasn't going to calm Tyler down, not even if he dumped it into his lap. It didn't have anywhere near enough ice in it.

Smothering or not, Tyler wasn't about to let her go to the bar without him. The cowboys of River-bend would take one look at her and drool all over themselves.

Sun kissed her legs and her toes, which were free of polish. Tyler tried to stop thinking about *himself* kissing her legs and nibbling on her toes, but it was tough.

Jess wasn't watching him, thank God, or she'd find him wiping a bit of drool off the side of his mouth. She looked down toward the ring, where Faith and Dominic, Faith's braided hair burnished by the sunshine, were hanging on the rail.

Faith had come home from school a little bit ago, rushed into the house, and rushed out again in her riding clothes. She'd waved for Dominic to follow her, which he'd done after looking to his mom for permission.

"You've really never ridden a horse?" Faith's voice came to them, her tone incredulous. "You mean, ever?"

Dominic scowled at her. "I live in Dallas. When did I have a chance? Have you ever ridden a BMX bike?"

"No," Faith admitted.

"You mean, ever?" Dominic mimicked her, then he dropped his mocking tone. "It's really fun. I have a BMX that I race at a track. Used to, anyway. If we stay here, I'll start doing it again. I'll teach you how to ride a course."

Faith pondered this. "My dad might say no. But I can teach you to ride a horse. Want me to?"

Dominic studied the tall horses wandering the corral, his back stiffening. There was no shame in being afraid to ride horses, Tyler wanted to tell him—the animals were big and could be danger-ous. Faith knew what she was doing though, and her horse, Dodie, was docile and good with kids.

"Okay," Dominic said, as though having weighed his options. "But don't laugh at me if I fall off."

Jess looked alarmed and set her iced tea aside. Tyler put his hand on hers to keep her from leap-ing up and running down to the ring. "Faith won't let him fall," he said in a low voice. "She teaches kids younger than she is, and Carter is down there. He'll keep an eye out. No one's more careful than Carter."

Jess sank back into her chair, watching as Faith took Dominic around the corral to the barn. The two fell in step, Faith casting a smile at Dominic.

"Shit, I hope that's not a budding romance," Tyler said with a qualm as he and Jess watched them go. "Carter will kill me."

When Jess spoke, her voice was soft. "No, let them have it. Let them have the romance, when it's fresh and innocent."

Her gaze was on the kids, not Tyler, her face relaxed and touched with the glow of afternoon sunshine.

Something changed in Tyler as he watched her. He mostly went through his life not paying attention to it—focusing on the horses and the stunts he did so he wouldn't harm his brothers or his animals. He made love to women for the fun of it, and the brief escape of orgasm. He cared about his brothers, mom, nephew, nieces, and friends without making a big show of it.

A part of him that had been silent a long time woke up. Tyler sat unmoving and let the new feeling ripple through him, wondering where it had been. His heart pumped, his blood flowed hot, and yet a wash of fear swamped him at the same time.

This wasn't wanting. This was a tender caring and a hope that the feeling would build into something else.

Tyler held his breath, waiting for the moment to pass, for him to return to his half-life of not giving a shit about too much of anything.

It didn't. The moment went on, stretching, as the sun slowly moved westward and the air cooled. The sensations inside him didn't cease. Something had awakened, and it wasn't going back to sleep any time soon.

JESS NOTICED THAT TYLER DIDN'T speak much as he drove Jess to the bar after dinner. Dominic, triumphant from his first horseback riding lesson—which consisted of him mounting, sitting, and dismounting a mare called Dodie—was staying in the main house tonight to watch movies with Faith, Grace, and Carter. Dominic was excited about the slumber party, except that there wouldn't be any boys his age around, he finished glumly.

Faith told him not to worry—when he started going to school, he'd meet lots of kids. Jess said nothing when Dominic gave her an inquiring look. Registering Dominic in school might be tricky, but it had to be done. That and getting her medical records so she could go to a new doctor would be the hardest part of this move.

Olivia had assured Jess, when they'd all returned to the ranch after pie that day, that she'd reached Mrs. Alvarez. The woman was fine and relieved to hear Jess was all right. Mrs. Alvarez had passed on the message that Jess shouldn't worry about any-thing—she would take care of the details so Jess could relax.

Jess nearly cried in gratitude. One day, she would pay Mrs. Alvarez back for everything she'd done. When Jess was certain Dominic would be safe, she'd give Mrs. Alvarez whatever she could, though she already knew Mrs. Alvarez wouldn't let her. Jess's life would have been ten times harder, she knew, if it hadn't been for the kind but no-non-sense woman who'd been volunteering one day at Dominic's school. Mrs. Alvarez had heard that Jess was desperate for a babysitter and approached her, and their friendship had been born.

Tyler was quiet at dinner, and he continued to be as they rolled into town. He drove the same pickup in which Jess had taken him back to his hotel room in Dallas. Where she'd unbuttoned his shirt, and he'd pulled her to him for a long, hot kiss …

Hot shivers ran through every limb. She'd never forget Tyler's hands on her body, how he'd held her while he leaned against the wall, kissing her more thoroughly than she'd ever been kissed.

Jess glanced at him now, his hands resting negligently on the wheel, his leg in blue jeans moving as he accelerated or braked. He had so much power, and now it was at rest.

She sensed tension in him though. He didn't look at her even as she stared at him, but kept his eyes on the road, not saying a word.

She knew Tyler was angry that she insisted on working at the bar. Jess didn't particularly want to, but she understood bartenders and they understood her. Even if she didn't get a job there, she could ask them for suggestions about where would be a good place to look for employment. Karen had mentioned AGCT Enterprises, saying she didn't think Jess would be happy there, but Jess would have to convince her otherwise. She wasn't afraid of work, or boredom, or Karen herself. She just needed a paycheck.

The drive wasn't long, and Tyler pulled into the parking lot that bordered the diner and killed the engine.

Jess expected Tyler to try to talk her out of going inside, but he only slid out of the truck and slammed the door. Before she could get out herself, Tyler was at the passenger door, opening it and handing her down like an old-fashioned gentleman. As Tyler's strong hand closed on hers, Jess decided she liked old-fashioned gentlemen.

It was nine, and the bar was crowded but Jess knew as soon as she walked in that Sam's was a far different place from the biker bar she'd just quit.

The layout was much the same—long U-shaped counter taking up one wall, wine and specialty liquor bottles on shelves behind it, glasses and mugs hanging overhead. Tables dotted the floor, filled already, and pool tables stood on the far left side from the door. A small raised stage occupied the end of the pool table area, empty tonight, but ready for a band.

The difference between the two bars was in the people. Hatted cowboys leaned on the counter or sat on stools, here to unwind after a hard day's work. Girlfriends and wives came with them, couples busy dancing to the country music that blared from speakers. The younger girls wore tight skirts and lots of makeup, and the younger cowboys eyed them.

As at the biker bar, the bartender here, a thirtyish woman, pulled beer or poured glasses of wine, not much drink mixing. No Pink Ladies tonight.

"I wouldn't mind the help," the young woman said over the noise when Tyler and Jess approached and Jess introduced herself. "Talk to Karen. I can put you to work."

Jess had feared that the bar would be too quiet in such a small town, but the joint was jumping. She could clear plenty of tips and not take too much away from the other employees. Besides, it would be enjoyable serving people out to have a good time.

"Not tonight," Tyler said, sending the bartender his best smile. "Tonight we're here to have fun."

Fine with her—Jess wasn't ready to run behind the bar and start pouring immediately. Her leg ached, which happened when she had too much stress, and she was tired. Taking the grand tour with Grace then lazing around the porch, plus jumping every time she saw a truck pull into the ranch, had worn her out.

The bartender grinned. "You stay, you have to buy something," she told Tyler.

"You got it, sweetheart." Tyler dug into his pocket and dropped a twenty on the bar. "Give us a couple of beers, and keep the change. Come on, sugar," he said to Jess. His hand was under her elbow, propelling her toward the dance floor. "I need you to dance with me."

CHAPTER 14

———

J ESS WAS ALREADY UNSTEADY TONIGHT, and being so close to Tyler didn't help. She wanted to tell him she'd rather sit down, but the noise in the room didn't allow her to explain.

The music thumped through her bones, catching her in its rhythm. She'd heard somewhere that humans responded automatically to music, something cellular reaching for the sound.

All her cells were gyrating by the time Tyler halted on the small dance floor and pulled her into his arms. The beat was rapid, but Tyler moved slowly, enclosing her in his supporting embrace.

Jess floated, her pain receding to a distant ache. It didn't matter how clumsy she felt tonight because Tyler had balance for both of them.

Instead of following the music's rhythm, Tyler stepped into a quiet, intimate pace. Jess was up against his chest as he put one arm firmly around her, his other hand guiding her in the dance she didn't know.

His vibrancy and grace came through his movements and his body. The athleticism he used with his horses and in his stunts made this man a fabulous dancer.

They went around the floor at Tyler's pace, Tyler avoiding the other couples with ease. When Jess looked up into Tyler's face, she found him gazing down at her at the same moment, unguarded.

What Jess saw in his eyes made her falter. There was an incandescence inside him, a flame buried deep. It confused her, almost frightening her with its intensity.

Tyler shuttered himself instantly, but the rawness she'd seen in him stayed with her, lighting a profound response in herself.

If the world were different—if Jess had nothing in her past and he had nothing in his—this would be beautiful.

It *was* beautiful. But Jess wasn't sure it could be real.

The song ended. Couples drifted back to their tables, arms around each other. One of the Malory brothers broke a clump of pool balls to start a game, the clack loud in the relative hush.

Tyler caught Jess as she started to turn away. He eased her back to him and leaned down and kissed her.

A melting sensation in the backs of her knees made Jess's body start to crumple, but Tyler caught her and lifted her to him while he kissed her with slow thoroughness.

Jess suddenly didn't care that they were in the middle of the bar, in the middle of the dance floor, with most of Riverbend around them. Her limbs tingled and her intimate spaces tightened, a wash of wanting gripping her.

Tyler didn't seem to give a rat's ass that they were

surrounded by the whole town either. He drew his hand up to tumble her hair, then let his thumb trace the curl of tatt that led from her shoulder to her breast. He didn't slide his fingers under her shirt; he simply touched, caressed.

"Oh, man." The deep voice of Kyle Malory boomed out. "Does every pretty woman in this town have to end up with a Campbell?"

The guys he played pool with laughed at him. "Tough shit, Kyle," one of them said.

"Bad enough my *sister* married one," Kyle went on in mock disgust. "What the hell was she thinking?"

Tyler didn't respond. He took his time ending the kiss, then he raised his head, his lips parted, his gaze lingering on Jess. After a moment, he turned slowly, sending Kyle a lazy look before giving him the finger.

More laughter. Jess sensed a rivalry that was part joking, part serious, forming a bond between them.

"Suck on it, Malory," Tyler said in a jovial tone. He put his arm around Jess and led her away.

"You know you'd love it, Tyler," Kyle said behind them. Whooping and jeers followed from his friends.

"Ignore the dickheads," Tyler said in Jess's ear, his breath warming her to her toes. "Too noisy in here. Want to get out?"

Jess did. She couldn't start work tonight even if she'd wanted to—her future had to wait until tomorrow. Then she'd find a way to talk to Karen and Christina, whom she hadn't met yet, about working in the bar. The Campbells were being very nice to her, but she wanted to stand on her own as soon as she could. They wouldn't be thrilled if she hung on them too long—there was an expiration date on hospitality.

"Sure," Jess said.

She preferred the ranch, with its quiet comfort, and the knowledge she wasn't alone there. Last night, whenever she'd woken in the dark, it had soothed her to think that over in the main house, more people slept—Carter and his family, Tyler's mom, Tyler.

Jess had spent plenty of time fantasizing about Tyler in his bed, wondering if he wore pajamas. He hadn't taken any clothes from his apartment yesterday afternoon, and she assumed he had things to wear in the main house, but maybe not pajamas. The thought of him bare against the sheets had sent her heart pounding and made sleep elude her.

The parking lot was a little quieter than the bar, but more people were arriving, and overflow from inside had groups standing around talking, joking, calling to one another. This was a friendly spot, not the territory of a gang who ran off anyone its members didn't like. The bar was a place to have fun, to meet up with friends after work, for guys to take their girlfriends and for young singles to try their luck.

Much more relaxed than Brent's Bar in Dallas. Jess hoped she never had to see that place again.

Tyler stopped at his truck, but instead of opening the door for Jess, he leaned against the fender and pulled her to him. He put his fingers under her chin, raising her face to his for another soul-satisfying kiss.

Jess kissed him hungrily, her hands finding the

sides of his waist and wandering down to his ass, tugging him closer. Jess was pressed against the length of him, the hardness behind his jeans a firm ridge against her abdomen. Flames that hadn't died rekindled.

Tyler broke the kiss, his eyes black in the darkness, and brushed Jess's lower lip with his thumb.

"You shouldn't keep kissing me," Jess said in a shaking voice. "People will think we're together."

"They can think whatever the hell they want." Tyler lowered his hand, taking his heat away, but his body was still tight to hers, his desire for her obvious.

"They hope we *are* a couple," Jess said. "They want us to be."

"I know." Tyler gently moved Jess aside, making her abruptly cold without him against her, and unlocked and opened the door.

No more words about it. Tyler neither declared they were together or stated that the rest of the world was wrong. No saying they needed to talk about it. Tyler simply helped Jess into the truck and walked to the other side.

He started the truck without a word, remaining silent as he drove out of the lot and the short way home. Jess still vibrated from the dance, from their kisses, from their closeness. Earlier today she'd rejoiced because she could stay near Tyler and get to know him, but now she wondered if that was a good idea. She'd drop dead of her need for him if she couldn't fulfill it.

For now, she enjoyed the quiet ride, liking that Tyler didn't flinch away when she placed her hand over his on the seat.

Jess loved the darkness out here—true darkness under a spangle of stars. No traffic, just an easy ride through the night to the ranch, the hottest cowboy in town taking her home.

Home. Jess wondered when she'd began thinking of it as such.

Dominic would be finishing his movie by now. Jess hopped out as soon as Tyler stopped his pickup in front of the house. She was a mom first, which meant hurrying inside to check on her son.

She found Dominic curled up under a blanket on the couch, in the circle of Grace's arm. Carter sat on an oversized chair next to them, Faith drowsing in his lap. Dominic's eyes drooped, but he was determinedly watching to the end of the movie.

Jess kissed him good night, said the same to the rest of them, and let Tyler walk her back to the apartment. She didn't miss the interested looks all four of them gave her and Tyler as they departed.

Everyone in that house, including Dominic, wanted her and Tyler to end up together. Jess could feel the waves of their hope all the way to the garage.

"I'm coming up with you," Tyler said as they reached the stairs. "I'm not letting you in there until I check it out. Deal with it, sweetheart."

"I'm so glad I have a big, strong man to look after me," Jess replied in a sugary voice.

"One you saw get his ass kicked," he said in a cynical tone.

"But you fought *really* hard."

Tyler turned from the step above her, coming back down to slide an arm around her waist. "You watch yourself, darlin'. Anyway, I did fight hard. There were just too many of them."

"I know," Jess said in her normal voice. "I was so scared they were going to kill you."

Tyler's tone gentled. "They didn't." He touched her lips with his fingers as he had when he'd finished kissing her at the bar, but to her disappointment, he let her go and headed up the stairs. "Now let me make sure no one's in here waiting for you."

He opened the door and walked inside, looking around the apartment with swift thoroughness. Then he signaled Jess to come in, and he shut the door behind her.

"You all right?" he asked her.

Jess was. More all right than she'd been in a long time.

Tyler made no move to kiss her again, to take her into his arms, to hint that they should move to the bedroom. He was going to be a gentleman, she realized. He'd bow out, saying he'd look after Dominic, leave her so she could get some sleep. He'd be gallant, and she'd be alone.

Jess couldn't stand it. She closed the distance between them and grasped the lapels of his shirt. "Stay," she whispered.

Tyler's throat worked. He rested his hand on her shoulder, thumb brushing her tatt as he studied her a long time, everything in his eyes. Then, slowly, he nodded.

"Yeah," he said, the word barely audible. "I'll stay."

THIS TIME WAS DIFFERENT, JESS thought. In Dallas, they'd been daring, exploring, strangers in the night. Tonight they slowed their touches, their kisses, learning each other. Tyler had been agile in the dance, and he brought that fluidity of movement to his lovemaking.

He undressed Jess with careful hands, next following the path his fingertips had taken on her body with his tongue. When he straightened again, Jess slid his shirt up his torso, pushing it aside so she could lean down to nip his chest, taste his hot skin.

Tyler glided his hands under her breasts, thumbs brushing her already tight nipples to firm points. He kissed her neck, her shoulder, her mouth, his lips and tongue bringing her to life.

A breeze stirred the wind chimes at the top of the stairs, another detail from his sisters-in-law. The sound flowed through Jess, resonating in her blood. Tyler's burning touch and his kisses on her neck joined the vibrations to make her body one point of fire.

He kissed his way to her breasts, his hair brushing her skin. He licked the end of her tattoo around her nipple then drew the point into his mouth.

Jess arched back, arms going around him to draw him against her. Once more, Tyler awakened her, Jess who had passion in abundance, but passion no one else wanted from her. Even her husband had told her flat out that she turned him off and had showed no interest in a physical relationship in the dying days of their marriage.

Tyler had plenty of interest. He caressed her as he suckled her, the roughness of his hands stirring need. The pull of his mouth on her breast made

Jess shift her legs open, her craving for him escalating into something raw.

He didn't make her wait long. Tyler opened her waistband and slid her jeans down her hips, his skilled hands removing her underwear in the next stroke. Jess kicked jeans and underwear away, impatient to be bare.

She started to speak but was silenced when he slid his hand between her legs.

Jess let out a moan, her feet moving farther apart, her hips rocking, her body wanting the crazed sensations he stirred. Her bad knee started to buckle, but Tyler caught her and held her in the curve of his arm, his kiss hard as he began to stroke her.

Not fair. Jess fumbled with his belt, finally popping it open at the same time he slid a long finger inside her. She gasped with it, but still worked to squeeze her fingers between herself and Tyler to unbutton his jeans and open his zipper. She managed to get her hand inside his underwear, closing it around his hot, stiff cock.

Tyler groaned in his throat but he didn't break the kiss. His fingers moved on Jessica, stirring her to climax, until she was gripping his cock hard, stroking him through her fist.

Tyler's hips moved with her rhythm, letting her make love to him with her hand, as he made her crazy with his. They held each other in the middle of the room, both making noises of pleasure as they each found ways to excite the other.

It wasn't long before Jess cried out, the white-hot sensation of his fingers inside her taking her over the top. She no longer remembered where she was or how she got there—all she knew was that she stood in the arms of a cowboy who made her body sing.

Tyler finally tugged her hand from his cock, lifting her to carry her swiftly to the bedroom. They more or less fell to the bed, Tyler landing on top of her.

Before Jess could draw a breath, he thrust himself inside her, the firm length of his cock taking the place of his fingers, renewing her frenzied need. She cried out, unable to stop herself, dimly hoping no one was below to hear them. Tyler caught her cries with his kisses, but his own voice soon joined hers as he rocked into her, his thrusts accelerating.

A hard-muscled, hot-bodied man was making love to her with skill but with a natural wildness that kept it from being rehearsed. Jess remembered the raw look she'd seen in his eyes at the bar, and that strength came to her now as he drove into her, his face set, eyes fixed on her. He had grace, but he had power as well.

As Jess came apart once more, Tyler rode her faster, finally giving one last thrust as his own climax hit him.

The world dissolved into a wash of color as Jess wrapped legs and arms around this beautiful, beautiful man. Tyler continued to love her, his movements quieting until they fell together, breathless and smiling, in the patch of moonlight that flooded the bed.

———

TYLER WOKE WITH HIS FACE pressed to Jess's shoulder. She lay on her stomach, her head turned from him, her breathing even. Her tatts were smooth beneath Tyler's lips, lines sharp in the morning sunlight.

Tyler thought over all she'd told him since she'd arrived in Riverbend—her ex, Elijah, her fears for Mrs. Alvarez.

Jess had so much love in her—for Dominic, for Mrs. Alvarez—and interest in her fellow beings, like Grace, and Tyler's brothers and niece. She shouldn't have to struggle to survive.

Tyler had so much. When he'd lost Lindsey and thought he would die, his family was there to hold him up, to take care of him until he was able to go on. Not *move* on, because Tyler had learned you never really got over losing someone—they were always a part of you. But you could continue, and laugh again, and live your life.

Elijah wasn't letting Jess move on, or live. He'd cornered her and was using her, in whatever game he'd decided to play. Tyler knew a man like that would not give up. He'd keep hunting for Jess until he cornered her again.

Tyler would never let that happen. He had brothers to help him protect her— Ross was already looking at Elijah's and Cade's records and seeing what he could do about keeping both of them out of River County, and maybe locked away, far from Jess.

Tyler could do something himself. It was obvious what the first step should be.

Jess woke. Tyler heard the change in her breathing, which was followed by a little groan.

She rolled over, shading her eyes from the sunshine that streamed through an open slat in the shutters.

"Is it morning already?" she mumbled in surprise.

"'Fraid so. Any second now, my brothers will be yelling at me to get my ass down to the ring."

"Oh. Damn." She sounded regretful, which made his heart sing. Tyler was definitely regretful and had the hard-on to prove it.

First things first. Tyler knew he'd lose the balls to do what he'd just decided if he didn't plunge right in.

He touched Jess's cheek, drew a quick breath, and said, "Marry me, Jess."

CHAPTER 15

———

JESS'S HEART STOPPED BEATING.

At least, it felt like that, because there was a long pause followed by a huge bang in her chest.

She sat up, the blankets falling away, her hair stinging her eyes. "What?"

Tyler regarded her without blinking. "I said, marry me."

She hadn't dreamed the words, nor the resolve in Tyler's voice. His eyes held determination, need, and … hope?

"Why?" came out of Jess's mouth. Her lips were numb—she hadn't meant to say that.

Tyler's half smile vanished. "What do you mean, *why*? I have plenty in my life, and I want to give it to you. We can live here, or we can find our own house. Our own place, I think—Dominic will need more room. You won't have to worry about slinging drinks for the horny men of Riverbend, and most of all, you'll be safe from your fuck of an ex and his best friend."

He was serious. Jess listened, open-mouthed, her limbs watery with shock.

Tyler wanted to save her, and so he held out

this offer. Become Mrs. Campbell, of the Riverbend Campbells, wife to a famous stunt rider. Be taken care of by him. Free to sit in the kitchen with Grace every day after she sent Dominic off to school while Tyler worked on the ranch and came home for lunch, dinner, and bed.

This amazing, sexy, generous man was offering ... himself.

It hadn't been easy for him. She saw that. Already his face was clouding as though he regretted the words.

"You barely know me," Jess choked out. "There are things about me you don't understand. I mean, I could be this creepy, sadistic black-widow kind of woman."

"You could be," Tyler agreed. "But you'd have gotten rid of Elijah a long time ago if you were." His brows came down. "Obviously you think it's a bad idea. Forget it."

He started to rise, the covers sliding from him, and Jess put desperate hands on his shoulders.

"I don't want to forget it. I just think we ought to think about it. Both of us. It's a huge thing."

Tyler sat back down, but he didn't relax. "Like I said, we should forget it."

"*No.*" Jess let her hands drop away. "But I'm serious that there are things you don't know about me. One big one you need to understand."

She stopped and swallowed hard, the words sticking in her throat. It had been hard enough to tell her husband six years ago, and he'd freaked out. Said he didn't want to deal with it, said she'd tainted his son, no matter how much she'd assured him no one had proved it was genetic. She'd already been prepared to leave Cade, and not long after that, he'd flung Dominic from him in rage, which had clinched it, and she had taken Dominic and fled.

What would Tyler do when he knew? Run away from her, far and fast? Take from her this tranquility she'd found?

But he had to understand. Jess couldn't lie to him—it wasn't fair after he'd been so wonderful.

She drew a long breath, her heart breaking, knowing her next words could lose him forever.

"Tyler, I have MS."

Tyler looked at her, going so still that the only movement was his chest rising and falling. Then he shook his head. "I don't know what that is."

"Multiple sclerosis. It's a neurological disorder. They believe." There were many unknown factors about MS, new theories all the time, ones that sort of fit, ones that were thrown out as fast as they were thought of. But no definite understanding, even now. "It's chronic, which means I need meds all the time. Basically the immune system attacks the myelin sheaths of the nerves—it's hard to explain. Sometimes I'm fine; other times it flares up and it's hell. I have to take one day at a time. That's why I was going on about keeping a job that has insurance—why I need a job again. So if you marry me … you get my MS too."

Tyler's only change in expression as she garbled this explanation was a slight pucker of his brows. When Jess trailed off, her throat hurting, Tyler remained motionless.

"Jess." He folded his fingers into his palms, forming fists. "Shit. I am so sorry."

Tears stung Jess's eyes. "I have a fairly mild form,"

she made herself go on. "It could be so much worse than it is. My left leg has the most trouble—it's weak and painful—and sometimes I'm too tired to do anything. Most of all, I need the medication to keep it under control, from getting worse. Injections, three times a week. They're hellaciously expensive. I have enough for another week, and Mrs. Alvarez is authorized to pick up the next batch and get them to me. But then that's it—that's the last; I'll run out at the end of September. Elijah … he was helping me pay for them. In return, I give him free drinks at the bar, run errands—nothing criminal, just annoying like doing his grocery shopping and stuff like that. This is how desperate I was to get away from him—I walked away from his money. The meds are thousands of dollars a month, and insurance only covers so much. But I …"

Her voice died, Jess unable to force out any more words. She had ceased crying about her condition years ago, realizing she could fold in on herself and exist in a ball of depression, or she could take care of what she could and get on with things. For Dominic's sake, she'd got on with her life.

"Damn it." Tyler's face reddened with fury. "No wonder Elijah had such a hold on you. The mofo. If he so much as comes near Riverbend, I'll kill him."

"I didn't want to tell you." Jess heard the profound sadness in her voice. "I didn't want to ruin this …" She waved a hand around the tumbled bed. "It's been so wonderful."

Tyler reached out and slid his hands over her arms, rubbing them as though worried she was cold. "You haven't ruined anything, sweetheart.

I'm going to take back taking back asking you to marry me. I still want to do it. But I guess *you* need to think about it a little more than I do."

Jess dragged in a ragged breath. "Don't you dare marry me because you feel sorry for me. I've figured out how to live. I'll need to see a doctor soon and tell him or her my life story, probably I'll have to go to Austin for a neurologist and my MRIs."

"Is there a cure for MS?" Tyler asked. "I genuinely don't know. If Elijah's been holding out on you ..."

Jess shook her head. "Not so far. It's still not a well-understood thing. It's like arthritis or lupus—not exactly like those, but something ongoing you just have to manage. You've been so damned nice to me, but I'm not going to marry you and dump my problems on you. And I won't let you marry me out of pity."

Tyler's eyes narrowed. "If it's okay with you, I can feel bad for you and want to marry you at the same time. When I asked you ten minutes ago, I didn't know all this. Knowing hasn't made me want to change my mind."

"But, I don't ..."

"Son of a bitch, Jess." Tyler released her and sat up straight, stark naked, fists balled, like a god readying himself to fight an enemy. "I'm not going to let you refuse me because you're scared, or let you think I'll toss you out on your ass for having something wrong with you. Hell, if being perfect was a requirement for living at Circle C, we'd all be homeless. If your husband gave you hell for it, I'll kill him too."

Jess said nothing, but Tyler must have read the

truth in her eyes. "That's it," he growled. "He's a dead man."

He opened his hand, his touch incredibly gentle as he cupped Jess's cheek. "So I've proposed. The ball is in your court. You said you'd think about it, so promise me you'll *think*. And not just say no because you feel sorry for *me*. I'm fucked up too—but I can take care of myself."

Jess let out a long, shaking sigh. Maybe, just maybe he was giving her something to believe in. "All right, all right. I'll think it over. You've lost your mind, but I'm not going to let you take it back—again." She gave him a severe look, as though daring him to tell her once more to forget it. Praying he didn't.

Tyler's grip tightened. He drew her closer and silenced any more words with a kiss that melted Jess into him, the heat of last night infusing it.

Down they went on the bed, Tyler's hand parting her legs, his thick cock sliding inside her a moment later.

They made love in swift silence, the only noise the creak of the bed, the whir of the air conditioner clicking on, signaling another hot day in Hill Country.

Tyler thrust into her, diffusing all the tension their words had caused. Jess surrendered to sensation, nothing else existing. There was no more pain, no regrets, no fear.

Jess clung to Tyler as she rose to another crazed climax, this one the best of all. Tyler laid her down when it was over, Jess out of breath. He touched her face as he withdrew, then he stood all the way up, retrieved his clothes from the floor, and strode out.

The door banged. Jess had risen to her elbows to watch him go, and now she collapsed onto the bed, flinging out her arms, and let out a strangled laugh.

"Damn," she said to the empty room. "That cowboy is *good*."

———

TYLER SHOWERED IN THE MAIN house, movements impatient, his body tight with emotions, and went to have breakfast. No one but Grace was in the kitchen so he told her a solution that had struck him in the shower.

Grace stopped and stared at him, eyes widening, before she said, "You know, that's actually a good idea."

"Don't sound so stunned," Tyler snarled and started shoveling huevos rancheros into his mouth.

Dominic came out and sat down, saying he was waiting for Faith who would give him his second riding lesson in the hour before she left for school—it was cooler in the mornings. Grace closed her mouth over questions and returned to cooking, looking thoughtful.

Tyler's mood lightened slightly as Dominic questioned him on the basics of horses—*How do you steer? Do you fall off a lot?* Tyler gave him pointers then slid his plate away and left for the stables. He liked talking to Dominic though. He'd do a lot more of that if he became the little guy's stepdad. Tyler enjoyed the thought.

His brief respite with Dominic didn't last, his anger returning as he tramped down to the ring where Grant waited with a new horse.

Tyler was mad at himself for springing the proposal on Jess, mad at her for not telling him how much of a hold Elijah had on her, mad at her for thinking he gave a crap about her disorder or whatever it was. Adam had burned himself all to hell and bore the scars, but he was still *Adam*. And Tyler was furious with Jess's ex-husband for putting that certainty in her eyes that Tyler would reject her.

He'd proposed not out of pity but because Tyler thought he knew how to fix everything. He always thought that, but in his defense, he was usually right.

No, that wasn't it entirely. Tyler had proposed because he wanted Jess in his life. The whole package of her.

Tyler stopped in his tracks halfway to the ring as realization hit him. *He wanted her in his life. Never wanted her out of it.*

He hadn't meant for this to happen. Jess had never been a one-night stand to him, he'd known that from the start. With her, there was no emptiness, no acknowledgment that their encounter would be temporary. No shrugging it off, no walking away.

A sweetness and a lightness had settled in his heart, a gladness that flared whenever Jess looked at him, when she spoke to him—hell, when she walked into a room. The moment she left Tyler's sight, he looked forward to seeing her again.

This had never happened before, not even when he'd been seventeen and engaged to Lindsey. He and Lindsey had been together for more than two years, and it was accepted by both their families, not to mention the whole town, that they'd marry.

What no one had known was that, underneath, Lindsey had wanted out. She'd hated Riverbend and hadn't wanted to marry a rancher. She'd already had someone else lined up to take her away. But she'd been too scared to tell anyone, including Tyler. Until one night …

Tyler shut down that thought, but strangely it didn't haunt him as much as it used to. He'd used sex and short relationships to keep himself from thinking too much soon after she'd died, and then it had become a habit.

Jess wasn't a palliative. She was real. Astounding all the way through. And Tyler loved her.

But what the hell had he been thinking? Of course Jess wouldn't want to jump into a marriage again, never mind the MS. Look at the crap that happened to her the last time. She was gun shy. Tyler should take it slow with her, like he would with a nervous horse, getting to know her, teaching her to trust and like him.

He'd jumped ahead, scaring the shit out of her.

Tyler knew he'd blurted out the proposal because he'd been worried he wouldn't have the opportunity to do it later. Jess wouldn't want to stay confined to Circle C. She'd find a job, leave the ranch, and start her life over, and Tyler would have missed his chance.

Her shock had made him feel like a dumb fuck. What had he expected she'd say—*Oh, yes, thank you, my knight in shining armor?* She'd already told him she didn't want one of those.

She'd tried to frighten him off by telling him she had MS, but it hadn't worked. Tyler had looked up what he could on his phone at breakfast—worrying stuff, but he wasn't about to abandon Jess because of it. She was strong and had faced a lot already. She wouldn't have to do it alone anymore.

"You look like hell," Grant said as Tyler climbed into the ring. The filly Grant had brought out was two years old and a firecracker, but smart and with lots of heart.

"Whatever," was all Tyler could think of to say.

Grant peered more closely at him and rumbled a laugh. "Sex hangover. I know the look."

"Yeah, yeah." Tyler took the longe line and snapped it onto the filly's halter. "Did you come to work or be a wise-ass?"

"She's a sweet woman," Grant said. "I know you know that. Don't fuck it up with her."

"Too late," Tyler said under his breath. Grant gave him a sharp glance, but to Tyler's relief, he dropped the subject.

Half an hour into the training, Jess emerged from the house with Faith and Dominic. Faith led the way to the big barn where the three of them disappeared for a time. By then, Grant had moved to riding in the covered arena, and Tyler worked the filly on the line, training her to respond to visual cues.

He had to pay attention, but watching Jess emerge from the barn in her leg-hugging jeans was seriously distracting. She leaned against the rail to watch Dominic already perched on Dodie, being led by Faith. Jess's backside faced Tyler, her strong arms bracing her on the railing.

The next thing Tyler knew, the filly stood beside him, watching too.

He sighed and gave up on getting anything useful done. If he screwed up this session, he'd have to start the filly's training all over again. Horses had great memories for routine—they'd remember the wrong one as easily as the right one. It was all the same to them.

Tyler led the horse back to her pen, gave her to one of the guys to brush down, and walked over to the training ring. Faith was explaining to Dominic how to use the reins, and then how to make Dodie move forward at a steady walk.

Dominic had the look of a man terrified but not about to admit it to his women. Tyler knew the feeling.

Jess glanced up as Tyler leaned on the railing next to her. "Morning," she said stiffly.

"Yeah, it is." Tyler looked her up and down, enjoying the sight of the tight top over her blue bra, her arms bared, sunshine on her tatts. "We need to get you a hat. You'll fry out here."

"A cowboy hat?" Jess asked, a glint in her eyes. She reached up and touched his, which he'd pushed back to look at her.

"Any kind." Tyler pretended that even that light impression of her fingers didn't electrify him.

"You're protective of your hats," Jess said. "I remember you fighting a guy for it at the bar. I'm surprised you gave one to Dominic."

Tyler shrugged. "He liked it."

"He insisted on bringing it with us," Jess said. "Refused to leave it behind. But I don't think he wants to give it back to you."

"That's fine. He'll grow into it."

Jess was silent as they watched Dominic and Faith. Faith was telling Dominic for the third time to keep his heels down, and Dominic scowled with concentration.

"Grace asked me to help her plan and then run her restaurant," Jess said after Dominic had walked past them, perched high on Dodie, awkwardly pushing the heels of his cowboy boots downward. "She said she'll need a lot of assistance once she has the baby—an understatement. I'm not sure she realizes exactly what will happen to her."

Jess smiled at Dominic, the look one of fondness, love, and understanding. It made her so lovely Tyler wanted to gather her up and never let her go.

"Grace has been planning that restaurant a long time," he said, just for something to say. "It's going to be on the square and feature Mrs. Ward's pies and Grace's pastries and cakes."

"She told me. She wants it to be a spot the locals can have a little time out and enjoy life. She's going to include gluten free and diabetic-friendly goods as well, so no one is left out."

"That's Grace. Feeding everybody."

"I think it's a wonderful idea. Grace already called Karen Marvin about me joining the team. Your nonprofit is helping her?"

Tyler nodded. "Grace's last business partner ran out on her, taking all her money. AGCT Enterprises is giving Grace a business loan and Karen's dealing with the permits and construction and that side of things. What does Grace want you to do?"

Jess ran a hand through her hair. "Management. Hire people, make sure everything's stocked—the grunt work so Grace can be in the kitchen and raise two kids at the same time." Another smile. "I also think she wants me to run interference with

Karen, so Karen doesn't take over. Grace didn't say that, but after meeting Karen, I'm deducing."

"Yeah, Karen is a force of nature." Tyler couldn't stop his shudder. Karen had pursued him a few times, wanting her insatiable appetite for cowboys fulfilled. It had taken all his powers of resistance to turn her away.

Jess saw the shiver and laughed. "I like Karen. A woman who knows what she wants."

"When she's eyeing me like I'm a choice steak on a spit, it's not so funny."

Jess didn't lose her amusement. "Now you know what it feels like."

"Hey, I never looked at you like that. You're gorgeous and I want to have as much sex with you as I possibly can, but you're not a piece of meat."

"Aw, how sweet. I didn't mean you. I meant guys in general, especially in bars. I told Grace I'd be thrilled to work for her. I probably won't be groped every second in a pastry and coffee shop. Possibly, sure, but not as often."

"Good." Tyler let out a breath, relaxing. "Glad you're on board with it."

"I'm going to meet with Karen tomorrow and sign everything. I'll start right away."

Jess sounded happy, and Tyler blessed Grace from the bottom of his heart.

This was the idea Tyler had approached Grace with at breakfast, realizing it was the perfect answer. It kept Jess away from bars and had her working with AGCT, which would also provide her health insurance, but preserved Jess's pride about taking charity from Tyler and all the Campbells. Grace truly needed the help and had been worried about postponing her dream after she had the baby.

"Means you'll be sticking around Riverbend," Tyler said, trying to sound nonchalant.

"I planned to stick around here anyway," Jess said. "No matter what."

"Good. Gives you time to do all your thinking." Jess flushed. "And you."

"I already thought about it. I decided I want to marry you." Tyler pinned her with a hard gaze. "So, like I said, the ball's in your court."

TYLER KNEW HOW TO KEEP her craving him. He stood close, the long, tall Texan Jess had first seen in the Dallas bar, with his charming smile and deep blue eyes, who'd softened her up in a heartbeat.

The fact that Jess had made love to him that very night, and now was with him on his beautiful ranch was like a fairytale. His T-shirt bared his tight arms, his hat shading his handsome and now-dusty face.

Jess touched his wrist, liking the sun-kissed warmth of his skin and the fact that she could reach for him and he was there.

Tyler looked at her with desire in his eyes, but something more shone behind that. He was lonely, Jess realized with a jolt. In the middle of his big, loving family and his ranch full of people and horses, there was no one solely for Tyler.

She remembered Karen telling her about Tyler and his "issues," the girlfriend who'd died. Tyler hadn't related the story, but Jess could be patient. He would tell her when he wanted her to know it.

Tyler covered Jess's hand where it rested on his

arm. The spark that jumped through her brought her close to leaping against him and bellowing *Yes!* to his proposal. She'd do it—she knew that. But first she had to …

Dominic rode by again, bravely taking his hand from the saddle's horn to wave. "Mom, look, I'm jogging!"

Dodie was moving at a very slow trot, barely bumping Dominic in the saddle. Dominic glowed, elated, while Faith watched with the look of a critical but encouraging teacher. The adult expression on a face so young made Jess want to laugh, her heart lightening.

Tyler's phone buzzed. He frowned at it, then answered. "Grace? What's up? … Whoa, whoa, slow down, honey. I'll find him. Don't you worry. You just sit down. Here, talk to Jess."

Tyler thrust the smartphone into Jess's hands then turned from the fence and cupped his hands around his mouth.

"Carter! Where the hell are you? Grant! Find Carter. Grace is having their baby. *Right now!*"

CHAPTER 16

———

JESS HAD TO ADMIRE GRACE'S poise. She barely remembered her own terrifying drive to the hospital when she'd gone into labor with Dominic, Cade both worried as hell and enraged at her for not quietly giving birth without interrupting his drinking with his friends.

Grace was much calmer. She was a little white about the eyes when Jess reached the kitchen, but seemed more unhappy that she'd messed up the kitchen floor than anything else. Jess read her fear underneath though—the baby was coming a few weeks earlier than expected, which could mean any number of things, or nothing at all. Babies arrived when they were ready, setting the precedent for the rest of their lives.

Jess sat with Grace on the porch, trying to keep her excited and not afraid, and watched Tyler be amazing.

Tyler took over with intense efficiency. He had Grant and the rest of the ranch hands out looking for Carter, who'd ridden off on a horse earlier and must be out of cell phone range. He got Dominic dismounted and Dodie given over to be unsaddled and rubbed down so Faith could hurry to the porch to be with Grace.

He had everyone else in the family contacted rapidly—his mom, Adam and Bailey, Ross, Christina. And he got his truck ready and pulled in front of the house so he could drive Grace to the clinic if Carter didn't show up in the next five minutes.

Carter did, racing up on his horse, dust flying from its hooves. He leapt to the ground before the horse stopped, as though doing one of his stunt routines, and sprinted to the porch. He was out of breath and looking wild, his dust-caked hair a mess, hazel eyes wide.

Faith hovered uncertainly, but Tyler had that covered too. As Carter half carried, half supported Grace to Tyler's pickup, too agitated to go for his own, Tyler lifted Faith in his arms.

"Why don't you stay with us, baby?" he said. "No need to go to school. When Grace is settled in, we'll head over and see her. Kids can take a long time to get born."

Carter looked over his shoulder, nodding in gratitude. "I'll call you first thing," he said to Faith. "Promise, sweetheart."

Carter eased Grace into the passenger seat. When he approached the driver's side, Tyler called, "Grant—drive them. Carter won't be able to see the road, and that's my truck. Bring it back in one piece, all right?"

Grant grinned at Tyler, shoved Carter through the driver's side and told him to scoot over. Grant climbed in after him, put the truck in gear, and gunned it down the drive. Dust rose in a thick white cloud, drifting into the light blue sky.

Jess's heart was pounding both in fear and delight. Grace was a sweetheart, having her first baby—she hoped everything would be all right.

Faith looked scared. Tyler hugged her hard and kissed her cheek. "Carter will take care of her, sweetie. So will Grant. Remember when Christina had her baby? Grant was running around like a crazy thing, put his boots on the wrong feet, his shirt on inside out. Remember that?"

Faith giggled. "Yeah. He was so scared."

"Christina and Emma were fine, and Grace will be too. The clinic will be nuts until they get her checked in."

Faith nodded, losing her smile. "We should stay out of the way."

"Uncle Grant will call as soon as we can show up. How about we have some lunch?"

Jess hastened to the kitchen door. "Let me clean up in there first."

Tyler caught her eye and nodded. "Sure that's okay?"

Jess had to laugh. "Seriously, I worked at a bar. You should see the kinds of things we had to clean up. You wouldn't eat for a week."

She hurried inside, listening to Tyler's rumbling voice soothing Faith and Dominic.

Jess had the floor scrubbed quickly, then she cleaned herself up and brought out what Grace had stocked in the refrigerator for the day—enchiladas, meatballs, and sandwiches. Faith didn't have much appetite, but Dominic ate enough for both of them.

As Jess cleaned up the dishes, Tyler's phone buzzed, and he grabbed it and dashed outside. He came back a few minutes later, holding up a hand.

"Don't rush out. Carter says Grace is comfortable but the baby isn't coming yet. It could be hours. But that's okay, plenty to do here."

"Like what?" Dominic asked, caught up in the excitement.

Tyler looked at Jess. "I know. Let's teach your mom how to ride a horse."

Jess gulped as cold flooded her. "Ride a horse? Are you crazy? I can't."

Tyler sat down at the kitchen table and gave her a challenging look. "You have a butt, don't you? Then you can sit on a horse."

Faith giggled, relaxing. Jess recognized that Tyler was trying to keep his niece occupied and calm, but watery fear rushed through her. "I'll fall."

"No, you won't," Tyler said. "I promise. Cross my heart."

"*Tyler.*"

A woman with balance issues and a weak leg shouldn't get on a horse. She'd slide right off into the dirt and bust her head open. Even if she survived, she'd be in no shape to help Grace or work for her restaurant and Karen.

Tyler met her gaze squarely. "I've put kids who couldn't walk a step on the ground on horses and trained them to be awesome riders. You need to trust me, darlin'." His blue eyes held conviction and something tender behind that. "I'll never let you fall."

———

JESS WAS AFRAID, TYLER KNEW that, watching her as one of the ranch hands brought out

Buster, saddled and ready. But she had the balls to walk out to the ring with him, knowing he was trying to keep Faith from going out of her mind.

He'd decided to have Faith stay home, because he knew Carter would have been crazy dividing his worry between Grace and his daughter. Faith would be scared at the clinic, in the way of the staff, and possibly pushed aside. Having her sit like a statue in the waiting room would be hard on her. At home, Tyler could distract her, and they could be at the clinic very quickly when it was time.

"This is Buster," Tyler said, introducing him to Jess. "He's a total shit on the ground, but once you're on him, he's a total pro. He won't let you fall either."

Jess's brows shot upward. "Isn't he the one who kicked the shit out of you? Your words."

"Yeah, but he did that on purpose. He likes *you*."

Buster had put his head down and nuzzled Jess's hands. Probably looking for a treat, but he then rubbed his nose against her arm.

"Does he?" Jess asked nervously.

"Yep. He hasn't drooled on you, shoved you, stepped on you, snapped his teeth at you …"

"Thanks. I feel better."

"He really does like you," Faith put in. "He's the sweetest horse in the world." She threw her arms around Buster's neck and kissed his cheek. Buster didn't look like he minded.

"He likes the ladies," Tyler said. "Only explanation. Now, let's get you up there."

Jess shot him a nervous glance but she allowed Tyler to wrap his hands around her left leg and boost her slowly upward.

It wasn't bad to rest his cheek against her back-side as he hauled her up, not bad to put his hand on her inner thigh and help her swing her leg over the saddle. Buster never moved, being the perfect riding horse once you were on him. Or maybe he just liked Jess, as Tyler and Faith claimed.

Jess had borrowed cowboy boots from one of the ranch hands who wore about her size. She looked good in them, the supple leather creasing at her ankles. She'd borrowed a hat as well, a straw one against the sun. With her short-sleeved shirt, her flowing dark hair, and her ink, she was sexy as hell. Buster was one lucky horse.

Tyler went around Buster's front side—Buster nipped at him—and adjusted her right stirrup, then came back around and did her left.

"You mentioned that this is your weaker leg, so I'm making this one a little shorter," he said. "You can hug this leg around him and not strain to reach the stirrup." Tyler patted her thigh, enjoying that too. "I'm going to be right next to you, and I'll catch you, but if you think you're going off, you grab the horn and hold on tight. We're not in a competition, and we're not roping, so I don't give a crap if your hand's on the horn. Hold the reins in your left hand, like this ..." He folded the reins and slid them through her fist and out between her thumb and fingers. "Buster neck reins really well, so you just push him this way, or that way, and you lean your weight in the direction you want him to go."

Buster obediently started to step to the right or left as Tyler guided Jess's hand. She froze when he moved, but gulped again and tried to relax.

"I'm going to hold the rein at the bit," Tyler said, "and we'll walk forward. Squeeze him a little with your lower legs, keeping your heels down. That's it."

Buster's ears pricked as he felt the faint command to walk, and he moved forward, Tyler right beside him. Buster seemed to understand that he was to be at his gentlest, because he moved quietly and not too fast.

"You can do it, Mom," Dominic said from where he and Faith watched at the rail. "*I* did it."

"He's a quick learner," Faith said generously. She spoke as though Dominic were much younger, though they had a year, maybe a year and a half between them.

Tyler led Buster around the ring, Jess's tension palpable through the reins. He knew that horseback riding was good physical therapy for neuromuscular disorders, and in fact, his mother held classes for challenged kids. Tyler also knew he spoke the truth when he said he'd never let her fall. He wouldn't. Ever.

Jess was stiff the first time around the ring but started to relax in the second. Buster felt the change and relaxed himself, moving more easily.

"It feels weird," Jess said above him.

"Just let yourself go with it." Tyler slowed to walk by her side instead of at Buster's nose. "Give into the movement. Horses walk using one foot at a time, never on the same side. Right front, left back, left front, right back. Let him move your ass."

Jess laughed shakily, but she started concentrating on Buster's gait, her legs becoming more pliable. Tyler caressed her knee, feeling her muscles calm.

"Looking good," Faith said.

"It's like being on a motorcycle," Dominic said. "Only totally different. Right?"

"Right," Jess answered. She sounded surprised.

They went around a few more times, Tyler guiding Buster. He'd wait until Jess had more confidence before she rode without him by her side. Give her time to get used to the saddle, find her equilibrium.

Not that Tyler was actually leading. Buster went where he wanted, and Tyler held on to the rein for show.

When Tyler decided the lesson was done, he showed Jess how to swing her right leg over Buster's rump, rest her pelvis on the saddle a moment, then push off to land on both feet. He helped her, which meant she landed in his arms, her back against his front. Again, not a bad place to be.

Jess looked up at him with her face flushed, her eyes sparkling. "That was fun. Can we do it again tomorrow?"

She hadn't asked that about sex. Tyler laughed at the thought and kissed her on the lips.

The kiss turned fierce, Tyler parting her dusty lips to kiss her deeply. Buster snorted.

"Are you two going to get married?" Faith asked in curiosity.

Jess started. She broke the kiss but didn't look angry when she glanced over at Faith and Dominic, who were watching in enjoyment. "I don't know. What do you think, Dominic?"

Dominic looked at her as though she'd asked a ridiculous question. "I think it's a great idea. Tyler's nice, and we wouldn't have to worry about stupid

Elijah."

Faith's brow puckered. "Who's Elijah?"

"A really bad guy. Mom only puts up with him because he helps her get drugs."

Now Faith's eyes widened. "Drugs?"

"He means medication," Jess said quickly.

"Which you don't need to be worrying about," Tyler said, his arm still around her. "I was looking up stuff this morning. There are organizations that help people who need the meds but can't afford them. Bet Elijah didn't tell you that."

Her eyes flashed irritation. "He did, and I looked it up too. But I wasn't qualified ... Or at least, that's what everyone told me."

"We'll get you qualified. Even if we don't, it won't be a problem. You're okay now, Jess."

Jess drew a breath. "You're being way too good to me—"

Tyler's growl cut off her words. "I do *not* want to hear your thanks or you saying how sweet I'm being to you. I can't help myself—I'm just one hell of a guy. Besides, I love you and want to marry you."

Jess went very still, staring up at him with her wide brown eyes, her lips parted. Tyler realized what he'd said, and said out loud, and his throat closed up. But he wasn't taking it back. Nope. She could deal with it.

"Yay!" Faith clapped her hands. Buster snorted, showering Tyler with mucus.

"Gross, you stupid beast," he snarled.

Buster raised his head and made a half neighing, half chortling noise. Jess jumped, startled out of her daze. "He really does laugh," she said.

"Yeah, he's hilarious. Come on. Let's go in so I can take another shower."

———•———

TYLER CONTINUED TO BE AMAZING throughout the long day and into the evening. Jess was still reeling from his declaration: *Besides, I love you and want to marry you.* He'd try to say it like it was no big deal, but she'd seen the tightness around his eyes, the near panic deep inside him.

Her world had stopped, then started again in a flash. Tyler Campbell had actually said he loved her. She wanted to stick around and make sure he said it again.

Tyler and Jess made dinner—warming up Grace's stocked meals—and Tyler thought of games to keep the kids occupied.

Carter called every hour to update them. Nothing yet. Olivia was at the clinic, there to keep Carter calmed down—at least, that was Tyler's opinion. Carter would never admit that over the speaker phone, especially with his daughter listening, he said.

They were in the middle of working a jigsaw puzzle on the living room coffee table when Christina and Bailey arrived with their little ones.

Faith flew at her aunts and her cousins, a look of joy on her face. More distractions for all of them.

Both babies were about six months old. Dale, named for his grandfather, was Adam and Bailey's son. He had a shock of dark hair, blue eyes, and a wide smile. The girl was Emma, belonging to Christina and Grant. She too had dark hair, but brown eyes and a look that said she was going to do and be whatever she wanted.

Faith sat down and held one baby on each knee. Dominic plopped next to her, studying the two children in fascination. He hadn't had much chance before this to be near babies.

Christina and Bailey both hugged Jess as though they were old friends. Christina and Bailey were sisters, Christina with a roguish look and short, curly hair, Bailey quieter but with the strength of steel.

"So," Christina said to Jess when the hugging was over. "How did you two meet?"

Jess slanted Tyler a glance, her heart warming, noting that he looked suddenly nervous. "I picked him up outside a bar," she said. "Literally."

Christina and Bailey, who must have heard the story from Adam and Grant, laughed uproariously. Tyler rolled his eyes and said, "Yeah, yeah," but he didn't look as embarrassed as he pretended to be.

"The Farrell Girls," as Tyler called them, soon had Jess sitting on a sofa between them. They wanted to know everything about her and her relationship with Tyler, why she'd decided to come to River-bend, and what she was going to do now. Christina asked most of the questions, but Bailey backed her up, watching Jess with a wise look.

Bailey and Christina liked Jess's honest answers, thought it was fantastic that she'd be working on Grace's restaurant, and laughed loudly about anything involving Tyler. He left them and went to kiss the babies, Jess's heart speeding as she watched how gentle he was with them. She also enjoyed studying his nice behind as he bent over the kids.

In the middle of laughter and teasing, Tyler's

phone rang. There was an instant hush, all attention riveting on Tyler as he answered.

The call was short. Tyler thumbed off the phone, and then threw up his fists and shouted, "There's a new Sullivan in the house!"

Faith burst into tears. She hugged her cousins close, sobbing against them while they looked bewildered. Dominic patted her shoulder, trying to comfort her.

Bailey and Christina squished Jess between them in a group hug, then dove apart when Tyler grabbed Jess and hauled her to her feet. He hugged her tight then danced her around the living room.

He twirled her, never letting her lose her balance, and then pulled her against him and kissed her hard on the lips. *I'll never let you fall*, he'd promised her, and his kiss sealed the bargain.

Tyler released Jess but pulled her into the circle of his arm and faced the others who were watching them in delight.

"All right, folks," he said. "Let's go say hi to the newest member of this crazy family."

———

TYLER HATED HOSPITALS, HAVING VISITED so many for all his injuries, but when he walked into the River County clinic he realized its advantages. The doctors had delivered Grace's baby, safe and sound, and both mom and child were doing fine, or so Olivia told them when she met them as they came off the elevators, happiness flushing her face.

They entered Grace's room to find Carter sitting beside his wife's bed, a look of profound peace on his face, and a tiny bundle in his arms.

Grace watched them both fondly, if tiredly, Carter's eyes focused on his new baby. The bundle had a shock of dark hair, a red face, and eyes squeezed tightly shut.

Carter raised his head when he heard Tyler lead in the troops—*quietly,* the nurses had warned them. Carter's hazel eyes held something Tyler hadn't seen in them before—complete happiness, the shadows of his past gone forever. Grace had erased most of those shadows, and now the last of them had disappeared.

Grant and Adam were already there, the brothers moving forward to surround their wives and respective kids. Olivia resumed a chair on Grace's other side, happy in her place as matriarch.

Jess pressed her fingers to her lips as she took in the scene. "Oh, he's beautiful," she said softly. She glanced at Grace for confirmation. "*He,* right?"

Grace nodded. "Zachary Campbell Sullivan," she said. "Zach for short."

"We wanted a Campbell in there somewhere," Carter rumbled.

Even his voice had changed, assuming a gentleness Tyler had never heard in him. The hard-eyed, cynical youth who'd been sent to Circle C ranch for rehabilitation had vanished. In his place was a man who was raising a sweet-as-honey daughter, had married the girl of his dreams, and now held his firstborn son. Tyler's eyes stung.

Carter held out one hand for Faith. "Come and meet your brother, sweetheart."

Faith approached without hesitation, giving Grace a big smile before she rose on tiptoe to peer at the small face against Carter's big arm.

"Oh, he's so cute," she crooned. "Hi, Zach." Her voice was as gentle as Carter's. "I'm your big sister. I'm gonna help take care of you."

Now Tyler's eyes were unashamedly wet. Jess turned to him, tears on her own lashes, and Tyler opened his arms to her. Jess came right to him, and he gathered her close, the happiness in the room embracing them all.

TYLER DROVE JESS AND DOMINIC back to the ranch, using his own truck once he found where Grant had left it in the parking lot. Faith remained with Carter, Grace, and Olivia, while Adam and Grant took their families back to Circle C to celebrate.

The only Campbell who hadn't made it to the clinic was Ross, who was on duty at the sheriff's department. But his absence bothered Tyler. Ross would have made an excuse to come—Carter was his favorite brother. The two had always been very close.

Ross not arriving when he heard about Grace having the baby—and in this town, he'd have heard in seconds—meant something was wrong, and Tyler didn't like that.

Jess, on the other hand, sighed contentedly as they pulled onto the straight road that led back to Riverbend. "That was wonderful. Thanks for letting me come."

"I didn't *let* you do anything. It's family."

Jess didn't appear to hear him. "I'm so happy for them. Grace deserves the best."

"Huh. She deserves a medal for changing Carter into a human being. Remind me to show you the battle scars from when we were kids."

Jess snuggled into the corner of her seat. "When you first talked about Carter, I was mad at him for being mean to you. Now I understand better."

"About what Carter is like? Or are you saying I asked for it?"

Jess laughed, a free and easy sound. "Both."

Dominic leaned forward from the backseat. "You guys were crying in there," he said. "I saw you."

"So were you, hotshot," Jess countered.

Dominic looked chagrined. "Okay, maybe a little. But only because everyone else was." He paused then said hesitantly, "Faith is cute."

Jess grinned. "I noticed you noticing her."

Tyler glanced back at him. "She is, but keep that to yourself for about—oh, ten years."

"Ten *years*?" Dominic looked aghast. "We'll be *old* by then."

"Decrepit," Tyler said. "But you'll be big enough to stand up to Carter when you tell him you like his daughter."

Dominic considered this. "Good point," he said, and vanished into the backseat again.

Jess sent Tyler a smile, then they were quiet until they hit the town limits. Tyler slowed and turned his truck along the square. It was about ten, everything dark except the bar across the way.

"Mind if I stop in at the sheriff's office?" Tyler asked. "I just want to make sure Ross got the news. He didn't answer his phone when I called at the clinic."

"Is something wrong?" Jess asked. She was

attuned to danger, too used to it, and she was picking up on Tyler's uneasiness.

"Probably not. He's likely out on a call, carting drunk drivers to jail. I'll leave him a message. 'Course, this is Riverbend. The dispatchers have probably already told half the county about Zach by now, with all the details."

Tyler spoke jovially, but he couldn't ease his trepidation. He pulled around the back of the sheriff's department and parked. They all went inside together, Tyler not wanting Jess and Dominic to wait in the truck alone. Tyler would take no chances until he had the Elijah problem resolved.

The moment they stepped into the foyer, the sergeant at the front desk called out, "Congratulations, Uncle Tyler!" Yep, everyone knew.

The sheriff's department had a long counter just inside the entrance with a small waiting room out front. A half-door in the counter led to the processing area in the back and kept the arrested riffraff away from any elderly ladies looking for lost dogs in the front. Anyone too dangerous—drug sellers or those taking bar fights to the violent extreme—would be locked in the cells downstairs.

Before Tyler could ask if Ross was around, the sergeant said, "Glad you stopped by. Ross is going crazy trying to calm down some people looking for your girlfriend."

"What?" Jess's face went sheet white, her eyes dilating with fear. Dominic shrank close to her, hands gripping her blue-jeaned legs.

"What people?" Tyler demanded. "If it's a guy named Elijah, arrest him now. He's dangerous and probably wanted all over Texas."

"No, no." The sergeant looked puzzled. "Nothing like that. It's ... Well, I'll let him tell you."

Ross emerged from behind a heavy door in the back wall as the sergeant spoke, saw Tyler, and made a swift path to the counter. "Tyler. What the hell? Is Jess with you ..." He noticed Jess and drew a breath. "Good. I—"

Before he could continue, the heavy door opened again, and a large woman with black hair and a colorful blouse and jeans charged through. "Jess—there you are! Will you tell this *idiota* to listen to me?"

Mrs. Alvarez. Behind her came three more women of the same age, forming a group behind her, all of them looking mad as hell.

CHAPTER 17

———

JESS'S HEART POUNDED AS MRS. Alvarez rushed around desks and out through the door in the counter, catching Jess in a fervent embrace.

Jess hugged her hard then pulled back. "What happened?"

Mrs. Alvarez's words tumbled out over hers. "I'm so sorry, Jessica. Elijah found me—I went to pick up your prescription, and he was there waiting. He must have thought you'd go back for it, but he was happy to grab me instead. He's flaming mad and is after you."

"Are you all right?" Jess asked worriedly. Mrs. Alvarez didn't have any obvious bruises, but Elijah could hurt a person so it didn't show.

"Yes, yes; he didn't touch me. My friends were with me, and we got away from him. He chased us, but we lost him. No one knows the streets of Dallas like me," Mrs. Alvarez finished proudly. "I would have called you, but I didn't want to stop a single second, and I wanted to tell what passes for the police in this town to shut the gates to Elijah. But honey, he's searching for you. And I have to tell you, your ex-husband is out and back in Dallas.

He wasn't with Elijah, but Elijah yelled after us that Cade was waiting for you at home. I'm so sorry."

Dominic clutched Jess's legs again, panic in his voice. "Dad's home? He used to beat up Mom. And me."

Before Jess could answer, Tyler leaned down to Dominic. "He won't ever again, son. I promise you that."

Mrs. Alvarez turned hard eyes on Ross. "What are you going to do?" she demanded. "Jessica needs to be kept safe from this man. What are you doing about it?"

Ross made a placating gesture. "First, we all calm down and take this somewhere quieter. You don't need to worry, Mrs. Alvarez. Jess is under our protection."

"For how long?" Mrs. Alvarez glared at him. "When Elijah and his bikers roll into this little town with their automatic weapons, how many of you will be safe?"

"She has a point," Jess said. "These are seriously bad guys, Ross. They're less volatile when they're hanging out for a drink or a game of pool, but when they go to war, it's no-holds-barred."

"And Elijah is their leader?" Ross asked. He didn't sound worried enough, but then, he'd probably had to deal with people like Elijah before. Small towns weren't immune to crime.

"Elijah and Cade, yes," Jess said. "I can tell you all kinds of dirt about them, if you want to know. Much of it is already in their files, but if you need more …"

Ross perked up. "You'd be willing to testify against them?"

Jess swallowed. Telling Ross about Elijah's criminal contacts or where she reasoned Cade must have stashed the mess of cash from the drug dealing he'd been doing before he went to prison was one thing. Standing up in court and testifying was another. She might never make it to the witness stand if Cade and Elijah had anything to say about it.

On the other hand, if she could send Cade back inside and Elijah with him, it might be worth it to get them out of her life.

Or, Elijah and Cade might send guys to find her and take their revenge. And unless Elijah and Cade were given life sentences with no hope of parole, they could be out after a too-short amount of time. The reason they'd never stayed in long was because their convictions had been for lesser crimes they'd plea-bargained for. Cade had never stood trial for drug dealing because his lawyers had proved there was no evidence—at least none the police had ever found. He'd pled his assault charge down because he'd been able to convince the judge he'd been acting in self-defense. The other guy had attacked first—he had witnesses.

"I don't know," Jess said. "I want them to go away, but testifying puts Dominic at risk. If it was just me ..."

Ross cut the discussion short and motioned for Tyler and Jess to follow him behind the counter. He asked Mrs. Alvarez to stay out front and look after Dominic—Mrs. Alvarez and her three friends surrounded Dominic without hesitation. Jess told him to stay put, giving him an encouraging nod. Dominic looked scared but was trying to be brave.

Ross led Jess and Tyler through the steel door in the back and down a hall into a room that held a wooden table with wooden chairs around it. Tyler closed the door and leaned against it, and Ross rested his uniformed hip on a corner of the table. The joking Campbell she'd met at the supper table her first night had gone. Ross's serious expression belonged to a man who was all business.

"Jess, we can protect you," he said. "Give you a new life, if you want. A new start, far from your past."

Jess stopped her nervous pacing as a chill washed through her. "Like WITSEC, you mean?" The mother of one of Dominic's friends, girlfriend of another of Elijah's bikers, had gone into WITSEC, or at least Texas's version of it. She and her son had vanished one morning, not appearing again until her boyfriend's trial. He'd gone down on multiple drug dealing charges, and she'd vanished again.

Ross nodded. "You'd be safe."

And could start over. They'd move Jess to a city far away, give her a new name and a new job, set her up with a bank account and a way to get her prescriptions. Elijah might try to trace her through those, but Jess wasn't the only one on the planet to have MS.

Going into witness protection would mean leaving Riverbend, the friends she'd started making, the opportunity to work with Grace, and most of all …

Tyler.

Her heart broke. Tyler didn't say a word behind her, and Jess couldn't turn around to look at him.

She'd have to leave Tyler. Never see him again.

She wouldn't marry him, share his life, go to bed with him, wake up with him. The best thing to happen to her since Dominic was born was meeting her tall, dark, and sexy cowboy, and she'd have to turn her back on him.

She'd have to forget she'd ever experienced a glorious time with him. Fallen in love with him. Heard him say he loved her.

Her throat closed up but she managed to get out the words. "What are the chances I could go into WITSEC *here?*"

Ross shook his head, as she'd known he would. "Elijah has met Tyler. Too many people already know you're here."

She understood that. This was a small town, where a new person was noticed, remarked upon, discussed, speculated about. Mrs. Alvarez and her ladies tearing down here hadn't helped, but they'd been afraid, and wise to flee Dallas. Elijah wouldn't hesitate to beat Mrs. Alvarez and her friends until they confessed all they knew. He was that kind of guy.

Jess would have to leave Mrs. Alvarez behind too. Everyone she cared about.

But could she risk Dominic's life? Jess could protect her son if she took him far from Dallas, Elijah, her former existence. If she'd only had to look after herself, the choice would be easier, but giving Dominic a chance to start again without having to look over their shoulders all the time would be golden.

If she stayed in Riverbend, defying Elijah and Cade, she'd put Tyler at risk too. Not only Tyler, but his entire family, including tiny Zach who was only hours old. Elijah was a monster, and Cade had trained him to be one.

Jess finally turned around and looked at Tyler. He remained against the door, his eyes holding quiet anguish.

"If it keeps you safe, Jess," he said, his voice scratchy. "You should go."

Tears burned her eyes. Ross was handing Jess a lifeline but a terrible choice. If she took up Ross's offer, she'd be empty for the rest of her life, knowing she'd held happiness in her grasp only moments before it had slipped away.

But could she deny her son his safety? A chance to grow up without fear?

She couldn't. Never.

Tyler understood that. Jess saw it in his eyes, read it in his heart. He was going to let her go, not demand she risk her life and her son's to stay with him no matter what.

It had taken a lot for Tyler to ask her to marry him. Jess realized that, both from what Karen and his family had told her, and what little Tyler had said about himself.

It took even more for him to say now, *Never mind. Go, and be safe.*

This fact separated him from the kind of man her ex-husband was, from every other man Jess had ever met—Tyler would never take what wasn't freely offered. He would always give.

She shared a long look with him, his blue eyes filled with sorrow and love. Jess wiped tears from her cheeks and swung back to Ross.

"Is there no other way? There has to be something else we can do."

"Yeah," Tyler said behind her. "Give us a rope, baby brother."

Ross's gaze rested on Tyler, understanding in his eyes, but also unhappiness. "I already did some research on Elijah and Cade. They're bad guys, but they're careful. Elijah has beat all his raps by paying his fines or doing his time and making sure he's not caught for anything worse. The guy Cade beat into a coma actually put in a good word for him to the parole board—said that fights get out of hand. What we need is new evidence. As it is, there's not very much to hang them with."

Tyler came forward, brushing past Jess to lean to his brother, resting his hands on the table. "What if they're caught doing something really bad? I can't believe Elijah wanted Cade released so they could go skipping down a beach together. I met Elijah— he's not a sentimental kind of guy. They must be up to something."

Jess nodded, folding her arms tightly over her chest. "Probably a lot of things. Elijah deals in drugs and weapons. He and Cade had a business going, but nothing could be proved—Cade even gypped guys out of money from a drug sale. That's why Cade got into the fight. But there was no evidence for the dealing, not enough to bring to a prosecutor, anyway, let alone a jury. I decided I didn't want to know what they were up to after Cade went to prison, but I've seen a lot of Elijah. I know in my bones that they kept their contacts, maybe were even keeping up the business, with Cade directing from prison. Elijah went to visit him a lot."

"Good." Tyler's animation returned. "So, Ross, how about if you talk to the sheriff and your cop buddies up and down central Texas and see if you can catch them doing dirty deeds? Fix up a nice sting operation? If you find direct evidence of arms or drug dealing, you won't need Jess. She can sit tight here and they don't ever have to know where she is."

Ross considered this, but Jess saw his skepticism. "It could work. I'm thinking one reason the prison system let Cade go is so they can catch him going right back to this old business. If this were a movie, it would be the perfect solution. But what if Cade and Elijah know that and decide to stay quiet for two years? Three? More? Like I said, they're careful."

"Make them an offer they can't refuse?" Tyler asked. "Set up something irresistible?"

"And then you have to be careful about entrapment," Ross said. "Defense attorneys can tear apart a great sting if cops get too impatient."

Jess joined Tyler at the table. Ross watched them calmly, an experienced man for his age of twenty-five. "Like I said, I *might* know where Cade's stash is," Jess told him. "You could set up someone to watch it until he comes to get it."

"Good idea," Ross said. "And we will. Again, he might wait two years."

Jess deflated. She'd have to leave Riverbend to find it, anyway. She had an idea where Cade had hidden money and possibly weapons, based on past experience, but she couldn't point to the place on a map. She'd have to ride there and check it out in person to make sure she remembered right.

She'd not tried to look for his money once he'd gone to prison, wanting to have nothing to do with anything he touched, and she wouldn't feel right not simply handing it over to the police. She hadn't felt certain enough to lead the police to it, and Elijah would have killed her for doing so. He watched her all the time. Besides, nothing might be there. Elijah could have moved the money for Cade while he was inside, or the two of them might have spent it already.

"Unless we motivate him to go get it." Tyler moved closer to Jess, his warmth bolstering her. "Make him worry it's gone, or make him need it."

Cade was greedy, that was true. Wherever he'd put the money, he might rush to grab it if he worried he'd lose it.

Jess began to feel more optimistic, made easier by Tyler so near, and his brother with the same strength in his eyes.

"I could meet with Cade," she offered. Not something she wanted to do, but anything to get him busted again. "Tell him I want to go back to him, but of course we need money. That I'm willing to help—"

"No," Tyler broke in, tone savage. "You're not going anywhere near the guy."

Jess turned to him, her whole body tense. "He doesn't think I'm very smart. Or strong. If he believes I'm willing to be under his thumb again, he'll be generous. He's like that. He didn't dump me when he found out about my MS, because I was *his*. Didn't matter whether he wanted to sleep with me or not, he didn't want me or Dominic away from his control. He'd jump at the chance to have it back again."

She didn't know whether Tyler had told anyone

else in his family about her MS, but she didn't care if Ross heard. No more hiding.

Tyler's eyes were quiet. "Not only no," he said. "But fuck no."

"Gotta go with Tyler on this one," Ross put in. "Way too dangerous. You might never get away from him again, no matter how many cops we have following you."

Jess faced them both, planting her hands on her hips. "You two have any better ideas?"

"Yes," Tyler said. "*I* go to him. Make him think I already know where his stash is. Taunt him. Make him run to it and check."

"Or he'll just kill you," Jess said. "Are you crazy?"

"I'd take muscle," Tyler answered, as though this was reasonable. "Carter knows guys who look like killers, and they'll do anything for him. I even had one of them keeping an eye on you at the bar—did you know that?"

Jess stilled. She remembered the biker who didn't talk much to the others, but drank his beer and didn't mess with anyone either. He'd been the one out in the parking lot having a smoke when Elijah had confronted her, the one who'd politely held the door for her when she'd gone back inside.

"You—" she spluttered.

Tyler broke in. "We can argue about it later. I wasn't about to leave you alone and unprotected, Jess. I won't do that now either. Ross could go with me undercover, and he's got plenty of training to make sure we don't get killed. I could wear a button mike or something. Our cousin Maddox up in Montana knows a guy who messes with all kinds of gadgets—Maddox sends us stuff in case it's useful in our shows or for protecting our horses on the road."

"I'd have to get this authorized," Ross said. "And that will take time. I warn you, shit like this can take forever to set up."

"Don't worry about making it official then," Tyler said. "I'll go with Carter's guys. You wander by, an off-duty cop. You see a crime, or evidence of a crime, so of course you have to call it in and investigate."

Ross started to nod, but Jess swung around. *"Tyler."*

He blinked, his blue eyes holding eagerness, a man ready to rush into battle. "What? I'm a good fighter, Jess. I know you saw me have my ass handed to me, but I was alone and half drunk and distracted. With backup, I'll be fine. Besides, if Elijah's as careful as Ross says, he won't kill me in front of witnesses who can get him dragged off to prison. I promise I won't go anywhere alone with him or Cade. I'll be surrounded by backup all the time."

"That's not the point!" Jess's voice rang out, resonating on the flimsy fluorescent lights. "I don't want to go into witness protection, because I don't want to lose you. I don't want you to confront Elijah and Cade, because I don't want to lose you. See a pattern?"

"Jess—"

She kept going. "So, yes, I'll marry you, Tyler Campbell. *Because I don't want to lose you!* Do you have that through your thick cowboy head? I want to marry you, because I love you!"

CHAPTER 18

———

FOR A MOMENT, TYLER COULDN'T breathe. A buzzing in his ears drowned all other sound, and he didn't think he'd heard right.

Jess McFadden couldn't have just shouted that she'd marry him, and that she loved him.

Tyler opened his mouth, making a little gasping sound as air rushed back into his lungs. "Marry me?" he croaked.

Jess's dark eyes glittered with tears. "I just said *yes*. How many times are you going to ask?"

Tyler's mouth worked, his lips forming and discarding words until he gave up. "Son of a bitch," was his hoarse whisper.

Ross whooped, sprang up, and pounded Tyler on the back. "Fast work, you lucky bastard."

Tyler swayed under Ross's thumping but barely noticed it. Jess started smiling, the smile growing wider and wider, and then she was in his arms, dragging him down to kiss him.

The kiss convinced him. Jess's mouth was hot, caressing, needing, giving, while her arms held him steady.

Tyler heard Ross quietly walk out of the room

and close the door. He'd probably gone off to spread the news, but Tyler didn't care. He pulled Jess closer, pouring every bit of longing into the kiss.

Fast work, Ross had said. Adam, Grant, and Carter had wooed their ladies, or should have been wooing them, for years. Screw that. Tyler wanted Jess *now*.

She was lithe against his body, her breasts cushioning him, her lips soft but skilled. He ran his fingers along her arms, already knowing the map of her tatts but eager to learn more.

Agitation worked its way through his euphoria, making Tyler reluctantly break the kiss.

"This is why I need to nail Elijah's hide to the wall," he said, cupping Jess's face in his hands. "And your ex's next to it. I don't want either of them giving you hell ever again. I want you free of them."

Jess's stubborn look returned, and she took a step back. "And this is why I don't want you anywhere near them. Let Ross and the police do the stake-out."

"While we hide for years, hoping Elijah doesn't figure out you've run off with the stunt rider from Riverbend? Maybe Ross is right, and WITSEC is best."

Tyler heard the sadness in his voice, saw answering sadness in her face. "No," Jess said firmly. "A minute ago I wanted that, to protect Dominic. I still want to protect him, but damn it, I'm tired of running, tired of hiding. We tell Cade where I am and that I have his money, and when they come after me, Ross and the sheriff will grab him."

"Hell, no." Tyler's words rang out. "Not using

you as bait. No way, no how."

"Because you confronting them wearing a button mike is more rational?" Jess glared at him. "I'm not letting you get yourself killed."

"I'm not letting you get yourself killed either!" Tyler roared. "I already did that to one fiancée. I sure as hell am not going to lose you, Jess." His voice dropped to a faint croak. "Sure as hell not."

He hadn't told Jess the entire story about Lindsey, but she would have heard enough in this busybody town. Jess's eyes softened, and she came to him, resting her head on his chest.

"You won't," she said. "You won't go through it again, I promise."

Tyler gathered her close and kissed her hair. He knew he wouldn't go through it again, because he would not let Elijah or Cade anywhere near Jess. He'd make sure they were locked away, no matter what he had to do.

He caressed Jess's chin and drew her up for another kiss, this one less fervent but just as heartfelt. Standing here kissing her was the best thing that had happened to him all day … apart from waking up with her and having sex with her. Okay, so that had been better.

The table that dug into his hip had a wide, sturdy surface. Tyler began to ease Jess down to it, his fingers sliding under the hem of her shirt, finding her warmth …

The door behind them banged open. "Is this true, Jessica?" Mrs. Alvarez asked in her stentorian tones. "You're marrying him? I certainly hope so. Take your hand out of her shirt, Mr. Campbell. Dominic is right behind me."

Tyler jumped away from Jess. Mrs. Alvarez's friends piled in, shielding the world from indecorousness until Jess and Tyler were upright and standing side by side.

Tyler slid his arm around Jess's waist, loving her warmth so close to him. "Yep, it's true. All right with you, Dominic, if I marry your mom?"

Dominic stormed in past the ladies and barreled into Tyler's legs, hugging him hard, then he looked up at them both, his face flushed.

"Well, yeah," he said, as though the question hadn't been necessary. "This is awesome. Faith got a new brother today, but I get a new *dad.*"

———•———

TYLER KNEW HE AND JESS wouldn't have any privacy back at Circle C with the massive celebration going on, so he resigned himself to sleeping alone. He walked Jess and Dominic to his apartment after the large after-hours feast and champagne to toast the arrival of Zach and the engagement of Tyler and Jess.

Tyler checked to make sure the apartment was safe, then kissed Jess good night at the bottom of the steps, regretting his decision to sleep apart from her as soon as their lips touched. He brought his hand up to cup her breast, the darkness shielding them from Dominic, who had already scampered up the stairs.

But no, Jess needed to rest, Tyler needed to calm the hell down, and besides, he had plans to put in motion.

"Night," he said as the kiss eased to its end.

Jess gave him a hungry look that almost crumpled his resolve. Then she nodded, as though as determined as he that they keep calm until things were settled.

Once Tyler knew Jess would be safe forever, he would take her to bed and make love to her until they were both unconscious and too weak to move.

Tyler cleared his throat. "Night," he said again.

"Night," Jess whispered back.

Tyler touched her cheek. "Night," he murmured.

Jess pulled him close and gave him one hell of a kiss.

When she released Tyler, he staggered back a step, his lips raw. Damn, when they let loose, it was going to be monumental.

He finally made himself leave her, watching her hips sway every step up to the apartment. His body hated him the moment she closed the door, shutting him out, but he forced himself to turn around and walk away.

Tyler took the rest of the night to make a ton of phone calls. Once Adam and Grant and families went home, it was quiet. Carter, Faith, and Tyler's mom had remained at the clinic with Grace and the new baby. Mrs. Alvarez and her friends had turned down the Campbell hospitality—they'd have had to squeeze into two rooms if they did—and were staying at a cozy B&B near the river.

That left Tyler alone to make calls and plan.

His thoughts strayed often to Jess, who would be stretched out in his bed in the apartment, sleep-warm and sexy. He imagined her curves outlined by the sheets, her lips parted as she slept.

Tyler's imaginings made him go hard, and then he experienced again the sensation of free falling when she'd said, *So, yes, I'll marry you, Tyler Campbell ... Because I love you.*

That had to be one of the best moments of his life. He'd say *the* best, but being inside Jess was even better. Now, if he could get her to say it while they made love ...

Tyler beat back his straying thoughts and made his plans. Tyler loved her, and he'd marry her. Now to keep her safe.

In the morning, before the sun rose, he went to the ranch's office and met Carter's friends and Jack Hillman, a local tough who was a friend of the Malorys as well as Carter.

"All right?" Tyler said at the end of his instructions.

"I heard all about Elijah," Noah, the man Tyler had sent up to Dallas to watch over Jess at the bar, said. His brother, Hayden, stood next to him, the two a solid wall of tatt-covered muscle. "Even before I saw him. He's one bad asshole. Sure you want to tangle with him?"

"Not sure at all. The idea is not to. I just want him to screw up enough that he'll get himself arrested, with enough shit to stick to get him convicted. So much that any plea bargain he makes will still get him a long stretch."

"He'll be armed," Jack warned. "So will his friends."

"I don't give a rat's ass." Tyler said calmly. "I'm not stopping until he's done."

He'd learned a long time ago that the best way to deal with bullies was to take them down. No bargaining, no hoping they'd go away; he'd learned to stand up and punch them in the mouth. Tyler knew plenty about fighting—he'd fought Carter when Carter had first arrived at the ranch, had learned a lot from him. Mostly that, in Carter's world and Elijah's, you fought for keeps. You didn't tangle with someone if you weren't prepared to fight dirty.

Carter, in fact, would be the best brother to back him up, but Tyler didn't want to pull him away from his family. He remembered the quietude in Carter's eyes when he'd looked up from baby Zach, and Tyler wanted that tranquility to remain with his brother always.

"First thing we need to do," Tyler said to his crew. "Is find them."

Jack shrugged. "Easy. Go back to where you found Elijah before. The biker bar."

"I was thinking somewhere less crowded," Tyler said. "Where he won't have twenty guys at his beck and call. Plus, I want to do this fast. Today. Before he starts a serious hunt for Jess."

"He runs a motorcycle parts business," Noah said. "Not far from the bar, but I don't know where. Heard guys talking about it." He shrugged. "Sorry I didn't find out more."

Tyler only nodded. Noah had been in place to run interference for Jess, watching over her when Tyler couldn't, and Tyler would be forever grateful to him for that.

"Call him." Jack spoke with conviction. "That will draw him out."

"Don't know his number," Tyler said. "But if I can find out where he lives or where this parts store is, we can corner him when he's not expecting it."

The other three nodded. "How?" Jack asked. "Since we're meeting at the butt-crack of dawn, I'm guessing you don't want your girlfriend to know we're doing this."

Tyler knew exactly how he'd discover where Elijah spent his days. "Saddle up, boys," he said. "Figuratively. A warning—where I'm taking you right now, don't say a word. You'd regret it. Look tough, but like you're soft on the inside. Can you do that?"

Jack chuckled, though Noah and Hayden looked puzzled. Tyler didn't explain as they piled into his pickup and he drove off to Riverbend's most popular B&B.

———

JESS WOKE IN THE MORNING, her fuzzy thoughts a mixture of elation and fear. At first she couldn't remember why she felt either one, and then memories poured at her.

Elation because she'd taken a leap of faith and told Tyler she'd marry him. She let herself swim in that thought for a few minutes, her pure happiness telling her she'd made the right choice.

Then the fear eked its way in. Cade was out of prison and he and Elijah might even now have figured out where Jess had gone, in spite of Mrs. Alvarez's assurances that she'd lost them. If so, they'd be on their way.

Next came nervousness, because Tyler's face when he'd talked about going after Cade and Elijah told her he hadn't been idly speculating. Tyler wanted to deal with the problem for once and for all, and she didn't think he'd wait for the police to act.

Her concern on this point made Jess hurry through a shower, throw on clothes, and rush to the main house, where Dominic had already gone. She found her son eating his way through a mountain of pancakes, Olivia Campbell, home from the clinic, taking over kitchen duty from Grace.

"Where's Tyler?" Jess asked breathlessly. She'd not seen him out in the rings with horses or anywhere in the house.

"Not here," Olivia answered. "He left early, or so Carrie—she's one of the ranch hands—told me."

"To go where?"

Olivia gave Jess a look of surprise. "Carrie didn't know. There's a lot to do on a ranch, Jess. Feed to buy and haul, constant repairs, negotiating with horse owners, dealing with farriers, vets, you name it. Everything happens early in the morning. I'm afraid you'll have to get used to that."

Olivia must not know what Tyler and Ross had planned. Jess closed her mouth over her babbling—having Olivia worried about her two youngest sons wouldn't solve anything. She didn't want Dominic worrying either. He was listening closely as he licked every drop of syrup from his fork.

The next minute, Dominic dropped the fork onto his empty plate and jumped from his chair, running to the door. "It's Mrs. Alvarez!" he sang out, and dashed onto the porch.

Mrs. Alvarez and her friends—Connie, Maria, and Virginia—had arrived in Mrs. Alvarez's big truck with its enclosed bed. They descended, arguing about something, but Mrs. Alvarez broke off when she saw Jess.

"Honey, I'm so happy for you." She enfolded Jess into her warm embrace. "Plus, I have a surprise for you," she said when she released her. "Didn't get a chance to give it to you with all the craziness last night."

She took Jess by the hand and led her around the back of the pickup, opening the door of the bed. Inside was Jess's motorcycle, her small Harley, gleaming black and chrome.

Jess's heart swelled with joy. She reached for the motorcycle, closing her hands around its handlebars as though she embraced an old friend, while Dominic punched the air. "Sweet!" he yelled.

"Thank you." Jess turned to Mrs. Alvarez. "I hated leaving it behind. I was so afraid Elijah would take it."

"I went and got it as soon as I could, so it would be gone when he came to pick you up. I'm just so sorry, honey, that I let him catch me at the pharmacy. I tried to have them deliver your meds to my address temporarily, but they wouldn't."

"We'll take care of that." Jess started to lift down the bike, and was joined at once by the other four ladies. Between the five of them, they had it on the ground without mishap. "I'll be starting a new job soon—I need to go see Karen, the woman who will be hiring me today. That is, once I figure out where Tyler went and make sure he's all right."

The guilty look Mrs. Alvarez flashed made Jess go still. Mrs. Alvarez tried to hide her face by bending to examine the bike, as though she'd never seen a speedometer before, but Jess knew she hadn't mistaken the expression.

Her voice hardened. "Do you know where he

is?"

Mrs. Alvarez wouldn't look at her, and Virginia, Connie, and Maria turned uneasily, pretending to admire the landscape.

"Mrs. Alvarez," Jess said firmly. "Carmina." Jess never called Mrs. Alvarez by her first name, respecting the woman's wishes, but this was a special circumstance.

Mrs. Alvarez at last raised her head, defiance in her dark eyes. "I'm sorry, Jessica. I think he's right. Such men will never stop unless we stop them." She lifted her chin. "Tyler asked me where Elijah lived and where he worked. I told him. Tyler had three tough men with him who looked like they could take care of themselves. And take care of Elijah."

Fear smacked Jess. She'd suspected when she didn't see Tyler around that he'd gone to confront Elijah. Tyler was decisive and didn't wait long between thought and action. Damn it.

Jess balled her fists. "Dominic, go back inside and stay with Mrs. Campbell." She moved to the motorcycle as Dominic reluctantly retreated to the porch, and swung her leg over the seat, a much more familiar action than climbing on a horse. She'd worried when she was diagnosed that she'd have to give up riding, but she'd not had as much problem as she'd feared. Like many people, she'd had the disease for years before she'd realized it, and she'd been riding so long that her body had learned to adjust when she went out on the bike. She'd never be the best rider in the world, but she could still do it.

She thought of how Tyler's hands had steadied

her when he'd hoisted her into the saddle, how gentle he'd been with her, knowing she was afraid. She'd do anything to feel his hands around her again, hear his voice comforting her.

Mrs. Alvarez grabbed onto the bike as Jess put her key in the ignition. "You aren't going after them," she said in agitation. "Alone? Do not be foolish."

"Not alone," Jess answered, and let the bike roar to life. The feel of it vibrating beneath her once more gave her confidence. "Tyler has a large family, lots of big, strong brothers who will be happy to help me drag him back home. Stay here and watch over Dominic. Please."

Mrs. Alvarez looked stubborn but finally let go of the handlebar she clung to and stepped back, relenting. "You be careful. Go get Tyler if you have to, but you stay out of the way and let the men fight."

"Don't worry about me," Jess said. "I'm good at taking care of myself, and Adam and Grant will be terrific bodyguards. I'll call you when Tyler's safe."

Mrs. Alvarez nodded, resigned if not happy. "God go with you, honey," she said.

Jess plucked her helmet from its place on the back of the bike and slid it onto her head, another familiar action that calmed her further. She was glad that Grace had showed her all over town, because she knew exactly where to go to find help.

"Counting on it," she said. Then she gunned the motorcycle, lifted her feet, and glided away.

———

TYLER WAS ALREADY INSIDE AND waiting when Elijah arrived to open his auto parts shop at ten in the morning. Tyler and his backup had decided to confront Elijah there, where he wouldn't have neighbors who might defend him, or who might even call the cops. Tyler wanted Elijah going down, not himself and Carter's friends.

The shop was on a back Dallas street, surrounded by similar places, older buildings with small businesses in them—a pawn shop, a tattoo parlor, and one that advertised massage, which Tyler was pretty sure didn't mean a spa with massage therapy. Elijah's auto parts shop seemed to contain mostly used bits from junkyards or broken-down motorcycles, though he had new products in stock as well. A small bay in the back of the store stood ready to fit parts on bikes right there.

Elijah worked this shop alone, so Ross had found out, hiring temporary assistance from time to time. He came and went as he pleased, and was late this morning, but then, there weren't hordes of customers beating down the door. He probably used the shop as a front for drug dealing or maybe stolen motorcycles and parts, though Tyler couldn't see anything in the shop that pointed specifically to illegal activities.

Elijah wasn't alone. He walked in with another man who looked nothing like what Tyler thought he would. While Elijah was unmistakable as a lifetime biker, the second man could have put on a suit and gone to work in a downtown high rise. He had dark hair cut short, a slim but muscular build, and was not much more than five and a half feet, five-six at most. On the other hand, he had the sun-bronzed face of a man who took his exercise once a day under glaring southwestern Texas skies, and the hard coldness of a criminal who had no remorse.

Jess had been married to this man. Tyler clenched his fists as he, Jack, and the other two rose from where they'd been relaxing behind the counter. He supposed Cade had a handsomeness coupled with an air of danger, something women seemed to respond to. He'd noticed that especially in women who had gone after Carter. Grace, bless her heart, had liked him because he was *Carter*.

Tyler reminded himself that Jess must have been very young when she'd met the guy. As young and stupid as he'd been at the end of high school, when he'd thought he held the world in his hands.

Elijah halted in surprise when he saw the four men, his hand going to the holster at his side. "Who the fuck? Oh, yeah, I remember *you*." Elijah relaxed as he looked Tyler over, but his hand remained on the butt of his gun. "The cowboy dumb-ass enough to come into my bar. I bet you want your revenge. You really are a dumb-ass."

"No, just came to talk." Tyler leaned his arms on the counter as though Elijah's gun didn't worry him. He kept his eye on Elijah's hand though. If that gun came out, Tyler would be on the floor in a flash.

He knew Jack had armed himself, and probably Noah and Hayden had too. Texas was an open carry state, which was why Elijah could walk around with what looked like a Sig in his holster. Jack and his friends chose to conceal, legal if they had a permit. Tyler hadn't bothered to ask to see those permits—Ross would know, and that was good enough for him.

Cade, on the other hand, didn't have a weapon in sight, but that didn't mean he didn't have one on him. He'd be barred from carrying at all, which meant he'd have to do it stealthily. He wasn't supposed to be anywhere near weapons, and probably nowhere near guys like Elijah, but Tyler didn't think Cade really gave a shit, as long as he wasn't caught.

"Talk about what?" Elijah asked easily. "How I kicked your ass? Did you want me to apologize? I told you about him, right?" he asked Cade. "Your wife was there that night, trying to get my boys to leave the poor cowboy alone. It was fucking funny."

Cade gave a nod, not looking very interested. Tyler realized with a start that these guys had no idea Tyler and Jess had left together that night, no idea Jess had gone to Riverbend to find him. That knowledge made Tyler relax a fraction.

"Talk to you about keeping out of prison." Tyler addressed Cade directly. "I know where I can find a ton of evidence that will put you right back in. It's what you came out to get."

He finally had Cade's attention. The man switched his ice-cold glare to Tyler. If Tyler hadn't been used to Carter staring at him like that all his life, he'd have flinched. As it was, he met the man's gaze with a cool one of his own.

"Tell me what the hell you're talking about," Cade growled.

"The cash from your last deal, your stash of weapons—those alone will put you back inside right quick. But your secret is safe with me. All you have to do is leave. The state—hell, the country. That would be the best idea. And not come back."

Cade watched Tyler in bafflement, a man used to commanding, and wondering why Tyler had tracked him down to be a pain in his ass.

Tyler saw the wheels turn inside the man's head as the bafflement slowly became realization and then rage. "She told you. The fucking slut. Jess told you about it, didn't she? Where is she? I'll kill her."

CHAPTER 19

———

TYLER'S BACKUP SURGED AROUND HIM in the small shop, looking like the dangerous men they truly were.

He didn't want bodies on the floor though. The goal was to get Cade and Elijah arrested or fleeing, out of Jess's life for good.

"You won't be going anywhere near her," Tyler said in a hard voice. "It's me you're dealing with now. But we can negotiate."

"Or, I can just kill you," Elijah said calmly. His hand remained on the gun, but he didn't draw.

"Then you won't find out what I did with the stash."

Tyler hoped his button mike worked well, and that Ross and his Dallas police buddies were getting every word. Cade said some choice ones.

"You fucker—you stole from me?" he bellowed. "You'll pay for that—you'd better fucking tell me where it is."

Tyler opened his mouth to continue the script he and Ross had cooked up, trying to convince Cade to rush to his hiding place and see if Tyler was lying. But in that moment, Tyler noticed that

Elijah's reaction was all wrong.

Instead of outrage that Tyler had robbed his friend—and probably part of the stash had been promised to Elijah, the loyal man who'd looked after Cade's wife—Elijah looked worried. He tried to hide it under his arrogant façade, but he was definitely troubled.

Stunt riding was all about careful planning, down to the last detail, but it also involved thinking on your feet when something went awry. Tyler had learned how to extemporize long ago, and learned it well.

"Or maybe Elijah knows something about it," Tyler suggested.

He didn't miss the color leaving Elijah's face. The man remained unmoved though. "Where's Jess?" Elijah countered. "I'm going to slap the bitch for ditching me."

Cade didn't look interested in Elijah's question. Tyler remembered Jess telling him and Ross how much of an asshole Cade had been about her MS, and had wanted her only so he could control her. If Cade had ever truly loved her, he'd have been by her side no matter what. The first thing a sane man would have done after being released from prison would be to contact her. Instead, he'd stuck with Elijah.

"Jess doesn't know anything about this," Tyler said, which was the truth. "But whoever you believe, if you want what I took back, get yourself the hell to Mexico, and I'll text you where I've put it."

"You took it to Mexico?" Cade asked, again baffled. He didn't seem to be the sharpest tool in the shed. "Wait—you're a liar. It's right where I left it."

"I'm willing to bet it's not," Tyler said.

"I could just beat it out of you," Cade said, taking a step forward.

Tyler didn't move. "You could. Or you could check. Or you could take my word for it. Tell you what, I'll give you those directions now. I know that by the time you find it, you won't be heading back north anytime soon." He held up his phone, showing them it was just a phone, and started to slide it open to start texting.

Elijah shook his head. "Don't listen to this stupid fuck," he said to Cade. "How could he have got hold of it?"

Cade scowled. "If Jess told him, took him there, he could. I wouldn't put it past her. She was always a shit to me."

"Makes me wonder why Elijah wanted to take such good care of her then," Tyler said to him. "Right? Maybe because she knew where the keys to your kingdom were. Or Elijah didn't want her to find out he'd been helping himself all this time and report it to you. Maybe hoping that, if she *did* find out, since Elijah has been helping her pay for her prescriptions, she'd take his side."

Made more sense now. If Cade was done with Jess and didn't seem to care about Dominic, why was Elijah so keen to look after them? Maybe Elijah had wanted Jess to go with him to Cade's release knowing she would protest and tell the prison's warden exactly why Cade *shouldn't* be let out.

"That's bullshit," Elijah said, his calm gone.

The biggest danger was that Elijah would pull out that pistol and shoot everyone in this room to keep his secret. Cade must have realized that too, because he stepped forward and grabbed the gun out of Elijah's holster so fast Elijah had no time to react.

"What the fuck?" Elijah asked Cade, wide-eyed.

Cade kept the gun pointed downward. "How about we take a ride, Elijah? See who's telling the truth?"

"It's what he wants you to do, dumb-ass!" Elijah's panic wasn't feigned. "I bet Jess sent him here to rob you."

Tyler spread his hands. "And I keep telling you, Jess has nothing to do with this. She doesn't even know I'm here." More truth.

"We're going," Cade said. He gestured with the pistol. "Come on."

Elijah looked hurt. "I've done everything for you, man. What the hell?"

"If this cowboy's lying, you don't have anything to worry about," Cade said in a reasonable tone. "Let's go." He pointed the pistol at Tyler. "*You*, stay here. Don't be here when I get back."

Tyler's heart stopped when he saw the barrel of the gun pointed at him, then pounded again when Cade withdrew and herded Elijah out.

"Shit," Jack said quietly. "Don't ever do that again, Tyler. I didn't bring a change of pants."

"What do you want us to do?" Noah asked.

"Follow them." Tyler lifted his shirt button to his lips. "You got that, bro? Follow him, but discreetly."

Ross couldn't answer—it was a one-way mike. Tyler waited until he heard a couple vehicles start up and drive off before he sprinted out of the shop.

Ross waited around the corner in a dilapidated

pickup, wearing a T-shirt and jeans instead of his uniform. "They're following." He touched the Bluetooth in his ear. "That mike's seriously sensitive. You almost blew out my eardrum."

"Yeah …" Tyler trailed off, catching sight of something he didn't want to see. Down the street a little way, halted in deep shadow, was a woman astride a black motorcycle. Her helmet hid her face, but her jeans and tight top hugged the curves he'd come to know and love.

Tyler strode toward her. His anger rose higher when he saw the truck parked behind her, containing the unmistakable forms of his two oldest brothers.

Jess took off her helmet as Tyler reached her, no shame or fear as she watched him. "Get on," she said.

Tyler halted in mid-stride. "What?"

"Get on," Jess repeated impatiently. "Do you want to catch Cade in the act or not? I know where they're going."

Ross, hearing, gave Tyler the thumbs up. Tyler glared at Adam and Grant, who didn't even look guilty, the shitheads then swung his leg over the back of the bike.

He'd ridden motorcycles before—Adam had taught him—but he had to grab on tight to Jess as she started out and expertly took off down the alley.

Not that Tyler minded. He hung on to Jess, the woman he wanted by his side for the rest of his life, as she gunned the bike and headed off with him to do battle.

—————

JESS WAS GOING TO KILL Tyler. What the hell was he thinking, confronting Elijah and Cade? She'd nearly collapsed in panic when she saw Cade walk out with a *gun*, damn it.

The cops hidden around could have pounced on Cade for simply holding that pistol, but Jess understood why they hadn't. Arresting Cade on the spot wouldn't solve the problem of Elijah—plus if Cade led them back to the evidence for that drug deal, both of them would be inside forever.

Jess couldn't see any sign of Cade as they went, but she didn't need to. She knew where he was heading. The back alleys and roads had become clear to her as she went along, these spaces she'd avoided for five years.

The difference this trip was that Tyler was wrapped around her, lending her his steadiness. The trepidation she'd undergone when riding these streets with Cade flowed away. She knew this town, and she'd use it against him.

Jess rode confidently through the back streets, knowing which ones ended abruptly and which ones snaked through. Tyler whooped as she took a hard corner, leaning with her to keep the motor-cycle balanced. "See? You can ride, darlin'! No wonder I love you."

Jess forced herself not to jerk the bike as his words poured over her. *Love.* From the sexiest man alive. Her heart filled, turning the last of her fear into iron strength.

The street she rode down appeared to end at a wall. Jess knew this was deceptive—a tiny alley turned from the wall to lead to another set of ware-houses. Cade had driven her here the first time before they married, a private place away from her mom's house where they could make love on the bench seat of his truck. Jess hadn't enjoyed it, which she'd thought was her fault. She understood now that Cade was just a jerk and bad at sex.

It turned out he owned a small storage space nearby where he'd kept spare parts for his truck and motorcycles or hid out when he needed to. Jess had never seen any sign of a stack of cash, drugs, or weapons the few times she'd been allowed to go in, but if Cade had hidden them, he'd hidden them here.

Jess halted her motorcycle halfway to the end wall, not wanting to announce their presence. She killed the engine and took off her helmet as she waited for Tyler to dismount. He caught her when she slid from her seat, pressing a brief and silent kiss to her mouth.

Jess felt the imprint of the kiss as they walked, keeping to shadows. The open area between buildings the alley led to was deserted when they reached it, but Jess knew where Cade's storage space was, memories rising as she went along.

Six doors in, Cade had told her when he'd first showed her the place. It was no wonder she wouldn't have been able to find it on a map though, even with satellite photos. It was a warren back here.

The sixth door along the brick building was black and beat up, paint scraped and rotting, the hinges rusty. The door was ajar, and from behind it, Jess heard voices.

Cade and Elijah were arguing. Their voices rang out as Tyler and Jess crept closer.

"What did you do?" Cade was roaring. "The second I turn my back, you rob me?"

"I still have it," Elijah returned, terror in his voice. Jess had never heard Elijah sound afraid before. "I moved it. It wasn't safe here."

"It damn well was! You said you'd take care of everything. I didn't know that meant screwing me over, you dickwad. You said you'd watch over Jess—were you fucking her too?"

"I never touched her," Elijah said with more conviction. "She's an ice queen. And she was yours."

"So is that money. Where the hell is it?"

"I took it to my place. It's still there."

"All of it?" Cade's voice was dangerous.

"No." The word was faint.

"You son of a—"

"Cade." Jess slid in through the open door. Tyler, after a startled curse, came rapidly after her. "If you kill him, you go right back to prison."

Cade upended the pistol in amazement. "Jess? What the hell?"

Elijah's hand went to his holster, the movement arrested when he remembered it was empty. "You bitch," he snarled at Jess. "You sold me out."

Jess's view of him was blocked when Tyler stepped in front of her. "You sold yourself out, asshole," Tyler said.

"What do *you* want?" Cade demanded of Tyler.

Tyler didn't answer, probably because he had no idea why Jess had rushed in here. Jess, on the other hand, had entered with a plan.

"Check your stash, Cade," she said. "Maybe Elijah didn't get it all."

Elijah glanced at her in astonishment. Cade looked puzzled but he didn't waste time with more questions. He took up a crowbar that lay on the cement floor, walked straight to the back wall, and started prying away bricks. Once he had a dozen of them down, he laid the gun on the ledge he'd made and continued to pull away bricks with his bare hands.

Behind the wall was a black garbage bag. Cade reached in and pulled it out, both he and Elijah regarding it in befuddlement. Cade thumped the bag to the ground and yanked it open.

"What the fuck? It's all here—at least ..." He started counting the wads of cash he pulled out, and then he tugged out a pistol covered with dust.

At the same time, the back and front doors of the storage unit burst open and blue and red lights and shouting blared into the dim interior. Ross, backed by about a dozen cops, trained their guns on Cade and Elijah. "Weapons down!" the Dallas cop with Ross yelled. "On your knees. *Now.*"

Cade stared at them, his hands filled with money and a pistol, the shock on his face comical. Elijah had the same look on his face, but he recovered much faster. He swung around and went for the loaded gun Cade had left on the bricks.

Tyler moved. Between one heartbeat and the next, he launched himself at Elijah, his boots connecting with the man's side the second before Elijah could close his hand around the pistol. Elijah grunted and went down, Tyler on top of him.

Tyler hadn't lied when he'd told Jess that he'd have been able to take Elijah if Elijah hadn't had twenty men with him. Tyler had him down on the ground in about three seconds, Ross rushing forward with four other cops to take charge of him.

A knife flashed in Elijah's hand, but Tyler pulled back and slammed his fist into Elijah's face. Elijah's head snapped back, and he went limp.

Ross held out a hand to help Tyler up. Tyler grabbed it, coming to his feet with agility, landing with a light touch. He spun around, crossing the floor in his swift moves, and swept Jess into an embrace.

He lifted her as he went around and around, laughing up at her. The cops had Cade on his knees, his hands on his head, and Ross was making arrangements to have Elijah carried out.

Jess barely noticed them. She only saw Tyler, his blue eyes on her, his smile broad as he spun her around the little space, letting her fly.

Tyler finally set her on her feet, and she landed softly, supported by his sheltering arms.

He towed her outside, a long way from the chaos of the police swarming Cade's storage unit, taking it apart.

"How the hell did you know that stuff would be there?" he asked.

Jess laughed, her triumph bubbling. "I put it there. Well, with the help of your brothers."

Tyler's eyes went wide. "My brothers? What are you talking about?"

Jess shrugged, trying to look modest. "I figured Elijah had stolen the money. It was too easy for him to pay for everything he did—he doesn't make near enough in his shop to cover expenses like that. Mrs. Alvarez told me you were going to his shop, so I took Adam and Grant to his house. When Elijah cleared out for work, we went in and found the stash—which he hid under some tiles in his kitchen—and brought it back to Cade's storage space. I figured Elijah's confusion would give the cops a second to run inside, and I wanted Cade to be caught with the stuff."

"Adam and Grant," Tyler repeated, his smile dying. "They are dead men."

"Now, Tyler, don't be like that," Grant said, coming to them. Adam was behind him, his big grin pulling at his scars. "You know Christina and Bailey egged us on. They thought it was a great idea."

Tyler scowled at them. "You could have done it without bringing Jess with you."

"No, they couldn't," Jess said calmly. "I had to show them where to go. And show you."

"Shit." Tyler started to say something more, then his face went bleak and he yanked Jess into a hard embrace. "Damn it. Don't scare me like that ever again."

"You don't either," Jess said into his chest. "Standing in front of a loaded weapon, jumping Elijah when he was going for a gun. What the hell were you thinking?"

Tyler pulled back and looked down at her, his blue eyes filled with heat. "Tell you what. I won't do anything more dangerous from now on than fall off horses and fight with my brothers. And you don't do scary shit that gives me a heart attack either. Deal? But first, we'll go home and not let anyone near us for a while. How does that sound?"

"Perfect." Jess shivered in sudden release. Her life was about to change, begin anew. She'd be in the beauty of Circle C and Riverbend, surrounded by friendly people. She'd be with her adorable son, and most of all, with this cowboy who'd saved her life, several times over.

"Perfect," she said again, softly this time. She leaned into Tyler, absorbing his vigor, hearing his heart rapidly beating. His hands on her back held her still, keeping her from all harm. "Let's go home."

CHAPTER 20

————

JESS LAY IN QUIET DARKNESS the next night, her head pillowed on her arm as she watched the rise and fall of Tyler's chest as he slept beside her. He'd fallen into hard slumber after their third round of lovemaking, and was sprawled on the sheets, his tanned body looking good against them.

Dominic was in the main house, liking to stay there, under the supervision of Olivia. She made a fantastic grandma, something Dominic had never really had. Something else she had to thank Tyler for.

Jess brushed Tyler's shoulder with her fingertips then kissed it, loving the smoothness of his skin beneath her lips.

"You're a beautiful man, Tyler Campbell," she whispered. "And I'm going to marry you."

Not because she was giddy and innocent, as she had been with Cade. Not for security—Jess would start work on Grace's restaurant in a few days with Karen, her salary dizzying her. Not for safety—Cade and Elijah had been denied bail that morning, and each was loudly trying to rat out the other, according to Ross.

Jess would marry Tyler because it was her choice, because she wanted to be with him. His family was a bonus, but even if she'd met none of them, she'd decide to be with Tyler. He was fun, loving, handsome, charming, and amazing at sex. Why the hell wouldn't she marry him?

Plus, he liked *her*. Not Jess the bartender fending off bikers for him, or Jess the mom protecting her son, or Jess with her disease that needed to be managed. Tyler wanted Jess the woman. Just her.

Tyler made a low noise in his throat, and his eyes fluttered open. He blinked when he saw Jess staring at him and then gave her a slow smile. "Hey there."

"Hey." Jess returned the smile, and his eyes softened.

Tyler stroked her arm, tracing her tattoos as he liked to do. "Where do you want to go on our honeymoon, sweetheart?"

Jess hadn't been many places other than Texas. "Hawaii?"

Tyler considered. "We could do that. Adam tells me there are spots where we could be completely alone. Just the two of us." He grinned. "We'd learn real quick whether this marriage will work or not."

"It will," Jess said, knowing it in her heart.

"Glad you're not worried about it." Tyler shook his head. "Neither am I. We'll have some good times, sweetheart. Even if you're two years older than me."

Jess widened her eyes in mock surprise. "Oh, wow. I guess I'm a cradle robber."

"A cougar," Tyler said. "A hot one."

"That would make you my boy toy."

Tyler spread his arms. "Fine by me. Play with me, darlin'."

His cock stood high, his body inviting her touch, her lips, her tongue …

Jess drew a ragged breath as she looked him over. "You'll have to wear nothing but a tiny bathing suit all day when we're in this secluded place in Hawaii."

"I will if you will." His eyes glinted. "You have great legs."

Jess became wistful. "One doesn't work very well."

Tyler sat up and wrapped one arm around her. "That doesn't matter. I'll hold you up."

Jess thrilled as Tyler curved over her to kiss her cheek, her neck, her lips. She ran her hands along his chest as she kissed him back, feeling his solidness, the steady beating of his heart.

She moved her touch downward, over his unyielding abdomen to the wiry hair at his cock, but he raised his head, gently moving her hand away.

"I need to be honest with you, Jess," he said somberly. "You told me your life secrets. You need to know mine."

Jess's pulse quickened, but she slanted him a teasing glance. "You mean *you're* a sadistic man-eating black widow?"

He gave her a flash of smile but shook his head. "About Lindsey. I want you to know the truth."

Jess's teasing died away. "I know she was killed. I'm so sorry, Tyler. You don't have to talk about it if you don't want to."

"No, I want you to know." Tyler sat up, keeping hold of her hand, his thumb rubbing the backs of her fingers. "Everyone figured Lindsey and me were madly in love. We were, sort of. We went together for almost three years, and decided we might as well get married once we graduated. It's what you think when you're seventeen—that you have to decide your life right then, and that's it. But it isn't. Not by a long way—you know that. Lindsey wanted to leave Riverbend. She wanted more." Tyler let out a breath. "Except she didn't tell me. I went on about us moving in at the ranch, me working with Adam and Grant. I was so excited. I wouldn't have to worry about finding a wife and settling down. That would all be taken care of by Lindsey, and I could just get on with my life. I was a stupid shit."

"Focused," Jess said. "So was I. I thought Cade would take care of me. I realize now I was looking for someone to replace my dad. Not in a weird way, but someone to watch over me and tell me what to do. It kept me from having to think for myself until it was too late."

Tyler nodded. "That's what happened to me—I stopped thinking. I just assumed, took her for granted. Then one night she tells me she's leaving with a guy she met in San Antonio, a guy she's been seeing behind my back for months. They're going to get married, she's going to go to school and learn fashion design. I didn't even know she was interested in fashion design. That's how much we didn't talk." He looked regretful. "I was furious. Looking back, I wasn't mad because she cheated on me. We'd been drifting apart, and I couldn't figure out why. I was mad because she hadn't told me.

We'd been friends for so long, and she couldn't tell me what she was truly feeling, or ask me how I felt about it, or for my advice. We shouted at each other for about two hours, and then she left. Jumped into her truck, raced off, went and picked up her guy who was waiting for her at the diner. They went down a back highway to San Antonio, and a semi swerved into their lane …"

Jess stilled his lips with her fingers while she laced her arm around him. "Shh, don't go on. Damn it, Tyler. I'm so sorry."

"It was a long time ago."

The sadness in his words tugged her heart, but that was all it was, sadness. That he hadn't been able to help Lindsey, hadn't been a good enough friend to her. He'd grieved for her, but not because he'd loved too deeply.

"Everyone thought you were brokenhearted," Jess said, understanding. "But it was guilt, wasn't it? You thought it was your fault."

"Yep." Tyler let out another long breath. "If I'd talked to her more, listened more, asked her questions, instead of focusing on my life, we could have agreed to break up, go our separate ways. We wouldn't have had that horrible fight, I wouldn't have said the things I said—most of which I don't even remember. But we were trying to hurt each other. Maybe she wouldn't have been so upset, her guy would have watched the road better …"

Jess closed her fingers around his work-roughened ones. "*That* you can't know. A lot of things came together at that moment, and *none of it was your fault.*"

"I figured that out after a while," Tyler said, his

eyes quiet. "But it's hard to get through your head, you know? Especially when you're seventeen. Everyone thought I started chasing women to forget my pain, but the truth was, I thought I sucked so much at connecting, why should I bother to try? So I picked women who didn't want to connect. Short relationships, not much emotion involved."

"And then you asked me to marry you," Jess said, squeezing his hand. "And didn't run when I said yes. I'd say that was progress."

Tyler looked into her eyes, his holding calm understanding. "Because right that moment, I realized why I never connected with Lindsey and didn't try with other women. Because they weren't you, Jess. I connected with *you*. I wasn't bad at it after all. Before, it just wasn't right, and something inside me knew that. Instinct, I guess. When you find the right one, it's not like settling for someone because they're familiar, or you're going after a sensation to make yourself feel better. You *know*. You're The One, Jess. So I had to ask you, quick, before you disappeared out of my life again."

Jess touched Tyler's face, putting her heart into her words. "I'm not going anywhere. I love you, Tyler Campbell."

"And damn it, I love you, Jess." He leaned to her, his breath brushing her lips. "Thank you for saving my ass."

"I couldn't fight Elijah's gang very well," Jess said, remembering her struggle to pull the bikers away from Tyler. "And you wouldn't let me take you to the hospital. So for driving you to your hotel and dabbing you with a washcloth—you're welcome."

The small curve of his lips into the charming

smile turned her inside out. "Not what I meant."

Jessica could say nothing more. He'd saved her life too, taking it from bleak and unending and landing her in this brand new world. With him.

Her tall, dark, sexy cowboy drew her into his arms. Tyler's next kiss seared her, sending her back down into the pillows. He licked her mouth, then her throat, then her breast, rolling his tongue along the curled end of her tatt.

"Love you, Jess," he whispered, all pain gone from his voice, his kiss erasing the hurt from her as well.

Tyler slid inside her, the love in his eyes opening her. Jess's old fears dissolved in the Hill Country breeze that danced at the window, rippling the wind chimes. Tyler had set her free.

She held on to him, and they rode together in the darkness, surrounded by beauty, the lifeline of family beyond these walls, and love.

EPILOGUE

———

October

A PERFECT DAY FOR A WEDDING. October in Hill Country could be warm and dry and it was today, with blue sky stretching forever.

Tyler turned from the arbor in the backyard, Ross next to him as a very proud best man, to watch Jess walking toward him on Adam's arm. Her white gown hugged her figure, and her shoulders were bare, white flowers in her hair.

Jess had debated whether to wear a gown that covered up her tatts, but Tyler had persuaded her otherwise. Her ink was part of who she was. The dress she'd chosen with the help of her new sisters-in-law and Karen showed off the colorful sleeve on one arm and the lines that curled up her other arm and around her collarbone, framing her neckline.

She held a bouquet of pink roses, which she handed to Grace as Adam delivered her to Tyler and took a step back.

The ceremony was short and sweet. The minister spoke the words, and Tyler repeated them, phrases he never thought he'd say.

With this ring, I thee wed ... To have and to hold ... All the days of my life.

Jess had tears in her eyes as Tyler slid the gold ring onto her finger, the one Ross had guarded with his life all morning.

The ring fit her perfectly, shining next to the diamond one Tyler had bought her a few days after she'd said *yes*.

A warm breeze blew around them, sending Jess's skirt dancing, as the minister announced they were man and wife.

Tyler snaked his arm around Jess and pulled her up for a long, long kiss. His brothers whooped and applauded, and the guests cheered.

Tyler eased back and looked down at his bride. Her brown eyes were full of laughter and happiness, the fear and worry she'd carried since he'd met her erased. She was free to simply be Jess.

As soon as they turned around, Dominic raced forward and flung his arms around both of them. Tyler bent down and lifted him, resting his new son on his shoulders. Cameras came up to take that picture, and then Tyler led his wife back down the aisle.

Photos, hugs, laughter, then a feast under the shade of a white tent, and toasts. Tyler held Jess's hand under the table, as though fearing she would disappear if he let her go.

He looked around at his family gathered at the main table—Adam and Bailey with little Dale; Christina and Grant with Emma. No, wait—Grant was now chasing after Emma, who could move with lightning speed.

Carter sat very close to Grace, Zach in his arms,

Faith hovering protectively over her little brother. Though Zach had been born weeks before he'd been expected, he had thrived and was robust. And damn, that kid had lungs. He was going to be an astonishing man.

Jess leaned against Tyler as Ross got to his feet and everyone looked at him expectantly.

Ross raised his glass. "We're here today to celebrate the marriage of my good-for-nothing brother, Tyler, and his radiant bride, Jess." Laughter and applause. Ross turned to Tyler, tipping the glass to him. "But seriously, you're looking at two people made for each other, meant for each other. Took them a while to *find* each other …" A ripple of laughter. "But Tyler was one lucky man. Of all the beer joints in all the world, he had to walk into hers. And got his butt kicked." The laughter grew. "Lucky for him, Jess was on hand to save him. I guess she decided she'd better marry him and keep him out of trouble." Cheers and applause.

Ross waited for the crowd to calm. He was the last unmarried Campbell, the little brother who'd idolized Carter when he'd come to live with them, looking for someone to be his dad. Ross had grown into a competent man and a good policeman, ready to take on the world.

"To my wild brother Tyler, and the gorgeous Jess," Ross went on. "I've seen in the last months that they are crazy in love with each other, but they have enough love left over for their son and their family and everyone else. Long may they know happiness." He lifted his glass higher, the champagne's bubbles dancing. "To Jess and Tyler."

"Jess and Tyler!" everyone shouted. Mrs. Alvarez,

sitting near the main table with her posse, wiped her eyes. So, to Tyler's surprise, did Karen Marvin, touching a handkerchief delicately to her cheek. She was sitting with Kyle and Ray Malory, which worried Tyler a bit.

Tyler turned and kissed Jess while everyone drank, which brought more noise from the guests.

On his other side, Tyler's mother seized his arm and reached up to kiss his cheek. "Thank you, Tyler," she said.

Tyler gave Olivia a hard hug and a kiss in return. "You are very welcome."

He knew why she thanked him. His mom had been sure, when Lindsey died, that Tyler would never settle down and lead a normal life—whatever normal was around here. Jess had brought hope and love back to him, trust and happiness.

A few well-meaning people had taken Tyler aside and advised him not to marry her because of her MS. She'd have to take care of that all her life, and it could become worse one day. Tyler had told them calmly that it was part of who she was, and he and Jess would deal with it. He wasn't going to abandon her because she wasn't in perfect health. They would live their lives, come what may. Together.

Jess's smile when Tyler turned back to her told him he had made the right choice.

Tomorrow, they'd drive to Austin and begin their plane journey to Hawaii—with Dominic—for their honeymoon. Tonight, they'd sleep in Tyler's apartment above the garage, not very romantic, but it was *theirs*. When they came home, they'd begin building a house on a piece of property adjoining the ranch.

For now … they needed to ditch all these people and have some time to themselves. Tyler knew a contingent of his friends would station themselves outside the garage and heckle, and he'd like to get Jess inside and out of sight before that happened.

First, they had to endure many toasts, drink, eat, and dance. Jess gave Tyler a look of trepidation when he led her to the middle of the cleared space, the band striking up a dance tune, but he held her competently in his arms. He hadn't been exaggerating when he'd promised he'd never let her fall.

It was Kyle Malory, in fact, who helped them escape. He got everyone going in a dancing contest, the band playing faster and faster to see who could keep to their feet, everyone plenty lubricated by that time. Mrs. Alvarez so far was winning. The lady had stamina.

Kyle tugged Tyler to a flap in the back of the tent and slid them through.

"You owe me one, Campbell," Kyle said. "I'll make sure Dominic gets back to the house with your mom."

Jess stepped to Kyle and gave him a kiss on the cheek, then a teasing look. "Thanks, Kyle. I might be sorry I met Tyler first."

Kyle laughed but flushed. "Yeah, sure, I am too. Don't screw this up, Campbell."

Instead of giving his traditional rival a derogatory brush-off, Tyler only shook his head. "I never will. I'm not that stupid. You're right, Malory. I owe you one."

He pulled Jess firmly away, and off into darkness.

Tyler's friends did show up later to heckle them, but Jess was already on the bed beneath him, Tyler buried inside her. He was not about to stop for something as annoying as his friends below the window.

"We'll outlast them," Tyler whispered. "No problem."

And they did. Jess was supple and warm under him, she holding him, all the empty spaces inside Tyler filling as he loved her. She wasn't a passive, blushing bride. Jess rose to meet his thrusts, her groans blending with his, her climax and his exploding together. After the third time of this, Tyler noticed all was quiet outside. His friends had given up and gone home.

They drowsed together, Tyler with his arms around the most wonderful woman on the earth.

"Love you, Jess," he whispered as he kissed her hair. "But you know that, right?"

Jess turned to look at him, her lips temptingly near. "I think so. But I don't mind you telling me. Every day—you'll need to remind me."

"Have no problem with that." Tyler kissed her mouth. "I love you. That's for tonight." Another kiss. "I love you. That's for in case I forget to say it later."

"I love you too." Jess's smile faded. "I'm so happy, I'm afraid to do anything else. I don't want this to go away."

"Oh, I can think of something we can do that's just as good." Tyler laughed softly. "This is just the start, darlin'. I promise you. We'll be off to Maui and our condo, and watch Dominic have all kinds of fun. And at night, we'll go to our room and see if we can't have some fun of our own."

"That sounds ... not bad." Jess grinned as Tyler

pretended to look hurt. "How do you feel about Dominic having a little brother or sister?"

Tyler had thought a lot about it, in truth, ever since Jess had floored him by agreeing to marry him. He'd seen the change in Carter when he'd held his son for the first time, had seen the change in Adam and Grant when their kids came. Had seen Carter's deep love for Faith, which had begun as soon as Carter had realized, at age eighteen, that the baby squalling in his arms was his. Carter had become a man at that moment, transforming from troubled teen to protective father in the space of a second.

"Well," Tyler said, pretending he hadn't already been hoping and planning. "I guess that would be okay. Is it okay with Dominic?"

"I asked him," Jess said. "He said yes. Which is a good thing."

"Yeah, it is." Tyler stopped, something in her voice making him give her a sharp look. "Wait, what exactly do you mean—a good thing?"

Her answering smile took his breath away. "Because next summer, he'll have a brother or sister. We'll have to make sure we have enough bedrooms in our house."

Tyler stared at her, his mouth open, for one heartbeat. Another, and another.

Then he propelled himself off the bed to land naked in the middle of the carpet, the yell escaping him rattling the windows.

"Son of a bitch! I'm going to be a dad? I'm gonna be a *dad*!"

Jess sat up, her smile bathing him in joy. "If those guys are still out there, they'll tell the whole town.

Or, wait—they probably heard you at the house."

"I do not. Give. A. Shit."

Tyler jumped into a handstand then pushed off to his feet again, springing from the floor onto the bed. He pulled Jessica down with him, joining her laughter with his, his love for her overflowing.

A thought cut through his elation. "Wait—will you be okay? I mean, with the MS and all."

Jess nodded. "I've already asked my doctors. I should be fine. In fact, a lot of women say the symptoms go away while they're pregnant."

Tyler blew out his breath. "No matter what happens, I'll be with you. Every step of the way. All right?" He rolled over onto her, looking down into her face flushed with happiness. "I love you, Jess Campbell. Thank you for saving my ass."

Jess caressed the ass in question. "Thank you, Tyler Campbell. For saving *me*."

She gathered him in a tight embrace, and Tyler slid back inside her, where he belonged.

Her eyes were stars in the darkness. Tyler kissed her, tasting joy, and the room went quiet—more or less—as they loved each other hungrily, touched by a cool Texas breeze.

Tyler loved, and was loved. The most beautiful thing in the world.

———

THE NEXT MORNING, BEFORE CLIMBING into the pickup that would take them to the airport, Jess's new sisters-in-law insisted she toss her bouquet. The guests who'd spent the night, including Karen and Mrs. Alvarez and friends, arrayed themselves to go through the ritual.

Jess winked at the impatient Tyler and Dominic, and Adam, who was waiting to drive them. She chose her aim, then turned her back and tossed the roses over her shoulder.

The bouquet landed exactly where Jess had wanted it to, in the hands of a bewildered Ross Campbell.

Tyler burst out laughing then helped Jess into the truck with his warm hand on her back. Dominic settled between them, and they left Circle C for a few days of fun and sunshine.

But they'd be back. Jess would always return to Circle C—to her family, her sexy cowboy, her new life. Her home.

AUTHOR'S NOTE

THANK YOU FOR READING! IF you are wondering why I chose to give my heroine, Jess, MS, I was inspired by my husband, who was diagnosed with multiple sclerosis a few years ago. Like Tyler, I had very little idea what it was or what it meant—we had to learn from the ground up. I asked my husband if he minded if I had a main character with MS, and he said, *No, of course not*, as though surprised I had to ask.

So, with my conviction that "everyone has a story," I wrote the tale of Tyler and Jess, two people struggling for a happy ending, each believing they'll never find one.

Multiple sclerosis is a frighteningly common disease, affecting more women than men, and most often diagnosed between the age of twenty and fifty. The cause is uncertain, to date there is no cure, and the disease itself is not well understood. Different people experience different symptoms, and the disease has various types of progression. Some, like Jess, have a milder form that is stabilized with medication; others have the progressive type that can be very severe. Research is ongoing, with amazing amounts of money poured into it, and the medication that's required is hideously expensive.

My hope is that someday, someone will understand the disease and halt it in its tracks. More can be found about MS on the following websites:

NATIONAL MS SOCIETY
www.nationalmssociety.org

MULTIPLE SCLEROSIS FOUNDATION
www.msfocus.org

MULTIPLE SCLEROSIS ASSOCIATION
OF AMERICA (MSAA)
www.mymsaa.org

———

I WAS HAPPY TO BE ABLE to return to Riverbend and the Campbell family! Next up is Ross, the cowboy deputy, and then we'll switch over to the Malorys and give Kyle and Ray the stage. I'm looking forward to writing about those two hot rodeo cowboys.

My newsletter will let you know when new books are coming out—you can sign up here! **www.eepurl.com/47kLL**

All my best wishes,

Jennifer Ashley

RECIPE:

MRS. ALVAREZ'S MIGAS

Migas is one of the simplest Tex-Mex dishes to make—all you need are crisp tortillas and eggs, and whatever peppers, tomatoes, onions, and chiles you have sitting around your kitchen. The word "Migas" means "crumbs," and these are delicious crumbs!

Ingredients (makes 4 servings)

Corn Tortillas: Four small corn tortillas or very good quality tortilla chips

Eggs: 6-8—broken into a small bowl and stirred together

Tomatoes: 4 chopped (any variety; can substitute canned plum tomatoes or diced tomatoes)

Bell pepper: 1 green or red or combo of both, cored and cut into strips

Onion: 1, sliced and diced

Chiles of choice: Jalapeños are great; a can of mild green chiles can be substituted

Cheddar or Jack cheese (or combo)

Cilantro for garnish (optional)

To Prepare

1. Cut corn tortillas into strips then cut the strips in half.
2. Fry tortilla strips in a frying pan in butter or oil over medium high heat until crisp and browning. Remove from pan.

Option: You can use very good quality tortilla chips and omit this step. Have about two cups of tortilla chips ready to use.

3. Add bell pepper and onion to the pan (add more oil as necessary) and cook for 3-4 minutes.
4. Add chiles and tomatoes, stir and cook for an additional 2 minutes.
5. Add fried tortillas (or chips) to pan, stirring in.
6. Reduce heat. Add eggs and stir gently to incorporate and scramble.
7. Once eggs are cooked, add cheese(s) and fold in.

Serve sprinkled with chopped cilantro and an additional sprinkle of cheese and a dab of sour cream if desired.

Enjoy!

ABOUT THE AUTHOR

NEW YORK TIMES BESTSELLING AND award-winning author Jennifer Ashley has written more than 85 published novels and novellas in romance, urban fantasy, and mystery under the names Jennifer Ashley, Allyson James, and Ashley Gardner. Her books have been nominated for and won Romance Writers of America's RITA (given for the best romance novels and novellas of the year), several *RT BookReviews* Reviewers Choice awards (including Best Urban Fantasy, Best Historical Mystery, and Career Achievement in Historical Romance), and Prism awards for her paranormal romances. Jennifer's books have been translated into more than a dozen languages and have earned starred reviews in *Booklist*.

More about the Jennifer's books can be found at
www.jenniferashley.com

Or join her newsletter at
www.eepurl.com/47kLL

Made in the USA
San Bernardino, CA
14 August 2017